To Gea,

Enjoy!

CATASTROPHE

BOOK TWO OF THE CAT LADY CHRONICLES

Susan Donovan
Valerie Mayhew

SUSAN DONOVAN & VALERIE MAYHEW

ADOBE COTTAGE MEDIA, LLC.

Catastrophe (Book 2 of the *Cat Lady Chronicles*) is a work of fiction. Names, characters, places, and incidents are the products of the author's imagination or are used fictitiously. Any resemblance to actual events, locales, or persons, living or dead, is entirely coincidental.

Copyright © 2022 by Susan Donovan and Valerie Mayhew
All rights reserved.
ISBN: 978-1-7379959-4-4
Published in the United States by:
ADOBE COTTAGE MEDIA, LLC.

Cover design: Elizabeth Mackey
Formatted by: Jesse Kimmel-Freeman

Cover image: Egyptian Bastet canopic jar by Veronese Design, www. Veronesedesign.com. Used by permission.

Cover photograph by Brian Jones Photography. Used by permission.

Printed in the United States of America

www.catladychronicles.com

ALSO BY THE AUTHORS

The Cat Lady Chronicles
Catalyst, Book 1
Catastrophe, Book 2
Cataclysm, Book 3, Coming soon…

*Cats know how to obtain food without labor, shelter without confinement,
and love without penalties.*
– Walter Lionel George

Book of the Dead – Judgment

Papyrus of Ani, Frame 3, c. 1250 B.C.E.
The British Museum, London, England
Image used with permission.

CHAPTER ONE

We're going to need a bigger trailer.

What an idiotic thing to say. Felicity was well aware that square footage was the least of their problems. She was stuck in Bastet's necklace and Tom was stuck on earth. The necklace would not release, no matter how many times they tried. Something was wrong. Seriously wrong.

"This has never happened before." Tom's mismatched eyes had flown wide a few moments before and seemed to be stuck that way.

"Try again. Maybe I'm just not concentrating as hard as I should. You know me, I can get distracted, go off on a tangent when I'm nervous and start rambling about unrelated issues and completely lose my focus. What was I saying?"

"You wanted me to try again."

"Right." Felicity turned her back to Tom, lifted her singed hair, and concentrated with all her might on the heavy gold jewelry collar around her neck. She envisioned it releasing. *Opening. Unlocking.*

Unclasping. Unhitching. Unfastening. Freeing...

This better work. She was running out of synonyms.

Tom cleared his throat, attempted to take a deep breath through the gauze-packed nostrils of his broken nose, and began the incantation again. She felt the cold edge of the ritual knife slide against the nape of her neck, slip under the back of the supple gold mesh, and exert pressure.

She closed her eyes and focused her mind on the endless loop of synonyms, realizing she'd completely missed *uncoupling*. Tom raised his voice and tried once more. And finally...

Not a damn thing.

He withdrew the knife. Felicity spun around.

Tom stood frozen, staring down at her with eyes as blank as they were big. "This has never happened before."

"I believe you've said that."

"Apep is defeated." His words were flat.

"Yep, we exterminated the rat bastard in Tasha's living room not six hours ago, extra-crispy snakeskin all over the wall-to-wall carpet."

"The necklace should release."

"Right, bucko, I'm with you on the 'should' part, so how about we move on to the 'why not' part?" Felicity noticed that Tom had gone pale, so she eased the sharp knife from his grip and gently placed it near the tiny Airstream sink.

At some point during their many attempts to remove the necklace, the weak light of dawn had given way to the morning sun, so Felicity moved to the window to let it warm her face. She needed a moment to think. If something had gone wrong, so what? When in her life had something gone right? She could handle another speed bump. She simply needed perspective. They had missed a step somewhere in the process, obviously. It was just another puzzle, and she was excellent at puzzles.

Felicity glanced at the wood cabinet over the sink, still plastered with taped scraps of paper scrawled with her notes. The last time she found herself overwhelmed by a mystery, she'd pieced it together until it made sense.

She'd do it again.

Felicity turned to Tom, excited to share her newfound determination, but found him slumped on the edge of the daybed, staring out at the overgrown garden. Mojo and Alphonse gently rubbed against his ankles and calves, attempting to comfort him by performing figure eights between his splayed feet. Tom didn't look comforted.

It made perfect sense that Tom couldn't cope with an unexpected turn of events. He was the guy who believed that if you did things the way they'd always been done, you would succeed as you always had. So this had to be a shock.

"Hey, are you OK?"

His empty gaze tracked slowly to the *usekh* around her neck. "This has never happened before."

Oh, for fuck's sake. "Snap out of it!"

That seemed to penetrate his stupor. He was about to respond when there was a loud knock at the trailer door.

Felicity had been expecting one or all of the posse to show up, so she called out, "It's open!"

The aluminum door rattled and creaked, revealing a stranger on the stoop. He was a tall man dressed in an elegant charcoal suit. His dress shirt was lavender, opened at the neck, no tie. He was probably just a few years younger than Felicity and carried a sleek leather briefcase. As she took all this in, deciding he must be an insurance salesman, his face lit up with happiness. His wide smile sparkled. Deep dimples appeared at the corners of his mouth and his eyes danced.

"Felicity Cheshire!"

OK, so he was a strangely charismatic insurance salesmen. "Yes?"

He reached inside the trailer to offer his hand. "I'm Alexander Helios Rigiat, and I am thrilled to finally meet you."

"Oh!" She shook the offered hand, a bit confused. "I didn't expect you. Please, come in. I'm glad to meet you, too!"

He stepped inside. His voice was mellow and resonant. "I spoke to Tubastet at great length last night and this morning, of course, but I wanted to give him time to say his goodbyes and complete his journey back before I—"

"Hello, Alexander."

Their visitor whipped around at the sound of that voice. Tom pushed himself from the daybed and entered his line of sight. Alexander shook his head, baffled. "Oh!" Then his eyes landed on the necklace at Felicity's throat. "I arrived too soon?" He glanced from Felicity to Tom and back again, his smile wilting.

"I think you're here just in time," Felicity said. Alexander would know how to fix this. She was sure of it. "We seem to be experiencing some technical difficulties and could use your help."

He gestured to her neck. "The Acolyte still wears the necklace." His tone was matter-of-fact, as if pointing out a detail they had failed to grasp.

Felicity pulled him into the center aisle of the trailer and guided him to the booth. "Please take a seat and let me explain. The *usekh* won't come off. It's stuck."

"Excuse me?" Alexander appeared lost. "What do you mean *stuck*?"

"I mean, the necklace won't release. It's stuck on my neck.

Fused. Affixed. Bonded. Fastened. We used the ritual knife and performed the incantation several times, and it didn't work."

Alexander forced the return of his smile, dimples dazzling. "It always comes off, Felicity."

For a lawyer, he seemed rather dense. She studied him a moment, with his genuine warm expression, his long masculine face. He had thick, black hair that sprouted from a pronounced widow's peak, with a touch of silver sparkling at the temples. His dark and thick eyebrows shaded a set of kind, blue-gray peepers. For a moment, Felicity was certain she'd met him before. No. It was more than that. It felt as if he was an old friend, someone with whom she'd spent so much time that she could predict his mannerisms and moods. But that was ridiculous.

"The *usekh* always comes off," Alexander repeated.

Lord love a duck. Felicity was so damn tired. She was so tired that she was about to lose whatever remained of her patience. She placed her hands on the booth table and leaned in to Alexander. She spoke slowly. She enunciated. "Not. This. Time."

Alexander blinked like an owl adjusting to daylight. Then his head swiveled toward Tom, then back to Felicity, and he nodded.

Finally! He got it. Relief washed over her. Alexander would now explain where they had gone wrong, and he would tell them how to make it right.

"This has never happened before," he said.

"Oh, for shit's sake!" Felicity threw her hands up in disgust, jarring her bruised ribs. She grunted in pain, reminding herself that getting nearly crushed to death by a giant snake could leave a girl mighty sore. "We get it. What we need to know is why it isn't releasing *now*."

Alexander agreed. "Exactly. You are exactly right, Ms.

Cheshire. We need to figure that out."

"Just Felicity, please. No need for formality."

"Of course, *Felicity*." The corners of Alexander's eyes crinkled. "So, let's start with the basics. Apep is dead, correct?"

"Yeah." Tom sounded about as perky as Felicity felt. "The six steps were completed—maybe not in the usual way, but there's no doubt he's gone. We all saw it. Not a speck remained of the bastard."

"Except that one little piece of him, right?" Felicity bit her lip, agitated. "You said Apep stashes a snippet of flesh someplace so he can regenerate. Maybe that's why it won't release."

"We've been over this. That's not how it works." Tom was tired and testy. Weren't they all? He began pacing. While limping.

Alexander intervened. "I do like the way you think, Felicity, but no." His eyes tracked Tom, back and forth, back and forth. "In each cycle, Apep hides a bit of his body before the final battle, just like the kings of old saved their organs in canopic jars for the afterlife. But as Apep's flesh begins a new regeneration cycle, the *usekh* always releases, without fail. Apep's flesh is not the cause."

Felicity let out a long, drawn-out sigh. "Fine."

Tom continued his pacing and limping.

"You're not looking so good, my friend," Alexander said.

"Trust me, I've looked worse."

"I'm sure you have, Tubastet."

"OK, so it's not Apep. Great. Then what the hell *is* it?" Felicity tried to concentrate, but waves of exhaustion slammed into her. She could barely keep her eyes open.

Tom stopped. He turned to Alexander. "It has always released, but there were times when the process didn't go smoothly, right?"

"Well, there was all that drama with the nineteenth Acolyte."

"Was that the Beatriz of Cadiz incident?" Tom squinted in an effort to remember.

"No, Beatriz was the eighteenth. I'm talking about the nineteenth, Alia, in 1230, during the Nasrid dynasty in Morocco, remember? She's the one who refused to give back the necklace, and you had to chase her through the Marrakesh marketplace." Alexander laughed. "Did you really run into a scimitar, pointy-end first?"

Tom winced. "Thanks for reminding me. That one hurt like a son of a bitch. Still hurts on cold days."

Felicity was impressed with Alexander's grasp of detail. "You have all the Acolytes memorized?"

"Of course, Felicity. This is not just my job, it's my life's sacred duty. And one day it will be my heir's sacred duty as well."

"Any news on that front, my friend? Found a wife?" Tom seemed to have recovered a bit from his distress. He walked past Felicity to grab a bottle of beer out of the small refrigerator, then returned to his slouch on the daybed.

Felicity almost mentioned how it was a little early to start drinking, but after all they'd been through, the urge was understandable. She would have joined him if she thought she could stay awake long enough to finish a bottle.

"Don't ask, Tubastet. I haven't been on a date in four months. Nothing since the breakup with Lola."

Felicity checked out Alexander's ring finger. "Hold up. So there's no Mrs. Rigiat?"

"No."

She was truly surprised. By any standard, Alexander was quite the catch. "Are you sure?"

He laughed. "Yes. I would have remembered if I were married."

"You'd be surprised," she said.

Tom took a long swig of his beer. "Sixty-two years, 364 days, and counting, my friend."

"I'll get on that."

"Literally," Tom said.

Both men laughed, then Tom downed the entire beer, went to the fridge, and opened another.

Felicity leaned against the cabinets and crossed her arms, watching Tom annihilate his latest brew. She wondered if the gulping was more coping mechanism than refreshment.

"You know, gentlemen," she said, "if we don't do something about the necklace, Tom will still *be* here in sixty-three years!" Felicity pushed away from the cabinets and walked down the trailer aisle and back again, all the while tugging on the heavy gold collar. It felt too tight, exactly the way it had felt the first few days she'd worn it.

She was filthy and singed and bandaged and about to fall over from fatigue. She needed a shower. She needed some sleep. But before those things, she really needed to get the necklace off. "Can we focus here, please?"

"You're right." Alexander gave a quick nod. "Let's get down to business. Felicity, sometime soon, we will sit down together so I can conduct your debrief."

Felicity looked at him, stunned. She was going to be debriefed? She'd never been debriefed before!

"In the meantime, I will search for anything I'm not remembering, anything that might have been omitted, perhaps some forgotten caveat applicable to your situation. After all, your calling was not strictly regulation."

He looked to Tom. "I'm sure we'll get this all sorted out eventually."

"Not eventually, Alexander. Immediately." Tom didn't bother to hide his irritation. "I need to get out of here. Right now." He nervously picked at the beer bottle label, then adjusted the bandage on his upper arm, not making eye contact.

Alexander cocked his head. "I'm not sure I follow you, Tubastet. I agree we have a mystery to solve and we will solve it, but the immediate danger has passed. Felicity has successfully vanquished Apep, and in the short term, that's all that matters. Think of it this way—for the first time in history, you have a moment to relax, take a deep breath, and simply enjoy time on the earthly plane." Alexander peered at Tom. "Why the desperate rush?"

They all heard a rapid-fire series of knocks just before the Airstream door flew open. Tom jumped to his feet again. Ronnie said, "Hey Felicity, do you want some—?"

She went still. She stared at Tom in puzzled silence. "Oh," Ronnie said. "I'm sorry, guys. I assumed you'd be done by now."

"We *are* done." Felicity said.

"I'm trapped here." Tom's voice was no more than a whisper. He directed his tortured gaze to Ronnie. Their eyes locked, and all the color drained from Ronnie's face.

A half-eaten leftover eggroll fell from her fingers and landed with a *splat!* on the linoleum. The cats swarmed. Valkyrie and Melrose got to it first, and snarfed it down. One tiny crumb had shot off toward Felicity's shoe, and Valkyrie snagged it. Silence settled over the Airstream except for the slurping noises.

Alexander jumped from the booth and broke the tension by standing between Ronnie and Tom. He offered his hand. "You must be Ms. Veronica Davis. I'm Alexander Helios Rigiat. I've heard a lot about Felicity's Goddess Posse."

His genuine smile seemed to give Ronnie permission to relax a bit. She shook his hand. "Sure. Right. You're the dude who likes to throw his money around."

"Well, it's not really my money. It's Felicity's."

Felicity jolted to attention so abruptly she had to grip the sink to steady herself. "Huh? What money is mine? I have money?"

"Not all of it, of course. Most of the fund is safely and wisely invested so that it is available for the next Acolyte. But that's one of the reasons I came this morning, Felicity, to have you sign the paperwork for your lifelong pension."

Felicity's lips had gone numb. "My lifelong what-the-actual-*what*?"

Alexander frowned and turned to Tom. "Tubastet, didn't you explain this to Felicity?"

Tom shook his head. "No time."

"Wow." Felicity was now full-on cranky and she didn't give a damn because, come on now, you'd think Tom might have mentioned at least *something* about a lifelong pension to the woman *without a fucking dime to her name*!

Alexander seemed at a loss for words.

"You know why he didn't tell me?" Felicity laughed. "He didn't think any of us would come out of this alive. Right, Tom? There was no need to explain what would happen after the battle, because you thought there wouldn't *be* an after. Right, Tom?"

She wanted that shower now. She wanted to sleep for about three days. In fact, she had assumed that by this point in the morning she would be under the hot water, reveling in the feel of the spray caressing her completely bare neck and shoulders, a sensation she'd not had for weeks.

But her throat wasn't bare. And Tom hadn't had faith in her to do her job. He didn't even bother to deny it. He simply resumed staring at Ronnie.

"All right, in that case, I'm happy to explain everything to you,

Felicity, just as soon we get this necklace issue sorted out and Tubastet is on his way." Alexander nodded sagely, as if he already had it all figured out. "We'll work as fast as we can. I promise."

Ronnie backed out the doorway, avoiding Tom's gaze. "Bye again, cat. Have a nice eternal life. I gotta hit the road if I'm going to get to Viper Apps in time." She was halfway down the aluminum steps before Felicity could stop her.

"No, Ronnie. Wait!" Felicity poked her head out the door.

"Why?"

"I'm a little concerned about everyone's…well, *safety*, I guess. The necklace isn't releasing, and I've got a really bad feeling."

Ronnie squinted at her. "What do you mean?"

"I worry there's still some kind of danger out there."

"Apep's dead. He was the danger and now he's no more."

"I know. I know. Just bear with me, OK? I'm nervous. And I don't think it's smart for you to go anywhere alone right now. It's too risky. Tom, will you…?"

"I'll go." Alexander had stepped up behind Felicity. "I'm quite familiar with computers, and I'm fully briefed on the situation."

Ronnie laughed. "I can take care of myself, thanks. I should get a move on." She was already at her Jeep when Alexander made a break for the door. Tom grabbed his arm.

"Watch out for her," Tom whispered. "Please." The desperation in his voice was painful to hear.

Alexander paused a moment, then nodded, and was gone.

Ugh. He wished to hell Felicity would stop staring at him.

He returned to the daybed, doing his best to avoid her laser-beam gawking. She was smart. Her intellect had saved the world. Surely, she'd already put the pieces together and saw he had feelings for Ronnie. Hell, she probably understood the situation better than he did. He just kept stepping in it, every time he turned around. He was fucking everything up. The *usekh* had failed to release. He'd failed to return to the Realm of the Gods. He was such a loser that Ronnie couldn't even look at him.

He had to go. *Now.* There was no other option.

Because of that kiss.

He turned his back to Felicity and stared out the window. It had been a goodbye kiss to end all goodbye kisses, given by a woman to a man who was already gone, given because fate was cruel and the rules could not be altered and because Ronnie was sure she would never, ever, see him again.

That was the only reason she had kissed him that way. He had to remember that. Under any other circumstances, a kiss that pure, that vulnerable, would have marked the beginning of something, not the end. A kiss that intense could change fate.

Oh, shit.

"You hanging in there, Tom?"

Double shit. He'd forgotten Felicity was still watching him.

"Fine." He was not fine. For the first time since he'd accepted Bastet's call to service, he realized the situation was not just out of his control but beyond his comprehension. Why had Ronnie kissed him like that? Why wouldn't the necklace release? Why did he think, deep down, that this was somehow all his fault? Because he truly did. He was certain he was being punished. What had he done? Why had the Goddess forsaken him?

He couldn't catch his breath. He reached up and yanked the gauze out of his nostrils, deciding he had to get out of there. The trailer walls were closing in on him.

"I'm taking a walk."

Felicity snorted. "Oh, yeah? Fabulous! I'm taking a shower! What do you think about that?"

He slammed the door on his way out.

Felicity grumbled to herself as she shuffled to the bathroom. She was angry at the world. She was angry at Tom and his angst-ridden, cranky-pants, truth-withholding behavior. What was the deal with him? Why hadn't he trusted her enough to tell her about the pension? He was being a complete jerk, and if anyone in this scenario deserved to be cranky, it was Felicity! She was worn down to the bone. She was smelly and singed. She was stuck in the *usekh*.

And speaking of the pension…how much was it? Would it be enough that she could get her own place someday? Felicity stopped herself from following that line of possibility. She didn't want to picture a fanciful dream only to be disappointed. She'd had enough of that to last a lifetime.

She opened the top two buttons of her shirt and had just reached for the shower curtain when Tasha and Bethany burst into the trailer.

"Why is Tom still here?" Tasha called out. "We just saw him stomp off down the lane like somebody stole his favorite toy."

Felicity stepped into the aisle.

"Hi, Felicity. Is this a bad time?" Bethany was always so polite.

Tasha slid into the booth and pointed. "You're still wearing the necklace. Why are you still wearing the necklace, Lissie?"

"It won't come off." How many times had she repeated that phrase, aloud or in her head, in the last hour?

"How come?" Bethany slid in beside Tasha.

"We don't have the foggiest idea." Felicity walked past them and collapsed on the daybed. Immediately, she realized she might never be capable of movement again. Gumbo took advantage of her stationary position and plopped down on top of her, stuck his huge tabby head under her chin, and purred. Felicity didn't even have the energy to give the poor guy a reassuring pat.

Tasha swung around in the booth. "Can't Tom just go back and check with Bastet or something?"

Felicity let her eyes close and sighed. "No, Tash. Turns out he needs to be wearing the necklace to get into the Realm of the Gods. And that's not happening if it's stuck on me."

"Well, damn. I didn't know that."

"Neither did I."

She laughed. "What—he just forgot to tell you?"

"Seems he forgot a few things. Now, if you ladies don't mind, I'm going to scrape myself off this cushion and get in the shower. You guys need to get some sleep too. Especially you, Bethany, for the baby." Felicity tried to leverage herself into a sitting position. She didn't quite make it. She decided to try again.

And that was when she heard it. The distinctive cry of a cat in crisis.

Oh, hell's bells! What now?

The cry came again, more urgent this time. Felicity hoisted herself up, rebuttoned her blouse, and staggered out the door. She stumbled a bit on the rickety steps, and then saw the little mama cat wobble toward her, the animal's eyes widened in pain.

"Oh, no." Felicity froze. "Not this. Anything but this."

CHAPTER TWO

Rrrraooooowwww-mmmaaowwwrrrr!

The scraggly calico paced between the Airstream and the garden. She panted through her mouth, fangs and tongue exposed. Her eyes were wild with fear and torment and Felicity couldn't help but notice that her heavy belly was lopsided. The cat released another desperate wail, which carried through the canopy of trees.

She heard Bethany's soft question behind her. "Siri, how do you deliver kittens?"

From Bethany's phone speaker came a cheerfully disembodied reply: "That is an interesting question!"

"Shut up, Siri." Felicity scanned the property. Yeah, Tom was long gone. And so was Ronnie.

Rrrraoww-maaowwwrrrr... The little mama's plaintive yowl tapered off at the end. She stopped pacing and hung her head. She took shallow breaths, quick and sharp.

Felicity slammed her eyes shut and stood rigid as the panic

twisted in her belly. No. She couldn't do this. She refused. Absolutely not.

And then what? The mother cat and her kittens would die.

"Dammit!" Felicity rolled up the sleeves of her shirt, cursing further under her breath, wondering when the universe might consider giving her a small fucking break!

Why didn't this mama cat show up a half hour ago, when Ronnie, the actual vet tech, was still on the premises? Or even ten minutes ago, when Tom was here. At least Tom spoke fluent cat!

"Why am I being asked to do more lifesaving?" Felicity said aloud. "I haven't even napped or showered since my last round, when I had to save the whole fucking world!"

Tasha patted her shoulder.

And why—Felicity raised her eyes to the morning sky as she continued her pity party in silence—this? It was true that the last couple of weeks had shown her that she was capable of far more than she realized. Slaying an ancient demon? Heh, why not? Fifteen sit ups? Bring it on. But even the Acolyte of the Goddess Bastet had limits, and for Felicity, she drew the line at the birth process. And for good reason.

She'd been ten when it happened. It was supposed to have been a routine fourth-grade science field trip, where they'd watch the cows getting milked and then learn how to churn butter like in the covered wagon days. But no. They arrived just as a cow unexpectedly went into labor with a calf. The kids and chaperones gathered around to watch the messy and loud ordeal, lots of "Ooooh, gross!" and "What's that?" coming from Felicity's classmates.

The poor creature groaned in agony as the vet shoved his arm into her body past the elbow, only to dislodge a stillborn. Felicity had stared in shock at the slimy blob in the straw, its eyes fused shut and its gangly legs unmoving.

She'd burst into sobs and tore off, running to the waiting school bus in a blind panic. Half the traumatized class was at her heels. It was a long ride back to the classroom that day, silent but for the crying and sniffling, and more than a few parents conveyed their displeasure to school officials. Many years later, when Felicity was in high school, her mother shared that Principal Olssen returned her phone call that same evening and gave her this sage advice: "Birth is ugly and messy and dangerous, and karma is a cold-hearted bitch. The sooner your daughter understands this, the better off she'll be."

Felicity's mother had added, "I always suspected that man smoked reefer, to tell you the truth."

In Felicity's married years, when she still hoped to have a child with Rich, she made her maternity ward requirements excruciatingly clear. She wanted fresh flowers and dim lighting. She wanted Enya's greatest hits playing in the background. And after those things were in place, she wanted a spinal block, a blindfold, earplugs, and a privacy sheet, with a healthy baby plopped into her arms when it was over.

In other words, Felicity was willing to go to extreme lengths to avoid the ugly, messy, and dangerous karma of which Mr. Olssen spoke. And, oh boy, that avoidance strategy had worked like a charm! After a decade of trying and a decade of fertility treatments, she never got pregnant and never had to face the ugly, messy danger she feared.

"This is one of the cats that showed up here for the feral feline convention a couple weeks back, isn't it?"

Tasha's question tore Felicity from her thoughts. "Yes."

"I bet she was here to scout you out, knowing she'd return when her time came."

Felicity couldn't believe what she was hearing. It was bizarre enough that Tasha remembered one of the dozens of cats who'd wandered onto the property that day to pay their respects to Tom. But it was astounding that Tasha would ponder what an individual cat might be thinking.

Just then, the calico lowered herself to the grass and rolled onto her side. She let go with a wretched howl and struggled to hold her head upright. Her tail slashed through the air.

"I think something's wrong with her," Bethany said.

Felicity took in a big gulp of air. Before she could second-guess her stupid decision to forge ahead, she barked out marching orders.

"Bethany, grab a couple of those big, sturdy cardboard boxes from the shed. You know, the ones from Kitty-Korner.com. And some string."

"On it!" She marched off, her perky blond ponytail swooshing across her shoulders as she made a beeline toward Tasha's garden shed.

"Tasha, gather whatever old towels and fleece blankets you have in the house, and I hate to ask this, but if you've got stainless steel tongs, you know, for turning hot dogs on the grill, please bring those."

"Ew. But OK." Tasha headed across the yard to her home, what was left of it anyway, after last night's good versus evil smackdown. At least the damage was mostly contained in the front rooms and the porch. The back bedrooms and the kitchen were fine. Sort of.

"Be right back," Felicity told the cat. She ran inside the trailer. She let hot water pour from the faucet into the dishpan while she grabbed her first aid kit. There was no one else to help. She had to do this. She had to at least try. But this was going to be a catastrophe. She just fucking knew it.

Back outside, Felicity lowered her knees to the grass and reached out to stroke the matted fur that covered the kitty's distended belly. The cat flinched at her touch. "It's OK, little mama. I'll do my best to help. Please try to relax."

Crazed, yellow eyes scanned Felicity's face. She watched the cat's belly roll and shift, an indication of the life inside desperate to survive. The cat panted through her mouth.

"Here's the boxes!" Bethany rushed toward her, cardboard banging against her knees. "Will baling twine work? It's all I could find."

Tasha returned, peering around a tall stack of old towels, blankets, and bedspreads as she navigated the yard. She dumped the pile on the ground. "And..." she said, reaching around to the back pocket of her jeans. "One pair of stainless-steel tongs, as ordered." She handed them to Felicity. "No need to give them back."

Rrrrraaaawwwwrrrr!

"Oh, my God. Poor kitty!" Bethany rested a hand on her own pooched belly, her pretty face twisted in worry.

"Hey, Tasha?" Felicity looked to her best friend. "Maybe now would be a good time for the two of you to get some rest. Like, right now. I'm going to need to concentrate."

"Absolutely." Tasha supported Bethany by the elbow and turned her toward the cottage. "Let's talk about backsplash tile until we fall asleep!"

That was a relief. First-time mother Bethany had no business watching this debacle unfold.

Felicity raised her face to the sun. Other people might take this opportunity to pray. Unfortunately, she'd never been big on prayer, and her concept of a supreme being had always been murky. As a kid, she'd envisioned the standard, white-bearded Santa Claus in the clouds. In adulthood, especially after a glass or two of wine, she would imagine God as an infinite collage of nebulae swirling into the vastness of all that is, a singularity of conscious energy.

But mostly she just drew a blank.

That lack of clarity was likely why her prayers never got answered. Not during the years of failed fertility treatments. Not when Rich cheated on her. Not when she lost her teaching job, when she got divorced and got cancer, or when she became homeless.

Felicity stilled, aware of a twinge low in her belly. It was just a spark of annoyance at first, but as soon as she acknowledged it and gave it a name, it began to grow and expand. Within seconds, the anger had crept up into her chest and burned her throat, exploding into a rage so white-hot it shocked her. Her temples throbbed with it. Her hands shook with it. Her mind melted with it.

Because she understood now. After all she'd experienced in the last two weeks, it was clear to Felicity that a deity really could hear her, even guide her. Bastet was goddess of the hearth, motherhood, family, and childbirth. The keeper of female secrets. She was the protector from illness and patron of music, dance, and sex. Bastet was mistress of the sun and moon, and, of course, the goddess of cats. And, as long as the necklace remained around Felicity's neck, she remained Bastet's Acolyte, the Goddess's earthly champion.

And this is how a champion gets rewarded? She'd hate to see what kind of hell awaited a coward!

The mama cat's breath got sharper, faster. *Mrrrp?* she asked, looking to Felicity.

And that's when it struck her, struck her like a tractor trailer hauling six tons of boiling-oil fury, jackknifing on a patch of black ice.

That bitch has abandoned me.

Here Felicity was, yet again, given no choice, forced to pull off the impossible, deal with a situation for which she was spectacularly unqualified. And why? Because there was no one else to do it! Yesterday, it was rescue humankind from annihilation. Today, it was usher kittens into the world.

And she was sick to death of it.

Her fingers trembled against the mama cat. "I get it," Felicity said through clenched teeth. "You're probably busy up there in Goddessville. Got other shit to do. Fine. But this is not right. It's not fair that you keep throwing one emergency after another at me! Why would you do that? Just to watch me suffer?"

Felicity paused, thinking she might be onto something. "Am I entertainment for you? Is that what this whole protracted shitshow has been—just a way to break up the monotony of the same ol' 'Acolyte gives Apep a beatdown' routine?"

Felicity went rigid. She felt a tear slither down her cheek. "How dare you?" she hissed. "A lot of people have been hurt trying to carry out your plan. Lives have been upended. And you let Boudica die! You took…" Felicity choked on a sob. "You took my special girl from me! You took her, and I hate you for it. Fuck off!"

Felicity dropped her head and cried, just let the sadness roll over her. Her shoulders heaved. Her nose ran and her stomach clenched and strings of spittle dripped from her open mouth onto the blades of grass. But so what? No one was there to judge her or comfort her or, God forbid, help her. She was alone.

She was always alone. Perhaps now more now than ever in her life.

Beneath her palms the kittens, pitched and kicked in the womb. It took a moment for Felicity to realize she'd been crying like an imbecile while her hands remained on the mama cat. How much time had she wasted on her own self-pity?

Mmmrrraooow…

"I know. Hold on. Sorry." Felicity reached for a corner of one of Tasha's old bedspreads and wiped her eyes and blew her nose. The thing was going to get trashed anyway. She took a deep breath and steeled herself. Her job was to get everyone through this alive, the babies and their mother. How she'd accomplish that, she had no idea.

"Here we go," Felicity said.

The first kitten was positioned head first but wasn't progressing. The mother cat would push, then stop. Push, then stop again. Felicity had no idea if this was normal or a sure sign that the mother cat was about to croak. Was she supposed to reach in there and pull? Should she use the tongs? The string? She had absolutely no idea what to do.

She touched the miniature kitten head, and it seemed to respond to the contact. The mama pushed again, and Felicity found herself guiding the tiny thing from the mama's body. When it shot out into Felicity's hands, she laughed in surprise and relief. She angled the matted and sopping wet creature's head down, then used a finger to remove goop and fluid from its little mouth and nose. But it wasn't breathing.

Blind. Panic. She needed to run back to the bus.

There was no bus.

But if there was anything she understood in this world, it was cats. She'd read everything there was to read about cats and experienced more feline health crises than she cared to recall. Come on now, Felicity. Just then, she remembered hearing something about how kittens often needed a kickstart, some kind of external stimulation to encourage breathing.

Wrapping the little one in a towel, she stroked its abdomen and chest, waiting one second, then another, changing the pressure and position of her fingertips. Finally, it wriggled and took its first breath, releasing a puny squeak.

"Yes!" Felicity used the first aid scissors to cut the umbilical cord, then used her fingers to pinch it closed near the kitten's body.

She wished she had more time to spend with this one, but the next one was on its way. Felicity gave kitten number one a quick rub with the towel, wrapped it snugly, and placed the bundle in the sunshine because she'd just remembered another tidbit: newborns can't regulate their own body temperatures. They can't shiver. They need direct warmth.

The second kitten was not as easy. Its head eased out from mama, but Felicity saw that the cord was wrapped around its pinky-thin neck. Terror shot through her. She began to hyperventilate and her fingers tingled. What was she supposed to do? Tug on the cord? Cut it? Slide a finger between it and the kitty's throat? Or just pull the baby out and hope for the best?

"You've got this, Felicity," she whispered to herself. "Stay steady. Don't freak out. Focus."

She paused a moment, took a deep and slow breath, and placed her hands beneath the kitten's motionless head. "Give me a little push, mama," she told the calico. "Just a little. You can do it. I know you're tired—hell, we're all tired—but it's important that you push this one, right now."

To her amazement, the mama cat complied, bearing down with enough force that the kitten's head pushed through. And that appeared to be the end of the maternal assistance. There was no more pushing. No more progress. And everything below the kitten's neck appeared to be stuck.

Not knowing what else to do, Felicity began moving the kitten in slow, alternating rocking motions, back and forth, at a slight downward angle, freeing one shoulder a bit and then the other a bit more, until suddenly the kitten squirted free.

She caught the baby with her hands, then moved the new life to one palm. With the utmost care and precision, she unwrapped the cord from the kitten's neck. Once that was dispatched, she repeated the same routine as with the first kitten. Felicity angled the tiny creature downward, cleared out its nose and mouth, and cut and pinched the cord. She immediately began stroking the kitten's belly.

Nothing.

Felicity blinked back tears. "You've got to breathe. Come on. You're here. You worked so hard to be born. Now's not the time to give up. Please, please just…"

It mewled! But there was no time to celebrate. She turned her head to a horrifying sight— protruding from the mother cat was one miniature calico foot and the white tip of a tail.

"Oh, hell no."

Felicity swaddled kitten number two in a towel and placed it next to its sibling in the sunshine, laughing out loud at her own ridiculousness. Hot dog tongs? Seriously? String? What was her plan— an abstract macrame project? Good lord.

Well, now she knew better. The next time, she'd know that helping a distressed mama cat give birth didn't require kitchen accessories. It required nerves of steel, steady hands, and a good, cleansing cry.

Not that there would be a next time. Ever.

The mother cat's eyes rolled back in her head, and her body went limp in the grass. Felicity knew she had to get this kitten out, and fast.

With the slightest touch of her fingertips, she massaged and coaxed and prodded. Once she could reach above one of the kitten's hocks, she tried what had worked with the last one—a gentle rocking back and forth. It was no help. Felicity then tried to rotate the kitten's orientation just a few degrees, followed by more back-and-forth easing, then another small rotation and more careful rocking. A second leg arrived, followed by a little bottom, and then the rest of the kitten plopped from its mother, horrifyingly still.

All she saw was the dead calf in the straw.

"Not on my watch." She got down to business, removing fluid and mucus from the kitten's unresponsive mouth and nose, sweeping her pinky along the baby's soft gums. The flesh was still warm. This little one would live. This little one must live.

Cradling the newest kitten in one hand, she tucked the towel-covered siblings inside one of Tasha's old fleece blankets and then raced up the Airstream steps and swung open the door. It took a moment for her eyesight to adjust from direct sunlight to mid-century paneling. "Hang in there. Don't die on me," she whispered to the tiny life in her palm. Felicity flung open cabinets and yanked out drawers. "I know I saw one the other day. I thought it was here in the trailer. Was it? Or did I just imagine...*yessss!*" Felicity ran back outside and fell to her knees in the grass. With the utmost care, she cradled the slippery kitten, its tiny spine tucked into her palm, and slipped the white and orange striped plastic straw between the kitten's unmoving lips. The straw was dented, a remnant from a long-ago fast-food order, but it would have to do.

Felicity slipped the opposite tip into her own lips, knowing this maneuver would be all about restraint. The lungs of this creature had to be the size of a fingernail. Any amount of air could be too much. Felicity had no idea what she was doing or even where this lamebrain idea had come from. But her only choice was to go with it, since she was fresh out of better ideas.

She produced a puff of air as soft as the breeze from a hummingbird's wings. It traveled down the hollow straw and into the kitten's mouth. Again. Each puff provided an infinitesimal dose of air.

"Come on, little girl," she said. "You can do it."

Nothing.

No. Felicity would not let this baby die.

Another puff.

"Breathe."

Puff.

"Breathe."

The *usekh* around Felicity's neck warmed her breastbone. A rush of calm certainty followed, settling into her bones.

That's when a pleasant, steady breeze rose up from the tree line and swept down upon the little group in the grass. Felicity felt the wind lift her singed hair and caress the raw skin at the back of her neck. It moved across her face like a kiss, tingling her skin. It wasn't an unpleasant sensation, but it was surprising. And it grew stronger, moving across her shoulders and over her breasts, down her solar plexus and abdomen, then racing down her legs until the very tips of her toes tingled.

She shook off the strange sensation and focused, breathing into the straw. She witnessed the kitten's itty-bitty mouth open wide to accept the gift of breath, of life.

The baby inhaled and exhaled. She squirmed and squeaked, and Felicity watched as one of her tears plopped right between the tiny creature's clenched eyelids.

She laughed as she carefully rubbed the little girl dry with a towel. And this was most definitely a she. Even though it was too early to be sure of these things, Felicity knew it.

She placed the kitty with her siblings under the towels and blankets and steeled herself to take care of the mama cat. She didn't know what she'd find but told herself that, should a worst case scenario unfold, she could handle it. She'd do a round of three a.m. eye-dropper feedings. She'd survive the worry while managing hot water bottles, measuring weight gain in grams, and counting the days until the kittens reached that do-or-die finish line at four weeks. If an orphaned kitten made it to four weeks, its odds of survival skyrocketed.

But oh, how she hoped the mama would be fine and all that wouldn't be necessary.

Felicity turned to the calico and gasped. She lay on her side, alive and well, cleaning herself and purring. The grass was a slimy mess of blood and mucus and fluid, but the mama was all right. She was absolutely fine!

"I clearly missed something."

She shaded her eyes to watch Tom power walk through the front gate, slipping his mobile phone into the back pocket of his jeans.

"Everything OK here?"

"Perfect timing," Felicity groaned, pushing to a stand, noticing that she'd fared no better than the grass. Her clothes and shoes were covered in goo.

She recruited Tom to clean up the yard and help her make a nest for the mama and her already latched-on babies, using one of the long and shallow Kitty-Korner delivery boxes lined with fluffy bedspreads and towels. They placed the new family in the shade of the Airstream, warm and protected but not in direct sunlight. Felicity brought food and water for the mother, and Tom placed a litter box nearby.

Then they stood together in silence, watching in awe.

"You are a wonder, Felicity."

"As in, 'I wonder how the hell she managed that?'"

"No." When Tom turned to look down at her, she saw he was just as exhausted as she was. He managed a gentle smile. "As in, you are remarkable, extraordinary, and wonderful."

She shrugged off the compliment. If she said anything more,

she'd likely blurt out that she'd just told the Ever-Living Goddess Bastet to go fuck herself. And that she'd actually planned to use barbecue tongs to deliver kittens. And now that the adrenaline had subsided and the exhaustion was creeping back, she could no longer ignore the heavy press of dread she felt.

The necklace wouldn't release. That wasn't a clerical error or a simple oversight. Not a sign of a minor disturbance in the order of things that could be easily restored. No. Felicity felt the weight of the worry now. She pictured it in her mind, black and thick, oozing up through cracks in the earth and swirling into the air. She felt it circling like Wepwawet's drooling jackals, waiting for the perfect instant to pounce.

The necklace wouldn't release because the danger intensified with each passing second.

Which was not wonderful. Not wonderful at all.

CHAPTER THREE

Felicity didn't mind that Tom took the first shower. She wanted to stand there a bit longer, just observing the kitties and their mama. Also, she wasn't sure she had the energy to make it up the stairs and into the trailer. The calico raised her head and made eye contact with Felicity, and they shared a moment of complete understanding, both exhausted but satisfied.

She wondered if Tasha had been right. Had the cat chosen Felicity to help her? Did cats plan ahead for major life events? Regardless, Felicity was glad she was here when help was needed.

She heard soft footsteps behind her and turned, expecting to see Tasha. But it was Bethany, walking with her head tilted to the side and her hands behind her back, tiptoeing as if she were afraid to interrupt.

"It's OK. Come see."

Bethany's eyes widened and she swallowed. "Are they…?"

"Everyone's fine."

Bethany exhaled in relief and sidled up next to Felicity, then stared in wonder at the mother calico and her kittens. She pressed her hands against her chest. "They're so tiny!"

"Yeah."

She knelt down to get a closer look, and after a moment came back to stand next to Felicity. "It's so weird, you know? A pregnant cat shows up and a little while later, *boom*, she's a mother, and that's what she'll be forever. She'll never *not* be a mother again."

Felicity knew Bethany's double-negative musing was more about herself than the stray cat, but she nodded. "That's what they say. Not that I would know."

Bethany fidgeted with the hem of her T-shirt and looked to Felicity, her eyes troubled. "Um, can I say something?"

"Sure."

"Well, it's just that, uh, I know how hard you tried to have children and here I am, preggers by mistake with your ex-husband, and, well, yeah, that's got to suck eggs." The timbre of her voice rose. "And you've been so kind to me, when you had no reason to be! So I just want to tell you that if my being here has caused you any pain, *I am so sorry!*"

The naked earnestness in that statement shocked Felicity, and she couldn't manage a response at first. What could she possibly say? *Hey, no biggie?* She took a moment to gather her thoughts. "Thank you, Bethany, but that part of my life seems so far away now. Your being here doesn't hurt me. In fact, I like you, and I'm glad we could be here for you."

Bethany's face lit up. "Really?" She moved in to hug Felicity, thought better of it, and laughed. "Maybe later."

Felicity looked at herself. She needed more than a quick cleanup. She needed a sand blasting.

"Think of it this way—you're a mother to cats, Felicity! A cat mom!" Bethany's smile was as broad as it was sincere. "I mean, you go out and rescue them and feed them and care for them and make sure they have a super nice life, right?"

Felicity chuckled. "I guess I do."

"And, I mean, look what you did!" Bethany gestured to the little family under the Airstream. "You literally brought these babies into the world, which is proof that you don't have to, you know, push something out of your v-jay-jay to be a mom."

She snorted at that, making a mental note to be sure to ask Tasha if she'd ever heard that expression, since it was funny as hell. Felicity touched the *usekh* around her throat and smiled to herself. Maybe Bethany was right. Maybe part of her strength was her maternal streak. In fact, if she hadn't been a rescuer—a *nurturer*—she never would have found Tom by the side of the road, brought him home, and saved the world.

"I'm making a bowl of corn flakes. Want one?"

"No, thanks."

Bethany was already marching back to the cottage. "I'm starving! I'm always starving!"

Felicity heard the crunch of gravel and turned to see a vaguely familiar, beat-up pickup roll through the gate. Her stomach lurched, at first thinking it was Hair Gel Jim coming back to make more trouble. But it couldn't be. And suddenly, Felicity knew why the truck seemed familiar.

She'd gotten a ride home in that truck one early morning a couple of weeks back. The truck belonged to Cass.

Felicity glanced down at herself. Her pants and shirt were filthy and ripped. There would be no saving these shoes. They were headed straight into the garbage can. She was smeared from head to toe with bloody afterbirth and sported a sexy new bald spot on the back of her head. This was not exactly the ensemble she'd imagined for a second date with her handsome dance floor partner.

Cass unfolded his long and lean frame from the driver's side of the truck, settling a rancher's hat square on his head. He took several lengthy strides in her direction. Then he stopped, slid his hands into the front pockets of his jeans, and frowned. His scowl deepened as he took a look around the property. Felicity imagined it would appear dire through his eyes.

Tasha's front picture window was boarded up with plywood and glass sparkled everywhere in the grass and weeds out front. Black scorch marks shot up the exterior siding and doorframe, licking at the front porch ceiling. The front door hung from its hinges and what was once lush shrubbery had been left charred and crunchy.

The extent of the exterior damage surprised Felicity. She'd not had a moment to take it all in. The flames must have shot everywhere when Apep got himself flambéed.

"Hi, Cass." She tried to smile. She limped toward him.

"I'm taking you to the hospital."

"I'm fine. We got home from the ER a few hours ago, in fact."

He examined Felicity's torn and stained clothing and the network of cuts, bruises, and blisters all over her body. His face contorted in equal parts confusion and worry, and one of his eyebrows shot high on his forehead. "I guess I've come at a bad time."

"Whatever gave you that impression?"

He blinked, then busted out in laughter. Felicity joined in. When their laughter subsided, Cass asked, serious now, "What the hell happened here, Felicity?"

"A fire… maybe?"

Cass narrowed one eye. "Maybe? You don't know?"

"It happened fast. It's all kind of a blur, really. The important thing is everyone is OK. And I just helped deliver kittens, see?" She gestured to the nest beneath the Airstream.

"Was that before or after the bomb...?"

Cass stopped midsentence. His face went stony and expressionless. Without turning around, Felicity knew that Tom must have emerged from the trailer.

She dared take a peek. Yep. It was bad. Tom wore nothing but a too-small towel caught low on his hips. His battle-scarred body glistened from the shower, and he stood rigid on the stoop. The aluminum door slammed shut behind him, like an exclamation point.

"Fabulous," Felicity mumbled.

Tom knew all about Felicity's wild, post-honkytonk, amazing one-night stand with Cassius Schwindorf, but Cass knew nothing about Tom. And what could Felicity say to explain away this situation?

"Cass, I'd like you to meet Tubastet-af-Ankh, an ancient shapeshifting warrior priest of the Egyptian Goddess of Bastet, though we just call him Tom. I found him injured on the side of the road when he was in cat form, but then he turned into a man, slapped this gold collar on me, and demanded that I rescue the planet from evil. Weird, right?"

Felicity doubted that would help matters, so she said, "Cass, this is Tom. Tom, Cass."

Tom lifted his chin in greeting, but didn't smile, "Ah, Cassius, the Roman dairy farmer! I've heard good things about you."

Felicity closed her eyes for a moment, fighting back anger. Why did Tom have to be so snooty? She was going to kick his ass, but good, as soon as she could move her legs again.

"Rrrrriiiight." Cass looked from Tom to Felicity and back again. "I should go. It was a bad idea to just show up without..."

"Let me walk you to your truck."

They stopped at the driver's side door. When Cass reached for the handle, Felicity had a flashback of those broad, rough hands all over her body. Those hands had held onto her when they tumbled, laughing, from the bed to the floor. They'd lifted her like she weighed next to nothing. They'd clutched her as they'd rolled across the bed, hot mouths on hot flesh. Those hands had been impossibly gentle one moment and aggressive and greedy the next. They'd laid claim to her for hours on end, until the sun rose.

"Wheeeew." Felicity undid the second button of her shirt again.

"Hey, at least your fancy necklace survived."

She glanced down. "Yeah. Turns out this sucker's indestructible. Can't get rid of it."

"Well." He looked defeated. "I guess I'll catch you later, then."

"Cass, wait."

She touched his forearm. Cass flinched. His eyes shot wide and he stared at her fingertips on his skin as if he'd been shocked, then looked at Felicity in surprise.

"What is it? Everything OK?"

"Yeah, but..." He shook his head. "Never mind. That was weird. What were you saying?"

Felicity removed her hand from his forearm. "I was saying that you're a wonderful man. I really like you, and I don't want you to misunderstand the situation."

He chuckled.

"I'm serious. Tom isn't my, you know, *lover*, or anything. He's living here temporarily, but it's not a... you know, a sexual situation. He's like a nephew to me."

"Uh huh." Cass narrowed his eyes at Tom, who remained posed like a Greek statue on the top of the steps. "Why did he call me a Roman?"

"Ah. Well, he's a history buff, especially ancient Egypt and Rome, and Cassius is an ancient Roman name."

"Sure." He blinked, skeptical.

"Cass." She hoped she'd find the right words. "My night with you was incredibly special. It was the best thing that's happened to me in years. It was the only thing that's happened!"

He couldn't suppress his grin, then sighed. "Go on. I know there's a *but* coming."

She nodded. "My life is pretty strange right now, and I need to sort out some things."

He used a forefinger to tip back the brim of his straw rancher's hat, opening his weatherworn face to the midmorning light. He was so handsome that her breath caught. How had she forgotten how attractive Cass was?

True, she'd had a lot on her mind, what with snatching humanity from extermination and all, but still.

"I don't want to add to the strangeness, Felicity."

"I appreciate that." Her stomach fell. She really didn't have time or space for him anywhere in her life, but it would have been nice if the man had put up more of a fight.

"So I'll pick someplace nice and normal when I take you out to dinner."

Yes! She couldn't help but smile. "I'll hold you to that. But, can you wait a couple weeks?"

"I can."

Cass leaned in to kiss her cheek, but stopped, scanning her face, which had to resemble a Jackson Pollock canvas of injury and afterbirth. "There aren't a whole lot of options for kissing you at the moment," he said.

"Yeah. How about here?" Felicity tapped a fingertip to the edge of her bottom lip, and Cass leaned in to deposit a quick kiss precisely where she'd indicated.

"Dinner. Two weeks." He got into his truck, turned the key, and looked back at her, a quizzical expression in his eyes. He was about to say something, but stopped himself. He hit the gas and was gone.

Felicity turned to find Tom slouched on the aluminum steps. She squeezed by him without making eye contact.

"I'm sorry about that, Felicity."

"Yeah, well, your outfit didn't help."

"I said I was…"

"Sorry. Got it." Felicity slammed the Airstream door. She headed straight for the trailer's tiny shower. She shoved her shoes straight into the trash bin and stripped off her filthy clothes—which smelled like a mix of bonfire and biohazard—and left them in a stinky pile in the narrow aisle.

Despite the fact that the trailer's shower was about as roomy as a pencil box, the warm water felt glorious cascading down her battered body. The blistered areas stung a bit and the shampoo made her scalp throb, but she was grateful for the water heater and Tasha's bountiful well and a place she could call home. She decided to focus on being grateful and allowed herself to enjoy the sensation of wiping the slate clean, getting a fresh start. A rebirth.

Birth—the kittens.

Death—her dear, sweet Boudica, in the end the bravest cat that ever was, dying so that all of them could live.

She found herself teetering on the edge of another sob. So much loss. So much stress. So little sleep. It was obvious that the exhaustion—emotional, physical, mental, spiritual—had her careening toward a meltdown. She felt jittery, shaky, and while still under the water spray, Felicity clutched her arms around herself and squeezed, as if she could prevent her broken pieces from flying off into space.

What was next? And why couldn't she shake that feeling that there was more lurking around the corner—more chaos, danger, and death? That was a rhetorical question, of course. She knew the answer.

Along with her pain-free knees and her quicker reaction time, Felicity's tenure as Acolyte had given her an unshakeable sixth sense, an intuition lodged in her bone and muscle and sinew, a knowing of things to come. And ever since the *usekh* refused to budge from her neck, she'd felt trepidation, a premonition that something was rising. Something extremely bad.

Maybe it had something to do with what Ronnie was doing. Maybe when the dangerous computer virus was destroyed, this feeling would go away. And then the necklace would release! That had to be it. For the first time all morning, Felicity felt hopeful.

She turned off the water, wrapped herself in a towel, and barely made it to her small bed before she fell deep into the empty void of the exhausted.

Ronnie and Alexander made their way down the alley behind the Viper Apps building in the Hawthorne District of Portland. The counterfeit key card slid into the reader, and with a satisfying click and a low buzz the heavy steel door opened. Ronnie allowed herself a small surge of pride that her plan had succeeded, even if this wasn't the original plan. She wasn't going in with the Goddess Posse to face the ultimate battle, as anticipated. She was going in the morning after to tie up any loose strings. Apep might be dead, but part of his plan still lived on.

It was early enough that Ronnie thought she could get everything destroyed before any of the staff showed up for work. But she had a backup plan just in case. She'd learned it was always wise to have a Plan B.

"I'll start upstairs in the big snake's nest. You start down here." She pointed Alexander to a set of desks. "First thing is to see whether any computers are hardwired into the Ethernet or connected to a modem in any way. You know how to do that?"

"Indeed, I do, Ms. Davis."

"I want these babies offline and totally isolated before I start pulling hard drives."

A deep voice from behind her answered. "The only computer online is Mr. A's."

Ronnie whirled around and rammed her body into a hard, male chest. In an instant she had dropped her bag, put the stranger in an armlock, and pushed him helpless up against the wall, his face squished against the plaster.

"Hey, hey, I heard what you said," he mumbled, his mouth distorted from the pressure. "I'm on your side. Really. *Ow.*" The dude wasn't struggling, but Ronnie didn't lessen the pressure on his elbow in the slightest.

"Who are you? What are you doing here?" She was in no mood to play around. If he gave her a bullshit answer, she would dislocate his shoulder.

"My buddy asked me to debug a chunk of his code, but something didn't sit right with me, so I inspected it at the hexadecimal level and..."

"You found a hidden execute order."

"Exactly."

"Stack overflow?"

"Not sure. Didn't get that far into the script."

"When was this?"

"Yesterday. I came back this morning to try to interrupt the final assembly." The tall guy groaned and attempted to adjust his position. "Hey, I can't breathe very well."

"Ms. Davis?" Alexander gestured to her painful hold on the man, and Ronnie forced herself to loosen her grip. She was running on adrenaline. She needed to take a few calming breaths, take it down a notch. She stepped away from the stranger as he turned around.

Alexander moved forward and held out his card. "Good morning. I'm Alexander Rigiat, and you are…?"

The man took the card, circling his shoulder to alleviate the pain. "I'm Niko Sweeney." He read the raised black ink on stiff white stock.

"Mr. Sweeney, I am here as a representative of the Viper Apps Board of Directors."

That was smooth. Ronnie wondered if he'd just made that up on the spot or if he'd been planning all this in the car. They hadn't talked much on the long drive, which was fine with her. Alexander had been on the phone most of the time, and she'd popped in her noise-cancelling earbuds and listened to music while she ran through all the possible scenarios of what awaited them at Viper Apps.

"We have a board of directors?" Niko looked confused.

"I'm sorry to be the bearer of bad news," Alexander continued, "but your employer was killed last night in a tragic accident—a gas explosion."

Ronnie had to choke down a laugh and turn away. True, Apep had gone up in flames, but it wasn't an accident and it sure as hell wasn't tragic.

Alexander's smile managed to convey caution along with his condolences. "Unfortunately, we received a tip that perhaps there was some—how shall I phrase this?—unethical work being done here. I've come as the Board's legal representative to shut everything down before the authorities are involved."

Wow. Ronnie was impressed. Alexander had just delivered a threat, but it rolled off his tongue as smooth as silk and as sweet as pie, and she wondered if Niko even knew what had hit him.

"Honestly, Mr.," he checked the business card, "*Ree-jee-at...*"

"It's pronounced with a hard G, *Rigg-ee-aht*."

"Right, so I'm not super choked up at the news of Mr. A's passing. He was, well..." Niko paused and risked a quick look at Ronnie. "Anyway, this job paid a ton of cash, but, yeah, it was starting to feel, you know, slimy. I'm used to slimy tech startups, but things around here were extreme. And, well, Mr. A was super creepy."

"You have no idea." Ronnie couldn't help herself.

Niko dared to keep his gaze on her. "I didn't catch your name."

"I didn't toss it."

Now it was Alexander who had to stifle a laugh. "Mr. Sweeney, we would appreciate any help you can give us to ensure that whatever illicit activity took place here does not come to fruition. In exchange for your cooperation, I'm sure the board would be happy to make it worth your while."

Niko stiffened. "You don't need to bribe me to do the right thing."

"I'm merely making sure you get what you deserve for your contribution." Alexander looked so sincere, but Ronnie could hear the steel in his voice. That guy was damn good.

"I hear you, Mr. Rigiat." Niko swallowed hard. Message received.

Ronnie got right up in his face. "Who's the black hat, Niko?"

"I'm not familiar with that term," Alexander said.

Ronnie grinned. "Our new friend here says today was the final assembly." She gestured to the large downstairs room with a half dozen desks and state-of-the-art computers. "So, all you code monkeys are innocent bystanders, churning out your lines, right, but somebody who knows all about the big, bad secret has to put it all together."

"Let me get on their computers and I'll find out," Niko offered.

She grabbed her dropped bag, pulled out a set of screwdrivers, and handed them to Alexander. "After you figure out who the black hat is, yank all the hard drives."

Ronnie turned and went nose to nose with Niko. "Alexander will be watching you. Fuck with either of us, and I will destroy you." She turned and started up the stairs.

She could feel Niko watching her and was a few steps from the top when she heard him say to Alexander, "Is it wrong that I find that incredibly sexy?"

"Save it," Ronnie and Alexander said in tandem.

Once on the second floor, Ronnie moved down a hallway and past a room that emitted a deep humming sound. She tugged open the unlocked door and confirmed it was the servers. A few steps more and she was at the heavy door of the expansive corner office. The door was locked, of course. She examined the mechanism. Lock picking was a skill she'd never needed, so she'd never bothered to master it. Since she might hurt herself trying to kick in this monstrosity, it was Plan B time.

She reached into her shoulder bag and pulled out her trusty SIG Sauer M18. She peeled open its Velcro storage holster, unlocked the safety, and pointed it at the doorknob. She fired two shots in quick succession.

"Everything good?" Alexander called up from the foot of the stairs.

"Stellar!" Ronnie had no problem pushing the door open since there was nothing but a big hole where the knob and lock once were.

She relocked and holstered her pistol, dropped it back in her bag, and took a deep breath. Gotta love Plan Bs.

She took a cautious step into Apep's office and stood a moment near the doorway. It was sparsely furnished but every detail was exquisite. The desktop was spotless. Underfoot was thick carpet. On the windows were velvet drapes. But the real thing of beauty was the dual ultra-wide curved monitor setup that dominated the workspace and the CPU on a wall shelf. *Holy shit*, what she wouldn't give for this kind of setup.

Ronnie sat in the leather ergonomic chair, which must have cost at least ten grand. She stroked the butter-smooth texture for a moment before relaxing into its depths. Then she rolled herself up to the desk and smiled big.

"All right, sweetie, let's see what you've got." She gently placed her fingers on the keyboard and began.

CHAPTER FOUR

One look down at her bare belly was all it took to know she was being eaten from the inside out. Her see-through skin, as pale and inconsequential as parchment, was the only thing that kept her writhing and twisting guts in place.

Something moved inside her, thrashing at the thin barrier. But what was it? Some kind of oversized worm? A parasite? Whatever it was, it swam through her bloodstream, jostled her organs, and used its tiny-razor teeth to tear at her flesh.

She tried to scream. Nothing came out.

"*They're back.*"

Felicity gasped and her eyes flew open. It took a moment for her vision to clear enough to make out the figure that hovered over her. She blinked, and Tom's face came into focus.

"Ronnie and Alexander. They're back. Otherwise, I'd let you sleep."

Sleep. Of course. She'd been asleep and that was just a bizarre nightmare, one she planned on never having again.

"You OK?" Tom frowned. At least he was dressed now.

"Yeah, just trying to wake up." She pushed herself to a sitting position, only to discover that everything from her scalp to her big toes throbbed in pain. "Be right there."

Tom left her alone. She took several deep breaths in an attempt to calm herself. It was only a dream. It wasn't real. But it was difficult to shake the hideous feel of that thing slithering around inside her.

"Ugh." She folded over, her stomach suddenly killing her. Well that explained the dream. She had indigestion, which was to be expected since she'd eaten close to nothing in the last twenty-four hours. She'd take a couple of antacids, maybe some Tylenol. It was no big deal. She could sure get herself riled up over nothing.

She found an old roll of chewable antacids in in her medicine cabinet, swallowed a couple, and splashed her face with water. She checked in the mirror to make sure there wasn't any dried drool on her chin and then gave up on doing anything with her singed hair.

She found Ronnie and Alexander already seated at the booth. Tom did his best to hover just out of Ronnie's sightline. At some point, when she had more energy, Felicity would insist that Tom tell her what had happened. But not right now. With her post-nightmare grogginess and churning stomach, she'd be lucky to stay lucid.

"So, how'd it go?" Felicity was heading to the booth when Tasha and Bethany came in through the door.

"What'd we miss?" Tasha stopped dead, her eyes widening. "And who the hell are you?"

Alexander scooted out from the bench and extended his hand, as he did with everyone he met. "I am Alexander Rigiat, and you must be Ms. Tasha Romero, Felicity's best friend."

Tasha scowled. She looked to Felicity with a bewildered shake of her head.

"That's Mr. Moneybags McMystery, Tash. The lawyer. Remember the cat with the backpack full of cash?"

Tasha's head whipped around again. "Oh. Hello."

"Hi!" Bethany extended her hand with enough enthusiasm to make up for Tasha's rather frosty reception. "I'm Bethany! It's so nice to meet you, Alexander!"

"And you as well. Won't you join us?"

Bethany squeezed next to Ronnie, and when Tasha backed up to lean against the door, Felicity slipped into the booth next to Alexander. Felicity gave her BFF a sideways glance. Tasha was acting like she needed to be ready to make a quick exit. Tom stayed near the bedroom, out of everyone's way. The twelve cats were distributed across the daybed, in the middle aisle, on the back window's ledge in the sunshine, and on Felicity's bed. Except for Melrose, who'd just jumped onto the tabletop and began grooming himself.

"Sorry," Felicity said, snatching the big gray tabby and setting him on the floor. "He likes to be the center of attention."

"Anyway, I was just about to go over everything that happened in Portland." Ronnie's eyes were shadowed in dark circles. She looked depleted. Felicity realized that while everyone else had eaten and showered and gotten some rest, Ronnie had been going nonstop for a day and a half. She was one tough soldier, but when she spoke, her voice was heavy and tired. "Before I say anything else, keep in mind that we got there in time. I found the rootkit before it was deployed."

"That sounds ominous," Tasha said from her position by the door.

"I'm afraid it was quite a serious situation. Ronnie did an outstanding job." Alexander beamed, as if he were proud of her. "Not only did she stop Apep's plan, she was able to identify seven employee

IDs and passwords that were going to be used in the attack."

"Employee passwords?" Felicity wasn't sure why that was important.

"What kind of attack?" Bethany plunked her elbows on the table and leaned in.

"The weakest link in any information technology security system is the human link," Ronnie said, rubbing her forehead. "I don't know if Apep bought them or stole them, but with those sign-on credentials he had the ability to throw us into the dark ages. He'd gained access to employees at the Eastern Interconnection transmission grid and two of the West Coast's largest power generators, plus several hydroelectric dams and the Palo Verde Generating Station in Arizona."

"Wait." Tasha had gone pale. "That's a nuclear power plant, right?"

"Yeah." Ronnie gave a sober nod. "At the very least, he was planning to cripple the entire North American power grid and start a cascade toward worldwide chaos. At the worst, we were only hours away from a planetary '404 Not Found.'"

Felicity shifted, trying to find a comfortable way to sit. "Did you find the... what did you call it? The black cap guy?"

"Niko did."

"What's a Niko?" It was the first time Tom had spoken.

Before Ronnie could answer, Alexander jumped in. "A Viper Apps engineer named Niko Sweeney. He'd become suspicious and was already there when we arrived. Turned out to be a straight shooter and a top programmer. A smart, good-looking young guy."

Felicity watched a vein protrude in Tom's neck.

"And you're never going to guess who our black hat villain turned out to be." Ronnie flashed an expectant look at Felicity.

"Wait—not the sweet nerd with the keycard I molested in the

frozen pizza aisle?"

"None other than."

"What happens now?" Bethany gave her tummy a protective rub.

"Nothing. It's done." Ronnie closed her eyes and leaned back in the booth. "The code is completely wiped. We even yanked the hard drives and double-checked for any backup in the cloud. Nothing. Oh, and the servers had a terrible mishap."

Felicity wasn't sure she wanted to know the answer but asked anyway. "What kind of mishap are we talking about?"

Alexander grinned. "Suffice it to say that it involved Ms. Davis and a heavy baseball bat from the trunk of her Jeep."

Bethany gasped.

"Gotta admit, it was cathartic." Ronnie almost smiled. Not quite, but it was the closest to a smile Felicity had seen from her in many days.

Alexander smiled for her. "I've been in touch with my cybercrime contacts at Homeland Security and the FBI. I'm afraid our frozen pizza friend's life is about to get very complicated."

"That's wonderful. Then it's all over." Tasha exhaled, and everyone followed.

"Tubastet?" Alexander looked to him. "Now that Apep's virus has been neutralized, you should be able to remove the *usekh*. I'm certain it was the computer program that kept the necklace from releasing."

Tom nodded and was about to retrieve the knife when Felicity jumped from the booth. "No."

Everyone stared at her. She wiped her palms on her jeans because they'd begun to sweat. She was dizzy and her stomach hurt again. She hated to bring everyone down from their moment of glory, but they had to know.

But know *what*, exactly?

She turned around to face the rear of the Airstream, all eyes on the back of her head. She had to get ahold of herself. She was breathing like she'd just run a marathon.

Mrrawwor? Circe lifted her head and blinked her blue eyes at Felicity. *Merp?*

She had no answer for her cat. She only knew this—Ronnie had shut down Apep's computer virus, but the dread was still there, stronger than it had been that morning. This meant the sinking, heavy feeling of looming disaster wasn't related to the computer virus. It was something else. Something that had dug its claws into her and wouldn't let go. She spun around to face everyone.

"It's not done. It's not over. Tom, you can keep trying to remove the *usekh* if it'll make you feel better, but it isn't coming off. Not yet."

"How can you be sure, Felicity?" He moved closer.

"I feel it." Her eyes moved from face to face. Ronnie looked dead serious. Bethany was worried. Tasha skeptical. And Alexander intrigued. Tom, however, was honed in on her, all his concentration focused on whatever she would say next.

"Tell us," he said.

"OK, OK. I don't have the perfect words, but I'm sensing—no I'm certain—that something else is lurking out there. Waiting." She swung her arms wide. "Look, I'm going to throw this out there one more time just to be sure. Are we *absolutely certain* that these bad vibes aren't coming from Apep's piece of flesh?"

Tom rolled his eyes. "Again, that's not the way this works. It takes Apep sixty-three years to regenerate to full power."

She turned to Alexander. "What if the process has sped up

somehow? Is that possible?"

Alexander gave a patient smile. "The laws of cellular reproduction on earth are unbending. It would take him nearly nine months to form a new body and then it would be immature, to say the least. In no way could he interfere with the *usekh* releasing."

"Ugh. This is so frustrating!" She balled up her fists. "I'm telling you, something is growing in power. It's not ready to strike quite yet, but it will be soon. The necklace won't release because the danger still exists."

"Tubastet, why don't you try again?"

Tom set the knife down and shook his head at Alexander. "If Felicity says this isn't over, then it isn't over. We wait. Together." Tom reached for Felicity's sweaty hand and gave it a gentle squeeze.

She was so moved by his trust and his loyalty that she had to blink back tears. She could almost forgive him for not mentioning the pension. And not correcting her when she'd pointed out that he didn't believe she could vanquish Apep.

Almost.

"All right. It's agreed that we'll all wait until this new threat makes itself known." Alexander scanned the crowded Airstream. "But not here. Not like this. Which brings me to our next topic of discussion."

"Oh, yeah?" Tasha crossed her arms over her chest. "Do tell!"

Alexander clicked open his briefcase and removed a shiny new laptop. He opened the screen and tapped at the keys. "Tubastet, of course, told me where he was staying, but somehow I pictured it being…more…" He stopped himself. "At any rate, I've made a few arrangements so that everyone will be comfortable." He looked to Felicity. "I've found a nice apartment near the beach for you until you can decide where you'd like to live on a more permanent basis."

"Huh?" She staggered backward, thudding into the daybed. One of the cats complained. "A nice apartment? At the beach? For me?"

"Indeed, if that's all right with you." Alexander's eyes twinkled.

"I can live with that." Her voice was steady, but in her head she was pumping her fists and screaming, *Oh, hell yesssssss!* But then she remembered. "What about my cats?"

"I'm working on it."

Alexander turned to Ronnie. "Ms. Davis, I'm assuming that you would rather not return to your apartment since it was breeched by Apep's hired goons. If you have a preference as to where you'd like to live, I'd be happy to arrange it."

"Here."

Alexander looked up from the keyboard, stupefied. "Excuse me?"

"If it's OK with Tasha, I want to stay in the Airstream for a little while. I dunno, I like it, I guess. It's become…special to me for some stupid reason." Her complete refusal to acknowledge that Tom was three feet away was almost comical. "Tasha, is that possible?"

She didn't hesitate. "Of course, Ronnie. You're welcome to stay here as long as you'd like."

Alexander made a few notes on his laptop before continuing. "Now, Mrs. Hume…"

Felicity jolted, almost answering. But then she remembered, with extreme relief, that she was no longer Mrs. Hume. She looked at Bethany, who twisted her fingers and chewed on her bottom lip. She was anxious, but then again, of course she was. She'd been through hell the last twenty-four hours. She was pregnant. Plus, she really *was* Mrs. Richard Hume, and it was a miracle she wasn't chewing off her own leg to make a break for it.

"You're going to be fine, kiddo." Ronnie pulled her close.

Bethany sniffed and nodded, then raised her gaze to Alexander. "Please call me Bethany. I know you're being proper and lawyerly and all, but I'd prefer you didn't call me Mrs. Hume."

"Of course. Absolutely." Alexander's response was gentle. "So, Bethany, how can I help you?"

"I don't really know if anyone can help me." She shook her head, trying hard to hide her trembling chin. "My life is sorta a mess right now, and I have a lot of decisions to make. I…I'm not really sure anyone can do anything, but I appreciate your kindness."

Alexander's eyes met Tom's. "Well, Bethany, I hope you'll forgive my presumption, but Tom mentioned that I might advise you regarding your marital status and any custody issues that may arise. I am, after all, already dealing with Mr. Hume on Ms. Cheshire's behalf."

Bethany's mouth unhinged. She stared at him for several long seconds. "Oh. Oh, my gosh," she eventually said. "You could really do that?"

"I'm an attorney."

"I know but…oh, my gosh! I think I'm overheating!" She began to fan herself, and when that didn't produce enough of a breeze, Ronnie reached over and grabbed a crossword puzzle book and got some air moving. "Thank you. Yes. Thank you so much. When I know what I want to do, I will be glad to accept your help." She looked around the trailer. "Not that I'm going to stay with him, 'cause I don't even like him, but I probably still need to be on his health insurance and I want some stuff out of the house. Oh, and I need a place to live too. Is it OK to ask for that?"

"I'd love it if you stayed with me." Tasha walked over to Bethany and touched her shoulder. "The bedrooms and kitchen are still functioning. You can help me renovate the place, since you really seem to have an eye for design. And a girl needs her posse when she's going to be a mother, right?" Tasha straightened, correcting herself. "Not that I'd have any personal experience with that, but, I mean, it makes sense, right?"

Bethany jumped up and threw her arms around Tasha, squeezing her tight. Felicity had to hide her shock when Tasha hugged her back without a hint of awkwardness.

"That brings us to you, Ms. Romero."

She released Bethany, eyeing Alexander with an arched eyebrow. "What about me?"

"A crew will be here tomorrow to begin the repair on your property, and, of course, to make any upgrades you'd like. The damage was done while defeating Apep, so, of course we'll be picking up all costs." He clicked open a new folder on his laptop and scrolled through what looked like a series of forms. "I took the liberty of getting everyone's hospital records."

Felicity was gobsmacked. "How in the world did you do that? Aren't they supposed to be private?" She was beginning to wonder if there was anything Alexander couldn't manage.

"Connections," was all he offered. "It looks like no one suffered any permanent damage, which is a miracle." He made a few clicks on the computer. "Except Ms. Romero. Again, my deepest gratitude for your service to The Ever-Living Bastet. I've made an appointment with an oral surgeon I know who will repair your teeth."

With a rubber band snap of her neck, Tasha stared at him. She backed away toward the door.

"And, Ms. Romero, I've arranged to have a state-of-the art double-wide manufactured home moved to your property where you can live in comfort while your historic home is being restored. I've sent schematics of your house to an architect known for his restoration of pre-war Craftsman bungalows. Perhaps you'd like to look at the preliminary schedule I drew up for demo and renovation?"

Tasha slowly turned to Felicity. *Yikes.* Tasha's mouth had contorted into a saccharine smile, but Felicity saw the upper lip spasm. Tasha blinked innocently, but Felicity knew flaming arrows were about to shoot from her pupils. No doubt about it. Things were about to get unpleasant in the Airstream.

"Before you continue, may I ask a teeny-tiny, little question, Mr. Helios Rigiat?" Tasha's voice was thin and high. To an inexperienced listener, she might have sounded meek. Felicity's trained ear told her it was time to duck and cover.

"Of course!"

"Super, because from where I stand, it looks like you just rolled up on my property in your Mr. Big bulldozer, took over like a know-it-all male-in-charge and started making decisions for the vulnerable womenfolk—decisions that aren't even yours to make!"

Alexander's smile collapsed.

"Oh, shit," Ronnie whispered.

"Because—weird, I know—but that just happens to be my absolute *least* favorite kind of man on the planet. So, I'm gonna say thanks, but no thanks to all your generous offers because I can handle my own shit. I've been handling my own shit since I was sixteen, and I certainly don't need to be rescued now, or at any time in the future, by some Courthouse Ken doll…"

"Ooof," Tom said.

"…who thinks it's OK to look at my private medical records and choose an oral surgeon to fix my *goddam teeth*! Are you serious? My body and my medical history are none of your concern, so why don't you kiss my gray roots and haul your prissy, perfect, Mercedes-driving ass outa here?"

Tasha spun around, yanked open the door, and was gone.

Alexander didn't breathe.

"Yep, it's a complete mystery why you're still single." Tom bent down and pulled the last beer out of the refrigerator.

Bethany jumped up. "Thank you, Alexander, for everything, really. You're the nicest man! It's just that sometimes, women don't like to be told what to do, especially a woman like Tasha. I better go see if I can talk to her." Bethany opened the door, took a step onto the stoop, and stepped back in. "The baby kittens are so cute, Felicity! But should they be left outside with your cats running around? I'll take them with me to Tasha's."

"Uh..." Felicity searched for the right way to say this. "Bethany, sweetie, maybe you should check with Tasha first before you take them over. She's not much for cats or dogs or birds or, well, any animal, really. And she's not exactly in the best of moods at the moment."

"Don't be ridiculous! Nobody can turn away a mother and her newborns!" They listened as Bethany made her way down the metal stairs and began a soft, singsong conversation with the little cat family.

"My money's on our girl Bethany."

"You may be right, Ronnie." Felicity worried that Bethany would get a tall glass of *nope* from Tasha, but who knew? The last twenty-four hours had changed everyone, in some way or another.

Alexander rose, tucked his computer away, already recovered from his Tasha beatdown. "Tubastet, you can come stay with me. I have plenty of room in my Beaverton house."

Tom's laugh was a bitter rebuke. Felicity had never heard him laugh like that, and it was disconcerting.

Tom tipped his chin in Felicity's direction. "The Acolyte still wears the *usekh*."

Understanding swept across Alexander's face, followed by a sheepish nod. "My mistake. Of course. I'll find you an apartment at the beach as well. Something very close by to Felicity. Perhaps next door."

"Thank you."

"It's sweet that you want to keep an eye on me, Tom, but you really don't have to. I'll be fine."

He and Alexander didn't respond.

"Why don't you walk me out to my car, Tubastet?" Alexander then addressed Ronnie. "It was a distinct pleasure watching you in action this afternoon. I hope you are able to get some well-deserved sleep." As he stepped towards Felicity to give her a warm and sincere hug, she noticed that despite his busy day of yanking hard drives, driving for hours, planning and plotting out everyone's lives—and being on the receiving end of Tasha's wrath—there wasn't a crease in the man's clothing. Not a hair was out of place and no cat fur clung to his clothing. His face was smooth and calm. It was fascinating.

"Felicity." He smiled. "You are as incredible as Tubastet said you were."

"Ha. Thanks, but right now I don't feel all that incredible. I feel antsy and out of sorts and I've got a wicked case of indigestion."

"Understood." He placed a hand on her elbow and smiled.

She examined his face again, annoyed that she still couldn't seem to place him. "You know, Alexander, it's the strangest thing. You seem so familiar, but I can't for the life of me figure out why. Have we met before or something?"

"No. I would have remembered a woman as wonderful as you."

Tom tossed his already drained beer bottle in the recycling. "Again, Alexander, how is it that you're still single?"

Ronnie chuckled.

"Maybe I'm a confirmed bachelor. Incurable." With a quick smile, he and Tom left.

And just like that, it hit her. Felicity's body stiffened with the epiphany. "*Oh, my fucking God!*"

"Are you OK?" Ronnie shot up from the booth.

"I just figured it out!"

"Figured what out?"

"I'm a confirmed bachelor. I'm incurable."

Ronnie scrunched up her nose. "I'm not following you."

"*Phantom Thread,* 2017, yet another of his Oscar nominations. Tasha's forced me to watch that film a hundred times!"

"And?"

"And, Alexander looks just like *Daniel Day freakin' Lewis*!" Felicity sank into the daybed, laughing.

Alexander's car was just across the yard, but they took their time getting there.

"Are you all right, Tubastet? This necklace problem seems to have really thrown you."

"It has. I don't like surprises. And I don't like mysteries. But most of all, I don't like complications." Speaking those words aloud caused him to tense even further.

"If you ask me, it seems as if this whole visit has been nothing but complications and surprises."

They reached Alexander's Mercedes, but instead of climbing behind the wheel, Alexander leaned his back against the door. "Are you worried?"

"Of course, I'm worried! This is an aberration. Completely without precedent."

"I'll do more research, and we'll figure out why the *usekh* won't release. There has to be an explanation somewhere, something more specific than Felicity's bad feelings." Alexander laid a comforting hand on his shoulder. "Is something else bothering you?"

He shook his head. "Not really. It's just that Felicity's probably right and there's some kind of new danger, and whatever it is, I'm to blame." He leaned back against the car, feeling himself deflate. "Man, I've fucked it all up, haven't I?"

Alexander let out a surprised laugh. "What are you talking about? You were victorious!"

He shrugged and looked down the lane, avoiding eye contact.

"You survived a near-lethal attack, found a worthy replacement Acolyte, bestowed the *usekh*, and led her to victory in an absurdly short amount of time. The Goddess' gratitude must be profound."

His bones ached with each of his two thousand years. "Then why am I being punished?"

"Why would she punish you, Tubastet? You've been an unwavering servant to her all these centuries. You've shown nothing but courage and resilience."

"But I chose Felicity myself, remember?" He looked to Alexander. "Was that an act of arrogance? Was there something else I should have done instead? Is the Ever-Living Goddess furious that I allowed Misty to fail? She certainly would have cause."

"Hold up, priest." He looked sideways at him. "Misty failed because she didn't follow your teaching. You selected Felicity out of utter necessity, and the Goddess couldn't have chosen better herself."

He managed a quick glance in his friend's direction. He hoped Alexander was right, though he couldn't feel sure. In fact, he felt just plain lost.

"Does Ronnie have anything to do with this?" Alexander's

voice was gentle.

"No. Of course not. How could she? Don't be ridiculous."

"Touchy much?" His friend paused, looked up at the first stars just peeking through the darkness. "I could never do what you do, Tubastet, living in fits and starts, grabbing connection wherever you can while knowing you must leave it behind, no exceptions, each and every time, like clockwork."

"It's my sacred duty." He shrugged. "I chose this path, all those years ago, as the Romans approached the temple and the Goddess asked for my service."

Alexander thought on that for a moment, then made certain to look him straight in the eye. "Thank you, Tubastet-af-Ankh, *hem-netjer-tepi* of the Ever-Living Goddess Bastet, temple guard of Per-Bast, warrior, and trainer of the Acolytes. Thank you for saying yes."

He almost laughed. He felt like a fraud. He didn't deserve those titles, and he sure as hell didn't deserve anyone's thanks. In fact, he didn't deserve the respect of a man like Alexander. "I didn't really have a choice, did I?"

"Of course, you did. She asked you. She didn't force you. You could have refused. But let me tell you, the whole world is lucky you didn't. There is no one more worthy of the call."

He looked away. He hoped there was a grain of truth in what Alexander said, but he couldn't be sure. All he knew was that whatever certainty he'd once possessed in his warrior soul had evaporated, and in its place, doubt had taken hold. He already felt its claws in him.

As any warrior knew, doubt was a death sentence.

Three-fourths of the Goddess Posse gathered at Tasha's tiny kitchen pub table, digging into just-delivered Mexican food. Ronnie maintained that she needed sleep more than *arroz con pollo* and was already unconscious on the Airstream daybed, snuggled under the blanket Felicity had provided. It was anyone's guess where Tom was, but she assumed he was taking another long walk after saying goodbye to Alexander.

Tom had taken quite a few walks that day, but as far as she could tell, they'd done nothing to improve his mood. He was a sullen mess.

Felicity stared at the greasy beef taco in her hand and hesitated. Maybe with her stomach acting up she shouldn't eat any more. She returned the half-consumed taco to its Styrofoam cradle and wiped her mouth with a paper napkin.

"Too bad Tom couldn't join us." Tasha stabbed her fork into her burrito bowl. "I'm sure he's busy restocking his beer supply."

Felicity decided to keep her concerns to herself, but nodded.

"I mean, sure, he's allowed to be upset," Tasha continued. "He wasn't planning on being stuck here, with us. I get it. If there's anyone who knows how much it sucks when reality doesn't meet expectations, it would be me, Tasha Romero."

"He seems a little angry," Bethany said. "Maybe discouraged."

"Yeah, and he's being a total dick toward Ronnie. Anyone else notice that?" Tasha grabbed a handful of tortilla chips.

Felicity leaned back in her chair. "I noticed that the two of them seem on edge today, but I haven't been able to put my finger on what's changed. They clashed something fierce when they first met, when we asked Ronnie to help unlock Misty's phone. But they seemed to get on better over time, even grow to like one another."

"Maybe they had a big fight when we weren't looking," Tasha offered.

"No. They kissed." Bethany took a bite of her enchilada.

"*What?*" Felicity and Tasha shouted in unison.

Bethany swallowed and nodded. "Yep, when they said goodbye this morning."

"Oh." Felicity chuckled. "You had me going there for a minute. You're just talking about a goodbye kiss, like a peck on the cheek, right?"

"Wrong. It was a full-on, you know, *clench*. Maybe with tongue and everything." Bethany took another bite.

Tasha's plastic fork clattered to the tabletop, and she gave Felicity a wide-eyed stare.

She needed some clarification. "So, wait. Ronnie allowed this to happen? She didn't try to, I don't know, *behead* him or something? Are you sure?"

"You have it completely backward, Felicity." Bethany blinked her huge eyes. "Ronnie kissed *him*. I saw the whole thing!"

"How?" Tasha asked.

"Well, remember when Tom said goodbye to us in the living room? You were vacuuming up glass and Apep skin and the front door was hanging off the hinges."

"Yeah?"

"And Tom and Ronnie walked out to the yard." Bethany pointed, as if they'd forgotten where the yard was located.

"Right. Then what?"

"Well, I think Tom was surprised by the whole thing."

"What makes you say that?"

"Because, without warning, Ronnie just reached up, grabbed him behind the neck, and yanked him down to her. She pretty much kissed the heck out of him, then just walked away. Tom stood there for a second, looking dazed and confused, then headed to the trailer."

Tasha's eyes met Felicity's across the table. Tasha mouthed *day-umm*. Bethany took another bite of enchilada.

"Well," Felicity tried to sound matter-of-fact. "A passionate goodbye kiss without the goodbye can definitely make things complicated. No wonder they've been acting strange."

"Ronnie's fine. It's Tom who can't handle it," Tasha said.

"Because Tom isn't fully human. I mean, he hasn't had the full human experience in a very long while." Bethany looked pensive. "Maybe he isn't as wise about matters of the heart as he is about weapons and battles and stuff. He might not know how to handle emotions."

Felicity blinked at her. Sometimes, that young lady was smarter than all of them combined.

"Ow!" Tasha raised a hand to her mouth, wincing.

"What's wrong?"

She shook her head, trying to free something with her tongue. "It's stuck."

Oh. Felicity felt bad for her. It looked like a tortilla chip got lodged in the gap left by her most recent missing tooth.

Tasha managed to get it loose and swallow. "OK. That hurt a lot." She cradled her cheek in her hand.

"Maybe you should take up Alexander's offer, Tash. Get your teeth fixed. You've been wanting to do that for a while, right? Now's your chance to get some fancy implants that someone else pays for!"

"I don't need anyone's charity."

Felicity laughed. "It's not charity. It's a settlement. You got injured protecting Bastet's Acolyte from Apep, and Alexander's job is to make sure you are compensated for your injury. The same goes for him offering to repair the house and provide a temporary mobile home while the work is being done."

"Yeah, well, you realize he didn't so much offer as command."

"But that doesn't make it any less beneficial to you."

Tasha rolled her eyes, but Felicity could tell she was already thinking about it.

"Well, I think he's super sweet and pretty hot for an older man, like, movie-star hot."

"Ha!" Tasha laughed. "Not sure what movie star that would be."

"You're kidding me, right?" Felicity could not believe her best friend was so blind. "How can…"

"Do you think Alexander will help me get a car?" Bethany perked up. "It doesn't have to be new or fancy or anything, but I'd really like to have my own transportation and not have to rely on anyone. I'd like to go to Portland to that shop where you guys found these bracelets." She held up her wrist and spun the silver Bastet bauble.

"I'm sure he'd help with that," Felicity said, "but in the meantime, you can borrow mine whenever you need it."

"If I weren't still mad about the kittens in my guest room, I'd let you borrow mine." Tasha raised a forkful of food to her mouth and took slow and cautious bites.

"Then just pretend they aren't even there, Tasha!" Bethany leaned in, like she had a plan to share. "I'll change the litter, wash the bedding, feed the mama, and make sure she has water. So, between their mama and me, you won't even know you have kittens in the house."

"Oh, I'll know."

"Besides, it's like an internship! I'm watching the mama cat and learning how to be a good mother so I'll know what to do when my time comes."

"Just don't go licking your kid's head or eating its afterbirth, all right?"

"Ewwww." Bethany's face fell.

"Ignore her, Bethany. That's a very sweet sentiment. I'm sure you and Little Mama will do very well together."

"Whoops. Sorry!" Bethany jumped down from her pub chair. "Need to use the bathroom. Again."

They watched Bethany toddle off down the hallway.

"I gotta admit that she's grown on me," Tasha said.

"It's nice that you're letting her stay here."

She shrugged. "Seemed like the right thing to do."

"The kittens will grow on you, too. You'll see."

"Yeah, don't hold your breath, Lissie. As soon as they're old enough, they're outa here, and I'm not kidding."

"I think your opinion of cats may be changing."

"You think wrong."

"Oh, shoot! H-E-double-toothpicks!" Bethany came hopping into the kitchen on one foot. She looked like a human pogo stick.

"What happened?" Tasha asked.

"Nothing. I just twisted my bruised knee."

"You have a bruised knee?"

"You know, when Apep tore my sweater, saw I wasn't wearing the necklace, and dropped me. I banged it super hard against the coffee table."

"Did you show the doctor?" Felicity patted Bethany's chair and, once seated, pushed up her loose pants.

"Yes."

"What did he say?"

"It's bruised."

Felicity saw several shades of purple and red, and a lot of swelling. She couldn't help herself and reached out to gently prod the edges of the bruise. "You got this because of me, and I'm sorry."

"That's ridiculous," Tasha said. "We battled that monster together. We made the choice to back you up. Right, Bethany?"

"Exactly! I don't blame you for anything, Felicity."

"Well, maybe you should." Felicity gave her knee a gentle pat.

"Yikes! What are you doing?" Bethany gasped. "That tingles. You're making it feel super weird! Stop!"

Felicity yanked her hand away. "I didn't mean to hurt you."

"Oh, my fucking gawd." Tasha pointed to Bethany's knee.

No bruise. No swelling. No purple. It appeared to be completely healed. Felicity sat back in her chair, confused.

"What did you *do*, Felicity?"

"I have no idea."

Bethany stared down at herself, then carefully bent her leg. "It doesn't hurt anymore."

The three women glanced at each other, baffled.

"I gotta admit, gals, I'm a little freaked out." Tasha stepped away from the pub table and paced between the refrigerator and sink. "Is there something you forgot to tell us, Lissie? Like, I don't know, you have magic healing powers now or some shit?"

"That's crazy. Of course not."

"Except my knee was all ugly and swollen and now it's not."

"Until Felicity touched it." Tasha grabbed one of Felicity's hands, examined it. "Looks normal. It's not shooting out gamma rays or anything."

Felicity pulled her hand away. "Of course it's normal."

Tasha leaned toward Felicity and pulled up the sleeve of her shirt. "Try it on me." The long, red streak on her upper arm wasn't deep enough to need stitches or even a bandage, but it looked sore.

Felicity examined the mark. "How'd you get this? Does it hurt?"

"Not really. It's from Apep's thumb nail, I think, from when he grabbed me."

Felicity was about to touch it, but pulled her hand away. "This is ridiculous."

"Right, but it's not ridiculous being the fifty-two-year-old chosen one called to battle the ancient God of Chaos? Do it, Lissie."

Felicity reached out and laid a gentle palm across Tasha's arm.

"Wow, that's tingly. Feels freaky."

Felicity yanked her hand away.

They all watched as Tasha's scratch faded and disappeared.

"Oh fuck." Felicity's stomach cramped.

"Do the cut on my other leg!" Bethany stuck out her right leg and pulled up her pants to reveal a tiny red mark on her shin. "It's from shaving yesterday."

Tasha looked appalled. "You took time to shave your legs on the day of the battle?"

Bethany rolled her eyes. "Well, I didn't know it was going to be the day of the battle, did I?"

"OK, I guess I could try." Felicity placed her fingertips on the scabbed nick.

"I don't feel anything." Bethany scrunched up her face. "Nope. No tingle."

Felicity tried thinking healing thoughts, but Bethany only shook her head. When Felicity moved her hand away the nick was still there. "It didn't work. Maybe the others were just freak coincidences."

Tasha was unconvinced. "You healed Bethany's knee and my arm, so it's not a coincidence. The question is, why can't you heal Bethany's cut?"

The three women lapsed into silence.

"Maybe it's because I did it to myself."

"Or it didn't hurt enough?" Tasha suggested.

Bethany shook her head. "It's how I got it that matters, not how much it hurts. Your scratch barely hurt, and shaving cuts sting like the dickens."

"That's ridiculous, Bethany..."

"She's right!" Felicity looked to Tasha. "You have other injuries you got from the battle, right?"

"Uh, yeah. Zip ties are the worst."

"Let me at 'em." When Tasha surrendered her left wrist, Felicity encircled the angry marks with her fingers.

"We're back in tingly territory," Tasha confirmed. When Felicity removed her hand, the welts were gone.

"That's it then. I can only heal wounds received in battle! Oh, my God!" Felicity paused, knowing she needed to verify this. "I need another wound *not* received in battle. Anybody?"

"I've got another one!" Bethany displayed the top of her left hand. "I burned myself on the kettle two days ago."

Felicity touched the small blister, and nothing happened. The burn was still there.

"When did all this start, Lissie? Was it when the necklace didn't release?"

"I have no idea, Tash." As soon as the words left her mouth, Felicity realized she *did* have an idea. That morning, when she'd delivered Little Mama's kittens—Goddess, had it only been that morning?—the *usekh* warmed against her breastbone and her whole body had vibrated. "The kittens."

Bethany squealed. "How cool is that? You saved the baby cats, and Bastet gave you a reward!"

"Or a warning." Felicity had a bad feeling about this.

"Why a warning?" Tasha asked.

"Think about it. If the *usekh* is about to release and my Acolyte days are numbered, why would she bother bestowing such a gift on me?"

Bethany's brows crinkled. "I think you're being paranoid, Felicity. You did a good and loving thing and she gave you a reward. Stop looking for the dark side of everything. Geez." Bethany got up, stretched, and produced a big yawn. "You worry too much. All righty. I gotta go to bed. We'll figure it all out tomorrow." She smiled and waved as she headed down the hall to the guest room.

Tasha sighed. "Maybe this really is just a simple gift to help with the aftermath of the battle, Lissie. Maybe everything will be back to normal before you know it." Tasha failed to stifle a yawn.

"It's possible, Tash." Felicity hugged her best friend. "It'll be clearer in the morning, I'm sure. Right now, we're all in desperate need of some sleep." Felicity wandered back to the Airstream, thinking that yes, she was sure she needed sleep, but that was it. Nothing else was clear.

Sleep didn't come for hours, and when it did, it was restless and fouled with nightmares of being eaten from the inside out.

CHAPTER FIVE

Felicity didn't need to announce her return to Tasha's place early the next morning since Tasha could see her coming across the yard. From her perch at the kitchen table, where she drank her coffee, Tasha stared through the gaping holes in the front wall of her house and the half-open door dangling from its hinges.

She managed a floppy wave. "Morning, Lissie."

Felicity stepped over the threshold and looked around. In the morning light, the house looked even worse. "I'm sorry your place got so trashed."

Tasha shrugged. "I call it Early Crime Scene Period décor." She took a slurp from her cup.

Felicity hopped on the raised stool next to her friend, hissing when pain stabbed her abdomen.

Tasha noticed. "What is going on with you?"

"Just indigestion."

"I guess I won't offer you coffee, then."

"Probably not the best idea."

Felicity decided not to share the nightmare she'd endured the night before, complete with blood and guts and see-through skin that allowed her to watch the needle-toothed worm rip at her organs. She might have to give up coffee. She might have to give up sleeping altogether if this continued.

"Any update on the healing thing?" Tasha poured herself more coffee.

"A bit. I was able to heal all the cuts and scrapes the cats got in the battle."

"That's great!"

"But I can't heal myself at all." Felicity held up one of her arms still full of cuts and bruises.

"That's bad."

"I'll check with Ronnie when she gets home from work, see if I can heal some of her battle injuries, and I'll try with Tom, too, if I ever see him again. I have no idea where he is, in cat or human form." Felicity popped two more antacids. "I'll do some research at the library as soon as it opens." She rose to get herself a glass of water from the kitchen, but the cupboard door came off in her hand. "Oh." She looked to Tasha. "Sorry."

Tasha's stare was blank. "Hey, can I ask you something, Lissie?"

"Of course. Anything. You know that." Felicity placed the door on the counter, filled her glass from the tap, and returned to the table.

Tasha studied the contents of her mug, shoulders slumped. "Why do you think I've never put any time or money into this house? It's been twelve years since I inherited it." She looked up at Felicity, the corners of her mouth turned down. "Is it some deep-seated denial?

Avoidance? Depression?"

"You've been busy and had other priorities. Maybe you just weren't ready to claim it as your own."

Tasha blinked, thinking, then took another sip of coffee. "How'd I get here? I mean, look around. I'm fifty-two, never married, living in a shit-hole shack with a pregnant runaway and a litter of newborn kittens. My best friend's morphed into Wonder Woman and lives in the camper in my yard with a shape-shifting warrior priest and the female version of Captain America."

They stared at each other, silence hanging between them for a moment. Then they exploded in laughter. They laughed so hard and for so long that Felicity had to wipe tears from her eyes.

Once Tasha caught her breath, she released an exasperated sigh.

The chirpy ringtone of Bethany's phone echoed down the hall. "She still asleep?" Felicity asked.

"The last time I checked." Tasha finished her coffee and took the mug to the sink.

"Wait. You *check* on her?" She swiveled on the stool to follow Tasha. "Keep that up and you'll have to turn in your cold-hearted bitch membership card."

"Ha." Tasha spun around and leaned up against the sink. "My membership applied only to my dealings with men, and I'm done with them."

"Your membership or men?"

"Men. In fact, let's make it formal." She placed her right hand on her heart. "I hereby swear off the male species for the rest of my days, forever and ever into eternity, and that includes giving out my number to anyone with a Y chromosome, amen."

Something about the tone of her voice indicated she really

meant it this time. "No exceptions?"

Tasha shook her head. "None. What's the point?"

"Even if you find a man who looks just like DDL?"

She snorted. "Like *that's* ever gonna happen."

Maybe it was time to mention the Academy Award-winning elephant in the room. "Uh, so, you've not noticed the resemblance?"

"Whose resemblance?"

"Well, Alexander. He looks just like Daniel Day Lewis."

Tasha reared back like she'd gotten a whiff of something terrible. "Courthouse Ken? In what possible way does he look like DDL?"

"Ohmigod, Tasha! How about the widow's peak, for starters? And the long face and square chin. The eyebrows and eye color and the freaking dimples! It's *him*! In the flesh!"

"You're delusional."

"Fine. Then just close your eyes and imagine him in buckskin, clutching a musket as he runs through the Adirondacks."

Tasha scoffed. "Not gonna happen."

"Morning!" Bethany shuffled into the kitchen, yawning, her hair twisted on top of her head in a messy bun and her long legs peeking from an oversized T-shirt. It was a mystery how a person could look that cute seconds after waking up. Maybe Felicity had possessed that gift at one point but hadn't capitalized on it.

"How'd you sleep, sweetie?" Tasha asked.

"Out like a light. I don't think I moved the whole night." Bethany set the kettle on the stove, found an herbal tea bag, and began looking through the cabinets.

"There's sugar in the bottom left."

"Oh, no thanks." Bethany found a mug and spoon. "I read that consuming refined sugar during pregnancy can lead to metabolism disorders and obesity risk in the child."

"I'll be damned." Tasha made eye contact with Felicity. "No wine. No refined carbs. A girl's gotta go Paleo-Amish just to gestate a baby these days."

Bethany filled the kettle and put it on the stove. "Thank you again, Felicity, for fixing my knee."

"Of course! I only wish I knew how and why I could do it."

They all heard the phone ring in the back bedroom. Bethany froze, then turned from the counter and cocked her head to listen.

"Not going to answer?" Felicity asked.

"No. It's Rich. I forgot to block him again."

"I didn't know you'd *un*blocked him," Tasha said.

"Well, yeah, I just did a couple of minutes ago. I knew he had to be worried sick. Three seconds later, he called."

"What did he say?" Tasha asked.

Bethany laughed softly, then released a big sigh. "It was sort of pathetic, really. A combo of threats and begging and crying. I was a little embarrassed for him."

"Threats?" Tasha and Felicity asked at the same time.

Bethany waved the spoon. "Nothing awful. I mean, he said I couldn't hide forever and that he'd track me down and stuff like that, but with all the crying and blowing his nose, honestly, I couldn't understand half of it."

"But he threatened you."

"Oh, gosh, I'm fine. Really, Tasha. And besides, I took care of it."

"Oh?" Felicity asked.

"I gave him Alexander's contact information and told him that from now on, he should talk to my lawyer." Bethany grabbed a banana from the fruit bowl.

"Well, good on you." Tasha raised her palm and Bethany gave her a high five.

"I do have a favor to ask." Bethany began to peel the banana. "I've got a doctor's appointment this afternoon, and since Rich isn't in the picture, can you can go with me?"

Tasha blinked and said, "Sure. I'm, uh, touched you asked."

Just then, the ground rumbled. Everyone turned to watch a procession of trucks and vans clamor down the lane and through the gate.

"Oh! We have company. I better go pee again and put on some pants." Bethany disappeared.

"What the hell?" Tasha headed for the front door and Felicity followed. No doubt this was Alexander's construction crew, and Felicity hoped he'd had the good sense not to show up with them.

The vehicles parked and workers climbed out, stretching, pouring coffee from thermoses, and lighting up cigarettes. An older gentleman in a pair of khakis and a button-down shirt had already honed in on Tasha and headed to the porch. He had kind eyes, Felicity noticed.

"Ms. Romero! I'm Janson Crenshaw, the architect." He stood on the grass, his gaze following the roof line. "I have to say, I'm a real fan of the Crafton model and I'm thrilled to have the opportunity to work on one."

That seemed to throw Tasha off. "What kind of model?"

"The Sears, Roebuck and Co. Crafton mail-order kit." He peered at the exposed insulation and lathe with adoration. "And this is the 1937 six-room version, model number. 33180."

"Well, no, you're wrong. My grandfather built this with his very own hands—"

"Of course he built it! He picked up the kit at the train station, brought it here, and assembled it." He looked back at the house. "What a beauty!"

Felicity thought that assessment might be a bit generous, given the house's current condition.

Just then, Bethany popped back onto the porch and waved to the assembled crowd. "Hi, everybody!" She studied the printing on the sides of the work vans, box trucks, and extended-cab pickups, her eyes widening with delight. "Excellent!" She pointed to the two men slumped against the electrician's van, who smiled and approached the porch as if summoned by the fairy queen.

Bethany seemed to have that effect on people.

"Hey guys! There's still some knob-and-tube in there, if you can believe it, and not a single GFI to be found!"

Tasha looked at her. "Huh?"

Felicity watched Bethany turn her benevolent gaze upon the heating and air conditioning crew. "Just a heads-up that there's a ton of infiltration in this house. It will need a total energy retrofit, HVAC too. Might even need asbestos abatement."

"You got it!" said one of the men.

"How do you know this stuff, Bethany?" Felicity was fascinated.

"I just remodeled my own house... well, Rich's house, or, I guess I should say *your* old house." She looked uncomfortable.

"You did a great job."

"Thanks. And remember that awful boyfriend I followed out here to Oregon? He was a general contractor. I used to help on projects, and I guess I just picked up on stuff."

She then zoomed in on the plumbers. "Oh, hey! Come around back and let me show you the leach field. Needs a whole new septic system and probably some percolation testing." Bethany descended the porch steps and disappeared into the side yard with several workers in tow.

Tasha and Felicity stood on the porch, watching as workers set up equipment and pulled down ladders. They saw the architect huddle with a crew of carpenters.

"I swear I said no. I said no, right?"

Three tractor trailers crashed down the lane and neared the gate. One carried an empty construction dumpster and the others hauled...

"Is that a *house*?" Tasha's mouth hung open.

"A really nice one." The double-wide had tasteful gray siding with white trim, an attached front porch, large windows, and what looked like a fireplace chimney.

"But I said no." She turned to Felicity. "You were there when I told him to get back in his luxury sedan and drive his know-it-all, bossy-assed self off my property. I told him no, right?"

Felicity bit her lip to keep from laughing. "Maybe you were too subtle about it, Tash. You're famous for that." Tasha produced a junior-high-worthy eye roll, which made Felicity snort-laugh. "Anyway, seriously, tell everyone to get lost if that's what you want. It's your place and your decision. The question is, are you sure you want to say no to all this wonderfulness?"

Just then, Tasha's front door decided to detach completely from its hinges and slam to the floorboards, shooting a plume of dust into the air.

She glanced over her shoulder. "I think my house just threw in the towel."

Felicity put an arm around her best friend. "For what it's worth, I'm thrilled for you. You deserve a beautiful home. I'm so excited!"

"Me too. And I just can't hide it." Tasha turned, stepped over the collapsed door, and entered the house, unbridled excitement oozing from every pore.

Felicity sat in her car in the library parking lot, waiting for the doors to open. Once inside, she dropped her bag on the table closest to the ancient Egypt section and headed into the stacks.

She wasn't entirely sure what she was looking for. All she had were questions without simple answers. She needed guidance. Like an advice columnist.

Dear Ancient Abby,

I'm a fifty-two-year-old Acolyte of Bastet. My usekh *won't release, and now I can heal wounds inflicted in battle with Apep. What does this mean? Is this normal? Am I crazy? Also, I'm sort of seeing a nice guy and the sex is phenomenal, but I haven't yet mentioned the whole supernatural calling thing. I don't want to scare him off, so how should I bring it up? Should I just not say anything and hope for the best?*

Sincerely,

Baffled Battler

The thought was almost enough to make her laugh. Almost. Felicity grabbed a few volumes on Egypt after the Roman annexation, a later period than what she'd been studying, which seemed like the logical place to start since that's when the calling of the human Acolyte began. Maybe there would be something, anything, that would point her in the right direction.

She added several tomes on Old Kingdom religion and a new arrival on the evolution of hieroglyphics. Just before she sat back down at the table, she found a beat-up copy of *The Book of the Dead*. She added it to her stack and took a deep breath.

She knew it was a long shot that her answers were in these volumes, but she had to start somewhere. The sense of dread was growing stronger by the hour, and despite Tom and Alexander's assurances, she couldn't shake the feeling that time was running out.

Tasha pulled into the North Coast Women's Health Partners parking lot, snagging a spot near the door. Bethany had been quiet on the drive, zapped of her usual bouncy energy. It was concerning.

"You ready?"

"Just a minute."

Tasha cut the engine and waited, but nothing was happening on Bethany's side of the car. There was no double-checking in the visor mirror, no sending of texts or smoothing of hair. Bethany just sat there, twiddling her thumbs and staring through the drizzle at the doctor's office entrance.

"Everything all right?"

Bethany swung her head toward Tasha, eyes brimming with tears. "I'm worried something's wrong with the baby."

"Oh, sweetie. Why? Has something happened?"

Bethany shook her head.

"Then what is it?"

"It's just a lot, you know?" She sniffled. "I'm responsible for everything with this little person." She rubbed her belly. "What I breathe, the baby breathes. Same goes for what I eat, drink, feel, hear…it's all up to me. What if I do something wrong or think negative thoughts? If something happens, it will be all my fault!"

Tasha was out of her depth and she knew it. "I can see how that might be overwhelming." She patted Bethany's knee.

"It is! Oh, my gosh, you're exactly right. It's overwhelming! I'm so overwhelmed!"

That hadn't gone as planned. Tasha tried a different tack. "How about you focus on all the things you're doing *right* for your baby, Bethany? You always put your baby first. I mean, every morning you're in the kitchen whipping up one of those hideous, I mean nutritious, delicious smoothies!"

Bethany narrowed one eye. "The recipe with kefir, flax oil, and kale provides excellent nutrition for the developing fetus."

"See? Exactly! So whad'ya say? Are you ready for this?"

"I guess." With a shrug, she opened the car door and they headed inside. Before they reached the door, she grabbed Tasha's arm. "Promise you'll stay with me."

"During the appointment?"

"Please. I can't do this by myself."

"Well, sure." She squeezed Bethany's hand. "I'd be happy to."

They waited about forty minutes for Bethany to get called back to an exam room. She changed into an examination gown, got her vitals checked, and chatted with the nurse practitioner. The whole time, Tasha sat in a chair and tried her best to be supportive. After that, they headed down the hallway to the dimly lit ultrasound room. Bethany got situated and was told the technician would be with them in a moment.

"Don't go, Tasha."

"I'm right here."

"I mean, pull the chair closer, OK?" Bethany patted the edge of the exam table, and without warning, burst into tears. "This isn't how I pictured it! It's nothing like how I thought it would be!"

Tasha snagged a few tissues from a box near the sink, then thought better of it and grabbed the whole box. She gave a handful to

Bethany, who blew her nose with gusto. "Have I made a mistake, Tasha? I mean, Rich *is* the father. He's my *husband*. He has a right to be here, doesn't he? Maybe I've been too hard on him." She dabbed her eyes. "Have I been too hard on him?"

Oh, shit. Don't say it. Don't call him a needle-dicked douche ninja.

"I've been too hard on him, haven't I?"

"Um..."

"Hello there, Mrs. Hume! Ready to see your baby?"

Bethany stared at the ultrasound technician and exploded in sobs.

The technician looked to Tasha. "Should I come back in a little bit?"

Tasha shook her head. "She'll be OK. She just needs something wonderful to focus on."

"Let's see what we can do, then."

A half hour later, Tasha and Bethany walked through the waiting room to the exit. Bethany was chatty and smiling, and some of the pep had returned to her step, but there was a faint undercurrent of shock in her expression.

"How could I have been that far off? I can't believe it!"

"Like the nurse practitioner said, they can't really pinpoint a due date until your first ultrasound."

"But a whole month? Wow! I'm five and a half months along already! That's—oh, my gosh, Tash! That's just crazy!"

"We'll just have to get everything ready a little sooner than expected, that's all."

"But that means I'm almost in my last trimester!"

"That's wonderful."

"The cottage will be done by then, at least."

"See? Perfect." Tasha held the door open for her.

"I didn't see a penis, did you?"

She's talking about the sonogram. Stay focused. "Well, I..."

"I know she said the baby might've been positioned in a way that the penis wasn't visible, but it could also mean it's a girl! Do you think it's a girl?"

"It might..."

"I'm sure I will love the baby no matter what it is, but wouldn't it be exciting if it were a girl?"

"Sure..."

"We could have another member of the Goddess Posse! Do you think she could be a member of the Goddess Posse?"

Tasha was starting to miss the quiet Bethany.

"So did you see a penis? In a way, I kinda hoped to get a peek at a little, itty-bitty penis today!"

Tasha faced her car, pointed the key fob, then came to an abrupt halt. She reflexively grabbed Bethany's hand.

"Hello, ladies."

It was Rich, which meant Bethany got to see an itty-bitty penis today after all.

Bethany stiffened and raised her chin.

"Like I said, you can't hide from me. Your appointments were on the refrigerator calendar."

"Oh."

He pointed at Bethany's belly. "How's my baby?"

"*Our* baby is healthy. I'm five and a half months along."

Rich didn't seem surprised. Probably because he'd not remembered any previously mentioned due date. He turned his beady eyes on Tasha. "What the hell are you doing with my wife?"

Tasha shook her head, not taking the bait. The last thing she wanted was to see Bethany sobbing again.

Rich grabbed Bethany's arm. "Are you in danger? Have they kidnapped you? Do you want to press charges?"

"Oh, for shit's sake, Hume. Do you have any idea how ridiculous you sound?"

"Don't grab me like that." Bethany pulled her arm away, but he hung on like a pit bull with a ribeye.

"Maybe calling the police isn't such a bad idea," Tasha said.

Bethany managed to free her arm. The sudden move caused Rich to lose his balance and nearly topple over the edge of the raised walkway.

Tasha placed a hand on her lower back and guided her to the car. "Let's go, Bethany."

"Get your hands off my wife! You and that fucking crazy cat lady have done something to her, haven't you? Brainwashed her. Drugged her! Got her involved in some kind of cult!"

"You're an idiot, Rich."

"Because under no circumstances would my beautiful, *young* wife willingly spend a minute with the toothless slut of Pine Beach and her homely hag of a best friend!"

Rich's face flared purple-red. His eyeballs bulged. Spittle gathered at the corner of his mouth. He looked like the poster boy for a stroke awareness campaign.

Bethany slowly turned her gaze to Tasha, a strange calmness in her expression. Maybe this was fortuitous. Maybe Bethany would never again ask herself if she'd been too hard on ol' Dicky Hume.

"Come with me, Bethany. Now. *Please.*" Rich was full-on begging. "I have a campaign event, and I need you to be in the audience so I can point to you. We'll go the house first so you can change into something more flattering."

Bethany looked down at herself, then back to Rich. "Have you contacted my lawyer?"

"No. Because you're not thinking straight. It's the hormones. You don't need a lawyer, honey, because you have *me*." Rich's teeth flashed hideously. Tasha figured it was supposed to be a smile, but, *ew*.

Bethany took a step toward him. She rose up on her tip toes. "Listen carefully, Richard. If you stalk me again, if you get anywhere near me and the baby at a doctor's appointment or at the grocery store or anywhere at all, I will file for a protective order and call every TV station and website and newspaper in Oregon. Do you understand what I'm telling you?"

He sniffed. He pulled back in shock.

"Time to go." Bethany turned and headed for the car. Tasha jumped behind the wheel and squealed out of the parking space as fast as she could. They both glanced out the rear windshield to see Rich running after them, arms flailing, eyes bugging, spit flying, as he screamed, "This is not over, Bethan-eeeeeeee!"

Once they were on the state highway, Bethany whispered, "Oh, it's *so* over."

CHAPTER SIX

Many hours later, Felicity shook her head at the ridiculous number of Egyptian history and archaeology books piled on the table before her. She'd been there all day, taking just one break to grab a convenience store sandwich she snarfed down in the car, which did nothing to help her tummy, and that was only after the librarian swore that she wouldn't let anyone touch Felicity's collection.

She'd been sitting too long and now had a charley horse. Just to double-check her theory, she tried to heal herself by placing her fingers on her inner thigh, closing her eyes, and thinking good, restorative thoughts. It got her nothing but an eyebrow wiggle from a retiree at the copy machine.

Every one of these texts had been a bust, leaving her with more questions than when she started. Even another careful reading of The Six Steps of Overthrowing Apep had yielded exactly zero clues about what could go wrong once Apep was overthrown. It made her wonder…did Apep have a buddy out there somewhere, a partner in crime bent on avenging his defeat? Because if there was a theme to be found in all these texts, in all these books, in all of Egyptian mythology, it was that the gods were big fans of vengeance. They were always on the lookout for any shifting alliance or betrayal, large or small, that would warrant an act of revenge.

But there was nothing of the kind related to the serpent god of chaos. Tom and Alexander had been right. When it came to Apep, you overthrow him and then you wait sixty-plus years to do it again. No muss, no fuss, and no exceptions.

One nugget of trivia really hacked her off, though. Felicity had read about this before, but after all she'd been through, the information had more bite. It was about how the cult of Bastet grew out of the earlier worship of Sekhmet, the fierce lioness goddess of war and protector of light. But the patriarchal powerbase decided Bastet needed taming, so they made her softer and less threatening, a goddess who encompassed both the loving aspect of the domesticated pussycat and the warrior nature of a lion.

Funny how little had changed in the millennia since.

Felicity did find many references to magical healing and the gods and goddesses who wielded that power, including Bastet in her untamed days. There was no mention of middle-aged cat ladies in Oregon who possessed that particular gift, however.

"Ah. I thought I'd find you here."

Felicity spun around to find Tom looming behind her. He'd not repacked his nose with gauze the way the ER doctor had instructed, but that was hardly a shocker. His nose had turned a fierce shade of purple and, from her perspective, seemed off kilter with the center line of his face.

"Mind if I join you?"

"Please!" Felicity caught herself and lowered her voice to a library-appropriate whisper. "Have a seat."

Tom sat and let his gaze wander over the books strewn across the table. He picked up the *Egyptian Book of the Dead*, gave it a cursory inspection, then set it down again. "A real page-turner," he said.

"But none of the pages were any help."

Felicity considered herself an expert in the many moods of Tubastet-af-Ankh. She supposed it was what happened when you spent every day with a person for weeks on end. But things were different now. She hadn't seen him since yesterday evening. And at that moment, sitting next to her at the library table, it was hard to read him. It was as if a wall of fog had risen up between them.

"What brings you here?"

Tom flicked a finger at the deckled-edge pages of a book. He shrugged. "You were definitely right that the danger hasn't passed."

"OK." She waited, but he had nothing more to add. "Thanks for being on my side last night, but you could've just called me to tell me this. You didn't have to drive all the way up here."

"No problem." He would not look at her.

"How *did* you drive all the way up here?"

"Alexander got me a pickup. It was delivered a couple of hours ago."

"Oh." Felicity chuckled. "I pegged you as more of a sports car kind of guy."

"Not very practical." Tom pulled two sets of keys from his pocket and set them on the table. "He sent over the keys to the new apartments. You're 302 and I'm 308. We can move in whenever."

Felicity picked up a set. "Thanks." She stared at him, but he didn't look up. "Is this what couldn't wait?"

When he raised his gaze she got an even better look at his battered face. Both of his mismatched eyes were cradled in a half-moon bruise, one for the turquoise and one for the greenish-gold.

"I thought you should know that *The Aken* remains docked at the municipal harbor."

It took her a second to follow, and when she did, she fell back into her chair. "Mahaf is still hanging around Pine Beach?"

"Yes."

"Why?"

"I guess whatever you're feeling, he's feeling it, too. The balance of the universe has not been restored."

Her stomach roiled. "I just don't understand, Tom. We watched Apep light up like an oily rag and reduce to a pile of ashes. The guy is an ex-evil maniac. D-E-A-D."

"I know. I was there."

"None of this makes any sense!"

"Agreed."

Felicity huffed. "Why won't the necklace come off?"

Tom stared at the library ceiling.

"We really have no idea what's going on, do we?"

"I'm afraid not."

"Did Alexander find out anything more today?"

Tom shook his head.

Felicity let loose with an exaggerated groan. "Listen. There's something else I need to tell you. I looked for you last night when it first happened, but you weren't around."

Tom shrugged.

"I don't know how this fits in with everything yet, but you need to know." She paused. "Maybe I should just show you."

"Show me?"

"Hold still. Don't move. Shut your eyes." He was about to complain when she stopped him. "Just do it, Tom. After all the crap you've put me through, the least you can do is sit there and be still for a minute. Sheesh."

"Fine."

Felicity raised her hands in front of Tom's face, then lowered her fingertips to his nose. She closed her eyes and left gentle touches at the bridge, down the sides, around his nostrils.

"That tickles."

"Shhhh."

Felicity focused. In her mind, she pictured Tom's face free of bruises and swelling, his nose once again straight and symmetrical.

"Whatever you're doing, it feels really weird. My whole head is tingling."

"Shhh!" She traced her fingers along his cheek bones to the sweep of his eye sockets, where she delivered a series of light taps. When she was done, she pulled away to inspect her handiwork. He was completely healed.

Tom's eyes flew open. "What did you do to me?"

"Here. Look." She picked up her mobile phone, clicked on the camera, and switched it to selfie mode. Then she held it up in front of his face. He went rigid. Then he grabbed the phone and moved it side to side and up and down, catching every angle.

"It started last night when I healed Bethany's knee. It was an accident—had no idea how it happened. Then I healed a nasty scratch on Tasha's shoulder. This morning I was able to heal the cuts and burns the cats got while fighting."

"You're saying that you can heal humans and cats?" Tom looked baffled.

"Only injuries sustained in battle with Apep, in Bastet's service. Nothing else. Oh, and I can't heal myself. Do you have any idea what's going on?"

Tom continued to examine his face in the mobile phone, pressing down on the bridge of his nose. Without any change in his expression, he slid the phone across the table to Felicity and said, "I have absolutely no idea."

"This has never happened with an Acolyte before?"

"Felicity, no Acolyte has ever remained in the necklace after defeating Apep."

"I'm pretty sure I got the power while helping Little Mama give birth. So, obviously, it was bestowed by Bastet, right?"

"Probably. Sounds like her."

"But...," she trailed off, not sure she even wanted to know the answer to the question she was about to ask, "do you think it's a gift, you know, like a reward? Or could it be a warning that bad things are coming and I'll need this power at some point in the future?"

Tom was silent, considering. "Like I said, I have no idea. We're in uncharted territory."

Felicity rubbed her temples, the exhaustion of the last few days swamping her. "I'm not sure I'm up for more uncharted territory right now."

"Tell me about it." And with that, Tom scooped up his set of keys and headed for the library exit.

The entire drive back to Pine Beach, he felt as if he would jump out of his own skin. He took no pleasure in the beauty of the seascape to his right, or the rolling fields to his left, or the sweet scent of freshly cut hay in his nostrils. In fact, he wasn't the least bit pleased that he'd regained his sense of smell, or that he could now breathe easy, or that his face didn't thump with pain. He didn't appreciate the butter-soft leather seats of this ridiculously lush pickup truck, with its surround sound system and backup cameras and lane-assist and whatever-the-fuck-else Americans believed were essential to get from one location to another.

Why had he been sentenced to remain here? He was of no use to anyone. He didn't have the slightest understanding of what was going on in the present, let alone what awaited them in the future. He had no knowledge of the order of things, or the historical precedent, or the expected cause and effect. He wasn't even sure he had the right to call himself a warrior priest. What war was he preparing for? What priestly texts was he supposed to follow? What orders from his mistress must he obey?

Alexander had been right about one thing last night. It was indeed brutal to make connections and then have to end them according to an external clock, lifetime after lifetime. But Alexander had been wrong about something too. The limbo in which he now existed had to be punishment, a punishment of the cruelest kind.

Because while he was trapped here, his relationships were growing and deepening in a way he'd never experienced before. These weren't some young teenage girls who battled and moved on with their lives, any memory of him fading as the months passed. These were women well into their adult lives, not easily molded, but already fully formed, with scars and strengths and joys and sorrows and loves and losses. His connection with them was new and terrifying. He didn't just respect them, he *liked* them. They made him laugh. They amazed him. They were his friends. They were more than that.

But inevitably he would be yanked away, and that would hurt. No. It would devastate him. Pure punishment.

It was ridiculous to track Felicity down at the library only to lie about why he'd come, but that was what he did. True, Felicity needed to know that Mahaf—that humorless automaton—remained at the dock, but he could have called her with the information, just as she'd pointed out. He'd almost told her the real reason he'd come, but he knew she would overreact. She'd smother him. She'd be afraid to leave his side. And right now, he didn't think he could handle that.

No. He wouldn't allow these attachments. He couldn't let the friendship with Felicity and her so-called Goddess Posse continue. He would keep his distance, for his sake and theirs.

He decided to pick up a couple of six packs to replace the Airstream stash. He'd been drinking a lot in the last couple of days and didn't want to leave an empty refrigerator for Ronnie since she enjoyed the occasional cold one.

Ronnie.

He found a parking spot at the market and turned off the engine, staring straight ahead into a line of trees. This was his fault. He'd dropped his guard. The rapport he formed with the women of Pine Beach had opened the door to her, and he'd discovered more than he ever intended, more than was prudent. And now, he could not unknow Veronica Davis, and she was right here, an everyday torture.

Her competent and steady hands soothed him when he'd been on the edge of death. Her slim fingers stroked his fur as she stitched his wounds. The vibration of her mellow voice moved through him like a balm. And days later, in the vet clinic parking lot, she was so perceptive that she saw the injured cat in the awkward man who stood before her, though such a prospect was far beyond her reality. At her apartment, she was too proud to be lied to and pushed for the whole story. She was strong enough to fight off two professional killers who tried to cut her throat, and brave enough to let her body to be used as a weapon against Apep.

Yet her kiss had been pure vulnerability. She tasted of longing, and loss. The smart, skilled, courageous Ronnie had let her guard down and allowed him in, if only to say goodbye.

Now what? *What the fuck* was he supposed to do with that? He could take what she offered, but then...? He had no control over his own destiny. It could be five hours or five weeks when the *usekh* released, and he would be snatched back.

And once he was there, he'd have an eternity to try to forget her. He already knew it wouldn't be enough.

Oh, yes, this was punishment. And he deserved it.

Moments after Tom left the library, Felicity's phone rang. It was Alexander, asking her to meet him at Kookie's Kitchen in Pine Beach. Though she hated to do it, she pulled herself away from her pile of reference books, got in her car, and headed south.

She found Alexander seated in a quiet booth in the back. He stood, waiting for her to slide into the booth. "I appreciate you meeting me on such short notice."

"Of course, but did you drive all the way here on the chance I was free for dinner?"

He laughed. "I had business in the area."

Felicity cocked her head.

"And, yes, I thought it prudent I be nearby on the first day of construction work at Tasha's. In case things got contentious."

"Gotcha." Felicity smiled. Alexander did, indeed, have very good sense.

"Are you hungry? Let's order." Alexander slid one of the menus in front of her, and, although her stomach was still bothering her, Felicity decided maybe something other than a convenience store sandwich would help.

After they ordered, Alexander opened his briefcase and pulled out a shiny and impossibly thin laptop computer. "This is for you."

Felicity accepted it, shocked at how light it was. "Why?"

"On it is the story of each of the Acolytes, her family and community, her hopes and dreams, and details of her success in battle."

"Whoa."

"Your own story is there too, at least the rough notes Tubastet has provided to date. After the *usekh* finally releases, we'll do a detailed accounting together."

"Do you think there may be a clue about what's going on with the *usekh* in here?" Felicity felt the day's first hint of optimism.

Alexander looked a bit uncomfortable. "I haven't been able to find anything, but I'm hoping fresh eyes might catch something I missed."

She nodded. "I hope so, too. I can't stop thinking—and *feeling*—that something or someone is coming."

"I hope you're wrong." Alexander attempted to smile.

"You and me both."

Their food arrived and Felicity dove into the bread, figuring that something bland would surely help her indigestion. Alexander took a big bite of his chicken parmigiana, which made Felicity wonder if he was aware of Tom's passionate aversion to Italian food.

"I know you're focused on other things right now, Felicity, but in the computer you'll find a series of files pertaining to finances—your health insurance options, investments, your bank accounts, pension, lines of credit, and estate planning. At some point, I'd like you to think about your preferences moving forward and whether you'd like to purchase a home or land."

Felicity's brain seized. *I have an estate?*

"Nothing has to be decided immediately, of course. Take all the time you need."

"But…"

"Remember, this is payment for a job well done, for the

brilliance, courage, and strength you displayed under extreme circumstances."

She smiled sadly. "You mean how I was the rando woman who couldn't run fast enough to escape the necklace?"

Alexander was quiet for a moment, mulling over her question. He put down his fork and leaned closer. "How are we to know, Felicity? It's possible that all has gone according to plan, but the plan is too vast and complex for us to comprehend."

"Well, if this is someone's plan, I'd like to file a complaint."

He produced one of his brilliant smiles. "You know what? I often feel that way, myself."

Felicity took another bite of bread. "I'm worried about Tom."

Alexander's smile collapsed. "I know. He's rattled."

"It's more than that. He's off somehow, not himself. He drove all the way up the coast to the library, handed me the apartment keys—thank you for that, by the way—and just ran off. Do you know where he was last night? Or where he is right now?"

Alexander shook his head. "No."

She swallowed. The bread hadn't helped her bellyache. And this chat with Alexander hadn't done anything to lessen her concern for Tom.

The Airstream was empty when he arrived. It didn't take him long to gather up his few possessions and shove them into a tote. He stood near the little sink and sucked down the last drops from his beer bottle, the one he'd allowed himself to enjoy while he packed. He was off to his new place tonight, and though he had no idea what lay ahead for him at Driftwood Village, he knew Alexander had arranged for furniture and necessities to be waiting for him and Felicity, and he had no doubt that they would be comfortable. After all, there was nothing that man couldn't pull off. In fact, right there, out the window, he could see Alexander's latest accomplishment.

A house had materialized on the property. The gray single-story sat on a temporary foundation, hooked up to utilities, and surrounded by pleasant landscaping. Tasha's cottage was already a work zone, with tarps and scaffolding and a dumpster in the side yard half-filled with old plywood, plumbing fixtures, and flooring. How Tasha had gone from calling Alexander Courthouse Ken to saying *Sure, do whatever you want* was anyone's guess.

He took one last look around. He would miss this quirky little trailer. But it was time to go. He didn't want to be here when Ronnie got back from work, or wherever she'd been all day. That was the last thing he needed—another uncomfortable Ronnie moment. But maybe he had time for just one more beer. He popped open another, and before he could bring the bottle to his lips, he heard a car pull onto the gravel.

He watched out the window as Ronnie exited her Jeep, checked out the shiny, new pickup, and headed up the Airstream steps. He tried to look casual.

She pushed open the door and stopped dead.

"Just picking up my stuff. I'll be out of your hair in a minute."

"Sure."

"I won't barge in on you again. This is your place now." He took another sip of his beer and tried not to drown in her eyes. He wasn't certain he'd ever known eyes that lovely or that intense. There was so much about Veronica Davis he wished he knew, had the time to know. They really needed to talk about the kiss, but he wouldn't know where to begin that conversation. Maybe he didn't have the courage for it.

"I'm sorry I kissed you."

Welp. That answered that. She was the braver of the two. "Why?"

"Why did I kiss you? Or why am I sorry?"

"Both, I guess."

Ronnie had almost healed from her encounter with Apep's errand boys, but she'd been freshly bruised by Apep himself. Despite that, he was certain he'd never seen a woman more beautiful. And that, right there, was why she shouldn't have kissed him. The awkwardness wasn't about her. It was about him, and he should man up and tell her so.

But he didn't. The doubt had taken hold. He was a coward now.

"I kissed you because I wanted to know how your mouth would feel on mine."

Oh, shit. She was really going there.

"I'd been wondering about that for a while, and I thought you felt the same way. I see now that I was wrong, and that is why I'm sorry."

"I'm not."

"You sure act like you are."

This woman was fearless, calling him out like that. She was magnificent. "Eventually we'll figure out why the necklace won't release, and I'll be gone. Ronnie, I don't know how long I'll be here."

"None of us know how long we'll be here."

She was right. And she was angry. He didn't blame her. "My concern is that you're going to want more from me than I can give. That's all."

"It's good to see that your ego hasn't been bruised."

"*Godverdomme!* I'm not talking from my ego. I'm just stating a fact."

"And you learned this from personal experience? Managing all those thousands of pretty young things in petticoats trying to change your wandering ways and asking for things the big ol' warrior priest couldn't give?"

"I wouldn't say 'thousands.'" That was not the right response and he'd known it the instant the words came out of his mouth. His thoughts were tangled. He felt out of balance. She had that effect on him.

Ronnie stepped closer. She got right up in his face. He breathed her in. He ached to touch her hair, her skin, her body...

"You don't know me, Tubastet-af-Ankh. You know nothing about where I've been, what I've had to face, or what I want. And the reason you don't know any of those things is because you've never bothered to ask. So don't you dare tell me you're protecting my delicate heart because that's just some sanctimonious bullshit right there—in any language."

"I didn't say I was protect..."

"I see you, all right? You're a tomcat on the prowl, footloose and fancy-free, accustomed to hittin' it and quittin' it, amiright?"

"I..."

"But this time, you feel something, and your badass warrior self can't deal. And you know what? I take back the whole 'sorry I kissed you' thing because I'm not sorry. I was right. You *do* want me. But you're not honest enough to admit it to yourself."

The explosion arrived without warning. One moment he was standing by the sink, sipping his beer, and in the next he had thrown the beer bottle at the Airstream paneling as hard as he could. Glass flew. Cats scattered. He grabbed her by the shoulders, not hard, but he knew he shouldn't be touching her at all.

"I'm going to say this just once, so listen to me." He spoke in a rough whisper. Ronnie's chest heaved. Her eyes were huge. "It does not matter what the fuck I feel. You get that? I don't have a choice here. When the necklace releases, I go. That's it. Period. And I stay gone until I'm slammed back down at some random location on this shitty planet and told to fight. Again. That's what I do. I serve. I fight. I leave. And I don't get a fucking choice in any of it."

"I understand."

"Do you, really?" It came out in a croak. He felt raw, all over. He couldn't help but stare at her—so much beauty, so much strength, so much of everything he could never have.

She spoke in a whisper. "I really do understand, Tubastet-af-Ankh, and I will only ask one thing of you—that for however long you're stuck on this shitty planet, you will not pretend I don't matter."

"You *can't* matter! Don't you fucking get that? I'm not allowed to let you matter!"

They stood nose to nose, breathing hard, and he wanted to kiss her more than he'd ever wanted anything in his too-long, goddess-forsaken life. But he didn't. Because he was weak. He was a coward. He did not deserve her.

"Then get your paws off me." Her voice was low and harsh.

He did as she commanded, let her go and stepped away.

"I feel bad for you, cat. You're just another mangy stray, too afraid to let anyone get close."

He'd had enough. More than enough. Without another word, he grabbed the tote crammed with his thrift-store wardrobe, turned, slammed the door shut, and climbed into his fancy new truck. He sped off down the lane, the shocks getting a workout, his mind remaining blank until he hit the state highway.

Ronnie was wrong. He did not want her. He couldn't. She did not matter to him. She couldn't. Because that was his life agreement.

He received three years for each Acolyte, training and battle. There was no time to want a woman who mattered. Three years was nowhere near enough time for a woman like Veronica Davis.

But there was time enough for a meaningless distraction. Because in many ways, he was nothing more than an ordinary man. He had needs. That was his problem, of course, why he'd been crawling out of his skin all damn day. It had been too long since he'd had release. He just needed to blow off some steam—hit it and quit it, just like Ronnie had said.

Ronnie, the woman who did not matter.

Hours later, he sat perched on a cracked vinyl barstool at The Gas Lite, the finest dive bar Pine Beach had to offer. It was located nowhere near the beach, however. That would have been too high-rent for a dump like this. But it was dark and the beer was coldish—he was on his third—and it was crowded with people who fell into one of two categories: those who didn't pay the slightest bit of attention to anyone else, and those who were on the hunt. He was squarely in the first camp, enjoying his anonymity, but open to suggestions from a woman from the second camp.

He sipped his beer and took a casual glance around the room. There were plenty of women there, but no one sparked his interest. Because he was only interested in one woman, the One Who Did Not Matter.

Nope. Fuck that. He wasn't going there, not ever again. He would evict her from his mind, kick her out of his head and be done with it. No more. She didn't matter because she couldn't matter and that was that.

The bartender announced last call. He downed the dregs of his beer and wondered if there might be another dive bar nearby, one that stayed open later, because he still had a point to make and an itch to scratch.

Just then, a woman sauntered up to the empty stool on his left. She had bleached blond hair and did an interesting thing with her hips as she walked. He appreciated her very tight jeans and her tall, black boots.

"Hey. I'm Cherilyn."

"I'm Tuba..." *Shit*. "I'm Tom."

She laughed. It was an easy laugh, well-practiced. But her smile seemed genuine. "Haven't seen you here before. You from outa town?"

"Yeah."

"Pine Beach is adorable. I could give you a little tour."

"I bet you could."

She sat down on the barstool, then scooted it too close. She smelled like she'd been marinating in bargain-bin perfume, and it took all his strength not to move away.

"In town for long?"

"I should've left yesterday."

"My favorite kind of tourist!" Cherilyn gave another sweet smile and leaned in to kiss him.

He pulled away, then realized he'd offended her. He reached out, put his hand on her thigh. "I'm not a big fan of kissing. On the lips, anyway."

"Ohhh," Cherilyn's eyes widened in comprehension. She leaned close again, placed her slippery-cool lips on the side of his neck, and executed a combination bite-and-suck technique that wasn't half bad.

"Let's get out of here, Todd," she whispered in his ear.

Chapter Seven

"Should I keep this?" Felicity held up a Beastie Boys concert tour T-shirt, a souvenir from the Hot Tamale days so well-loved that it was see-through in the late afternoon light.

"Why?" Ronnie asked. "The armpits are totally ripped."

"But so are the memories," Tasha said, snickering.

"OK. Keeper pile it is." Felicity shoved the tattered cotton shirt into the expandable trash bag on her bed, which contained the clothes she would haul off to her fancy new digs at Driftwood Village. The contents of the other two bags were destined for either donation or the landfill. It struck her as kind of sad, really, that all the collected treasures of her life took up no more room than the surface area of a double bed and a booth tabletop.

"What are these?" Bethany held up a pair of Felicity's high-waisted compression briefs.

"Tummy control panties," Tasha said.

Bethany's otherwise flawless forehead gathered into a crinkle.

"You mean, like, to squeeze you in?"

"Pretty much," Felicity said, adding yet another unmatched sock to her growing pile.

Bethany examined the underwear, then held the garment against the front of her body. "But it goes all the way from your ribs to your knees. That can't be comfortable."

"Comfort is not the goal, sweetie," Tasha said.

"And it helps with thigh chafing," Felicity added.

Bethany looked to Tasha, then Felicity, a slow-moving terror taking hold of her expression. "When… I mean… will I…?" Her chin trembled. "I'm going to need a pair of these after the baby, aren't I?"

"Of course not," Tasha said. "You'll snap back like rubber band. Besides, neither Felicity nor I ever had children, so motherhood isn't the causal factor."

"Then what is?"

"Middle age," Felicity said, cramming old towels into the landfill bag. "And a decade of in-vitro bloatification."

"Junk food," Tasha added. "And beer. And the wrong man, followed by an even wronger one."

"Or it could be a lack of cardio and weight-bearing exercise," Ronnie suggested.

"Yeah." Felicity let her gaze wander out the window above the head of her bed. "That, too, for sure."

"But your new complex has a fitness facility, doesn't it? And a saltwater pool?"

Ronnie was obviously trying to motivate Felicity, and she appreciated it. "Yep. It's pretty swanky."

She'd seen it for the first time earlier that day. The apartment had a lovely ocean-view balcony that looked right out to Pine Beach's claim to fame, the Seal Sisters sea stacks, a trio of rock formations jutting from the waves about a football field from the beach, dotted with evergreens that grew at such strange angles that they seemed to defy gravity. Though Felicity knew these rocks like the lines of her own face, the balcony elevation gave her a new perspective. In last evening's sea mist, they looked magical. Downright otherworldly.

The rest of the place was a two-bedroom, two-bath, off-white wonderland. But for all its beauty and comforts, Felicity wasn't convinced she'd be happy there. Because of the cats.

She looked around the Airstream to find each of them doing what they did best, which was whatever they wanted. Breakfast had come and gone, so they were now scattered on the daybed, on the windowsills, the booth benches, and the bed, curled up or stretched out according to their preferences, cleaning themselves, sleeping, playing, or plotting. It was almost impossible for Felicity to picture her eleven cats anywhere but here.

But Alexander had somehow convinced the apartment complex board of managers to bend their no pets rule for Felicity, giving her permission to have six cats at a time in the apartment. But that was just half of her crew, and though Ronnie had volunteered to watch whoever stayed behind in the trailer, which was sweet of her, Felicity still hadn't decided who would stay and who would go.

Would she relocate only the bonded cats, to keep social units intact? Valkyrie and the kittens—Scratch and Sniff—had to stay together. That was nonnegotiable. But then, so did P. Diddy and Circe. And if she added Rick James and Teena Marie, who were utterly obsessed with one another and couldn't be apart, that would make seven cats, which would put her over the limit.

So, instead, would she take just the remaining four to the apartment—Mojo, Alphonse, Melrose, and Gumbo? But that would mean four males together, and since Mojo still had his cojones and liked to boss everyone around—she really needed to find the time to fix that—the dynamic could get dicey. Besides, Mojo would resent being confined to an apartment, where he wasn't allowed to roam the woods, and might even resume spraying the furniture, a bad habit Felicity had worked months to correct.

"Looks like you're still twisted up in the *Sophie's Choice* drama, huh?" Ronnie got up from where she'd been perched on the corner of the bed. "I was serious, Felicity. It's no problem to take care of them. My professional recommendation would be to leave them in the Airstream until you make a permanent move. They'll experience far less stress by staying in their established environment."

"But I'll miss them so much."

Tasha laughed. "C'mon, Lissie. It's not like you're doing twenty-five to life in a women's prison. You'll be ten minutes down the road and will probably be here every day anyway."

"I guess you're right."

"In fact," Tasha added, "you don't even have to move if you don't want to. The double-wide has three bedrooms. You can bunk with the mama and newborn kittens."

"I know, and thanks. But I think I need to do this. It's me learning to stand on my own two feet again." Felicity sighed, dropping one of Richard's old cardigans into the "donate" bag. Four years out of that marriage, Felicity couldn't remember what it felt like to have a spouse. Did they once stand in front of the bathroom mirror and brush their teeth in tandem? Was there really another body next to hers in bed every night? She couldn't recall what it was like to share a morning pot of coffee with someone. And she'd forgotten that she once had a man in her life whose cardigans were fair game.

Not that she wanted a husband again—absolutely not. And if she had a hankering for a menswear cardigan, she could go out and buy one. Felicity was just fascinated that she'd found one of Richard's sweaters mixed in with her things, like an archaeological find from an ancient lifetime.

The sound of footsteps made everyone cock their heads to listen. Someone was coming up the aluminum stairs. The tread was heavy, faltered. Then came a knock at the door.

Ronnie opened it. It was Tom, or what was left of him. He looked like he'd slept in a storm drain. His eyeballs were bright red and his short hair stuck up in every direction.

"Hi, Tom!"

He winced at Bethany's overly enthusiastic greeting. It didn't take a detective to see he had one helluva hangover.

"Excuse us." Tasha had already grabbed Bethany by the elbow and ushered her to the door. "See you ladies later!"

Everyone heard what Bethany said on their way to the modular home. "He smells terrible!"

"Hey, Tom," Felicity said, tying off her bag. "Wondered where you've been. Haven't seen you since yesterday at the library."

"Yeah, it's been twenty-three hours and twenty-nine minutes."

"That's... precise."

"I figured you'd be collecting more of your stuff. Just came to, you know, check in." He moved to the sink, grabbed a glass from the cupboard, and filled it with water. He drained the whole thing and refilled.

"You look like you just woke up."

"I did."

"It's 4:30 in the afternoon, Tom."

"Couldn't get to sleep 'til this morning."

Ronnie shifted her stance, and when she spoke her voice was tight. "Thought you weren't going to pop in anymore."

"Sorry. Just looking for Felicity." He closed his eyes against the puny light over the sink, as if it was too bright for him to bear. Felicity saw Ronnie stiffen and followed her gaze to...

Oh, shit. The right side of Tom's neck sported a large, capillary-speckled hickey, complete with unmistakable teeth marks. It seemed Tom had spent the previous evening with a lamprey.

"Do you have any aspirin?" He didn't seem to notice them staring.

"No." Ronnie might have appeared smooth as glass on the surface, but Felicity felt her vibrate with hurt and anger. It was time to get Tom out of there. She swung her "keep" trash bag into the center aisle of the Airstream. "Let's go, dude." Felicity grabbed his wrist. "I have aspirin back at the apartment."

He spoke to Felicity while staring at Ronnie. "OK. I'll follow you back."

"You sober enough to drive?"

"I haven't had a drink in hours. Unfortunately." After one last glance Ronnie's way, he headed out the door.

Felicity hesitated, then turned back. She found Ronnie standing at attention, shoulders back. It broke Felicity's heart to see how that idiot had hurt her. "If you ever want to talk, I'm here."

Ronnie gave a tired shake of her head. "Nothing to talk about." She lifted her chin, exposing the tight tendons at her throat. "But thanks for having my six."

Because Felicity was not Tom's mother, thank the Goddess, she was fine with handing him her bottle of aspirin and dumping the sorry, misbehaving, hickey-covered priest at his own apartment. She suggested he might want to get his shit together, then slammed his door.

Once she was rid of him, Felicity had planned to kick back in her new place, maybe read a book or cook something in that fancy, ultramodern, fully-stocked kitchen of hers. The double ovens tempted her to start baking again. She couldn't remember the last time she'd made her famous chocolate cake.

But now was not the time for baking. She needed to be in a good mood to bake, a humming-to-yourself kind of good mood, and she was miles away from that at the moment. Felicity just couldn't settle. She wandered through the apartment, unable to shake the feeling that disaster was headed her way and she wasn't doing enough to prevent it. So she grabbed her sweater and a scarf and decided to walk along the beach. If she were lucky, walking would tire her out enough that she could get some sleep, and her thoughts were always clearer after a good night's sleep.

She walked, allowing her limbs to stretch and her lungs to expand. Kids played in the liquid-gold tidepools of sunset, and parents ran after toddlers who ventured too close to the white, frothy waves. Happy dogs chased Frisbees and tennis balls. It was the close of a normal summer day, and she was grateful for it. She was grateful that all these nice, fun-loving people and creatures were still alive, and that the world and all its beauty remained intact because Apep had been defeated.

She raised her hand to the woven scarf around her neck, feeling the necklace beneath. Worry once again cut into her thoughts like cactus spines through the skin, but Felicity refused to acknowledge it further. Instead, she focused on the rhythmic thud of her footsteps and the squish of cool, wet sand between her toes. True, no one knew why the necklace remained around her throat, but it did. She was still the Acolyte. She would figure it out.

Back in her apartment, Felicity enjoyed the most over-the-top shower experience of her life, with four heads massaging and twirling and beating water against her flesh from a variety of angles and directions, like an automated car wash.

She opened the double doors to the closet, intending to toss her garbage bag of clothes inside, but instead froze where she stood. Sometime between last night and this afternoon, Alexander, or someone on his behalf, had assembled a new wardrobe for Felicity, and every piece was well-made and obviously expensive.

Felicity grabbed a pair of jeans and a soft sweater, then put them back. She rifled through the contents of the built-in drawers until she found a silky-soft pair of cotton pajamas. They fit like a dream. And since she couldn't solve anything more tonight, she peeled down the luxurious duvet of her new king-size bed, settled down into a mattress that cradled her like a newborn, and pulled the cool sheets and fluffy comforter up to her chin. The lullaby of the sea just outside her window sang her to sleep.

Felicity woke in the morning covered in sweat, her stomach gnawing and grinding. Had she had another one of those nightmares? Maybe. No. She couldn't remember. But the pain was getting worse.

She rooted around in her purse for her roll of extra-strength antacids, only to find it empty. She rifled through the bathroom cabinets and kitchen cupboards, but found nothing. She threw on some clothes, left her apartment, and went three doors down to Tom's, hoping maybe Alexander had stocked his place with first aid supplies. She knocked on the door of Apartment 308 West and heard a shuffling noise inside.

"Tom?" Felicity pressed her ear to the door and waited. "Hey, Tom! It's Felicity. Do you have any antacid?"

"Go away."

She pulled back, surprised at the frosty tone of his voice. She'd had it up to there with Tom's self-pity-palooza. "Open up. We need to talk. I'm worried about you."

"Go the fuck away."

Felicity tried the door and found it unlocked. She stepped inside. Tom didn't bother to look up. He was slumped in the middle of the mostly bare living room floor, surrounded by beer bottle empties and papers strewn every which way. She saw his profile, head dropped and shoulders hunched. He looked like he'd been up all night, doing whatever *this* was.

"You've got to get it together, my friend." Felicity closed the door and moved to stand over him. He didn't acknowledge her so she dropped to her knees. "What's all this?" She reached for one of the pages. He tried to snatch it from her grip, but she was too quick for him.

That's when she saw what lay under all those papers—Misty's sparkly, pink phone. "Where'd you get that?"

"Alexander found it when they emptied Viper Apps."

Felicity glanced down at the paper in her hands and a few on the carpet. These were printouts of emails and text messages between Misty McAlpin of Clackamas, Oregon, and her teenage friends. There had to be a hundred pages or more fanned out in front of them, each one a complaint or a whine.

"Why are you doing this to yourself, Tom?"

His mismatched eyes were still rimmed in red, but at least he'd showered. The hickey, however, was there for the long haul. "You know nothing, Felicity."

"Then how about you fill me in?"

Air sawed in and out of his nose. He glared at her in defiance. "That girl *haaaaaaated* me. Absolutely despised me."

"She was young. You told me yourself…"

"No. You've got to hear this shit, Felicity. Hold on a second. I just had it." Tom fanned through the papers until he found what he was looking for. He held the paper out in front of him, cleared his throat and read, in what had to be an imitation of his former Acolyte, *"Oh. My. God. Sorry I can't go out tonight. My parents hired some totally sus tutor. Can't stand to be in the same room with him."*

Tom glanced up. "Suspect! She called me *suspect*. And she called me a tutor! I am trainer of the Acolytes, not a tutor!"

Felicity sighed. She decided to sit cross-legged on the floor next to him. She might as well get comfortable since this would probably take a while.

"And this one!" Tom shook his head in disbelief, then read. *"Dude is such a selfish asshole. I swear five minutes with him and I'm lowkey suicidal."* He blinked. "Training with me made her want to kill herself."

"Come on, Tom. She was a teenager. She was exaggerating. It was just her way of bitching to her friends and besides, she had to tell them you were her tutor, right? Like I had to tell Tasha and Ronnie you were my nephew."

"Yeah? Then she was the world's most prolific bitch because there are hundreds and hundreds of these messages!" Tom chose a random page. *"He thinks he's the GOAT and that he knows everything and I'm just an idiot. I could yeet his ass to the state line if I wanted to."*

"How did you get these, anyway?"

"Alexander. After he found the phone, I asked him to copy all her correspondence, hoping there'd be something helpful about why the *usekh* didn't release. Everything was here last night, waiting for me."

She narrowed an eye at him. "And was there anything helpful?"

He let go with an angry laugh. "Absolutely chock-full of helpful examples of how I'd bossed her around. Never listened to her. Expected her to behave like a robot. Was cold and distant and how, over time, she'd come to loathe my loser-old-man existence. Apparently, I ruined her life."

Felicity began collecting the papers.

"Looking back, I'm sure all the Acolytes have hated me. It's just that they didn't live in an era when technology could capture their every random thought and keep a record of it into perpetuity."

"That's utter crap."

"How would you know, Felicity?"

"Well, first off, I'm one of your previous Acolytes, you dipshit! And I don't hate you."

"Riiiiiight."

"And I've been reading the Acolyte records that Alexander gave me. So far, I haven't found a single one who hated you."

"Yeah? How many have you gotten through?"

"Not many. Mostly skimming. It's thousands of pages."

He laughed. "Get back to me when you're done."

Felicity rose to a stand, the pages tucked under her arm. "Listen, Tom. Sure, yes, you pissed me off on a daily basis and pushed me beyond where I thought I could go, but the last I heard, that's your job."

His mouth curled into a snarl as he looked up at her. "Thanks for the pep talk, but none of it matters. I failed. My actions caused Misty to hate me with such a passion that she went off and got herself killed. Then I failed to remove the necklace from her replacement. By definition, that makes me a failure. I'm such a disappointment to the Ever-Living Goddess that I wouldn't blame her if she struck me down where I stand, exterminated me like the insect I am."

"Phew. That's a relief, then."

He glared.

"You're safe at the moment, right? Because you're on the floor, wallowing in spineless self-loathing, not strong enough to stand on your own two feet. You should probably just stay down there, you know, out of an abundance of caution."

Whoops. She might have gone too far. Tom's expression and body language radiated pure disgust, an ugly loathing the likes of which Felicity had never encountered in a human being. Even Rich hadn't been able to muster that kind of repugnance while looking at her.

"You have overstepped, Acolyte."

"No. You're the one who's overstepped. The drinking. The dramatic self-flagellation. The hickey from Loulou the Lamprey. And the disrespect of those who care for you. You're better than that, Tubastet-af-Ankh, *hem netjer-tepi* of the Goddess Bastet, temple guard of per-Bast, warrior, and trainer of the Acolytes!"

He leaned away, blinking.

"And you are *needed*. I need you. Something is wrong, and we'll soon be called to fight again. I just know it. And the man I'm looking at right now is no warrior. He's worthless to me, worthless to his mistress, and worthless to the world."

She wasn't sure what she expected from her teacher. Maybe a grunt of acquiescence or a shrug of *I'll see what I can do*, or perhaps even a snarky comeback about Loulou, but this was what she got instead:

"Get. The fuck. Out."

CHAPTER EIGHT

Felicity was prepped and ready to face whatever danger lay just around the corner. She'd practiced her spins and kicks and even tried a few sit-ups. But she'd done it alone, in the apartment complex fitness center. Because since the night she found Tom with Misty's cell phone and printouts, he'd either been absent, disinterested, or worthless. So she'd done the best she could. She was focused. She was ready.

And nothing happened.

For ten days, nothing.

Finally, Felicity realized she was driving herself, and the posse, crazy. So she was happy to accept Cass' dinner invitation. She deserved a night out. She would not allow a sense of uneasiness to stop her from living. In fact, maybe Bethany had been right. Maybe she really *was* paranoid, looking for a dark side in everything.

So she chewed an antacid and paced in front of the walk-in-closet mirror, nervous as Circe confronting a cucumber. She hadn't prepared to go out on an actual date with a man for… she turned to

Tasha, who sat directly behind her in a tufted, pink velvet wingback chair. Felicity never thought she'd have a closet so chic it had its own chair. "Hey, Tash. When was my last date?"

She drummed her fingers on the chair arm. "If it was that car salesman in Oceanview, then three years ago, right before your diagnosis."

"No." Felicity wracked her brain for the details. "The car guy was right after Rich kicked me to the curb. There was someone in between him and my diagnosis, but I can't remember his name. I can't even remember his face."

From her perch on the bed, Ronnie said, "Must have been a bomb-ass date."

"If you can believe it, he made me pay for my own ice cream cone."

"Now, that's low," Ronnie said.

Felicity may not have remembered the man, but she remembered the moment. The Creamery Creations cashier had been terribly embarrassed when she handed Felicity her chocolate-with-sprinkles waffle cone. "Uh," the girl's eyes tracked to Felicity's date, who had sauntered out the shop's front door, busily licking his butter brickle. "He didn't actually pay for yours." Felicity dug into her purse and made good on her debt, and once outside, she walked right past her date, tossed her cone into the trash can, and made a beeline for the parking lot where she'd left her car. "Hey!" he'd called after her. "What's your problem?"

But tonight, she was going out with Cass, who wasn't like that. Cass was one of the good guys. She didn't know him well, yet she was certain of it.

Too bad her stomach wouldn't settle. She grabbed another chewable out of her purse.

"Are you feeling OK, Lissie? Is your stomach still bothering you?"

"I'm fine, Tash. It comes and goes."

"You should see a doctor," Ronnie said. "It's likely nothing, but it would be smart to rule out anything serious."

Felicity shook her head. "I'll be fine." She stood before the floor-length mirror, unable to decide between the tailored linen skirt she'd put on and the palazzo pants on the hanger she kept holding up to her waist, then pulling away, only to repeat. She questioned whether she had the panache required for these silky, wide-leg trousers.

"Those pants are super cute!" Bethany poked her head into the bedroom. "You should definitely wear those—so fun and flirty!"

"That's me all right!" Felicity shimmied out of the skirt and into the pants. She chose a pair of wedge-heeled espadrilles with a tie at the ankle, then buttoned up a striped cotton dress shirt and knotted it at her waist. She stared at her reflection. "I think this will work."

"Seriously, Lissie. You look fabulous." Tasha beamed.

"Agreed," Ronnie said. "But I can't get over how Alexander just went ahead and stocked your closet without asking."

"The man has a complex," Tasha said. "A certified control freak."

"Said the other certified control freak." Felicity straightened a button.

"Funny." Tasha said.

Ronnie scootched her way up to the head of the king-size bed. "The weirdest part is you actually like the stuff he got you, and it looks great on you. What are the odds of that? I mean, he was so spot-on it's scary. If a man ever tried to buy me clothes, I'd punch him in the throat." Ronnie changed the subject. "Did your dairy farm dreamboat tell you where he's taking you?"

Felicity giggled. "Nope. Isn't that exciting!" She turned to check her profile. She'd pulled her hair up into a relaxed bun and let a few loose curls fall around her face and against the nape of her neck, a style that looked good *and* covered the still-visible bald spot on the back of her head—a win-win!

"What's that god-awful smell?" Ronnie asked.

Tasha rolled her eyes and lowered her voice. "Bethany's smudging again. She's gotten deep into the woo lately. There's herbs and tarot cards and astrology charts all over the double-wide. She's spending a lot of time at the occult store on Hawthorne, where we got these." Tasha held up her Bastet bracelet.

"Hey, Bethany!" Felicity waited until her head popped in the door again.

"Yes?"

"Out of curiosity, why are you saging the apartment? It's a brand-new building, not a haunted Victorian mansion or something."

"Oh, well, interestingly enough, I've learned that negative energy has nothing to do with the age of a structure. What I picked up here is fresh. And very intense. There's a lot of low-frequency negativity near the front door. Darkness and pain. Felicity, how have you been feeling?" Bethany straightened her right arm, raising the smoldering bundle of herbs high, then used a feather to direct a curling tendril of smoke to trace the shape of the bedroom doorway.

"Might want to stay clear of the smoke detector," Ronnie said.

Felicity didn't say as much, but she knew Bethany's observations weren't far off the mark. The source of all that negativity had to be Tom. It's the only thing that made sense to her. He'd singlehandedly changed the dynamic of everything.

He'd even changed Felicity's perception of time. She now saw history in two distinct eras, Before the Hickey and After the Hickey.

In the BH era, she was sure everyone was on the same team, that they were all in this together and the Goddess Posse and their immortal priest could work together to find a solution to any problem.

Now, in the AH era, Tom was collapsing before their eyes, drowning in a cesspool of self-absorbed misery. She never even saw him anymore, except for his "visits." Every single day, right at or just before noon, Tom would simply show up, wherever Felicity happened to be. He never had anything specific to tell her. He'd simply say hello, then turn around and leave.

That very afternoon, he'd come by the apartment. Felicity opened the door to find him staring at her with hollow eyes. He shook his head when she invited him in for a cup of tea, then turned around and walked back to his place. If she were honest, the whole thing was weird as fuck.

Though the AH era had begun just ten days before, it felt like ten years. She missed Tom. She missed who he used to be. She missed her friend.

Felicity grabbed her bag. "I should go. I don't want to be late." Bethany saged the path, leading everyone out the front door and into the hallway, where she extinguished her smudge stick. The posse escorted Felicity down to the lobby to wait for Cass.

His pickup pulled into the semicircular drive right on time. He got out, his face lighting up when he saw Felicity.

"Wow! You look incredible."

"I thought I'd try a slime-free look tonight."

He laughed, making his way around the front of the truck, then leaned in to kiss Felicity on the cheek. He pulled back and locked his eyes on hers, a puzzled expression already in place. For whatever reason, she seemed to puzzle the man on a regular basis. Cass then moved to stand before the posse. "Great to see you again, Tasha." Cass kissed her on the cheek too, then Tasha introduced him to Ronnie and Bethany. After a few moments of small talk, they were on their way.

"Have fun!" Bethany called out.

"Call if you'll be late!" Ronnie added.

Cass turned to Felicity, his hands on the wheel. "She's kidding, right?"

"Absolutely."

"Good. Because what I have planned will get you back very late indeed."

The last rays of sunset burnished his face, highlighting his crow's feet and the weatherworn lines at the edges of his mouth while the candle flame flickered in his eyes. He was an exceptionally handsome man. He was an unusually polite and thoughtful one, too. And the idea that he'd gone to all this trouble for her—the private table for two on the pier, the wine, the flowers, the delicious meal—was almost too much to process.

"I'm pretty sure this is the most romantic night I've ever had in my life."

Cass seemed pleased to hear that, folding his hands on his lap and relaxing into the high back of his dining chair. "Good. That was my evil plan."

No one had ever done something like this for Felicity. Sure, she'd been out to dinner at fancy places, but Cass had created an entire experience for her this evening. And she knew he'd done it for *her* and not for her bank balance or line of credit, because he knew nothing of those things. He'd asked no questions about her sudden upgrade in wardrobe and housing, either.

"So. Aren't you the least bit curious?"

His mouth hitched. "About…?"

She laughed. "It's fairly obvious that my life just got bumped to business class."

He nodded, amused. "I figured you'd tell me when you were good and ready. Whatever's happened—the lottery or an inheritance or cryptocurrency or whatever—I'm happy for you because you look...," he paused. "I guess the word is settled. You are a lot more relaxed than when I saw you last. That's a good thing."

Felicity took a sip from her wine glass, enjoying the mellow Willamette Valley pinot noir on her tongue. "It *is* a good thing. I still have a few complications I'll need to deal with at some point."

"Ah, yes, all the strangeness. And your nonsexual, sort-of nephew."

"That's part of it, yes." She smiled at Cass, relieved for his low-key acceptance. "In the meantime, I'm just trying to be grateful and appreciate life, especially tonight, here with you."

He tipped his head and studied her. It wasn't an awkward or invasive kind of staring, though. Felicity saw thoughtful curiosity in the way he looked at her. Not long ago, such frank admiration would have sparked a cascade of negative thinking, sharp suspicion, and a sinking mistrust. Felicity would have already started the countdown for the proverbial shoe to drop. But not tonight. Not with this man. And the difference, she supposed, wasn't only about Cass. It was about her, too.

She trusted herself now. Whatever happened and however and whenever this ended, she had faith that she would manage her part wisely and would emerge whole and strong, instead of broken.

Which made dating a lot less intimidating.

"Something else is different about you. I mean...," he chuckled and fidgeted in his chair, grasping for what he wanted to say. "It's not the clothes or the apartment. You're lit up from the inside, Felicity, and I'm really happy to see it."

She wanted to respond but was dumbstruck. And flattered. And impressed with how attuned Cass was to the world around him, and to her. She fiddled with the napkin in her lap until she managed to say, "That's sweet of you."

"I didn't mean to make you uncomfortable."

She looked up into his eyes and realized she'd never really appreciated their color, a misty, muted green, like a shore pine in the fog.

"I'd like to kiss you, Felicity, if you're comfortable with kissing in public."

Her belly did a little nervous somersault, but she was determined to keep her cool. "It's been so long, I can't remember where I stand on that issue."

Cass stood, took his time moving around their linen-draped café table, and stood over her. He offered his palm, and she slipped her hand in his. Cass eased her to her feet and guided her out onto the pier. Facing her, he gently lifted one of her arms and placed it around his neck, then pressed his palm to the small of her back. Cass began to sway with her, slow and smooth, in sync with make-believe music. The whole time, his green eyes glittered.

"Cass?"

"Hmm?" He lowered his forehead to hers and kept swaying.

"I should point out that this is dancing, not kissing. You didn't ask me how I felt about public dancing."

His chuckle was low and warm. He lifted his head and smiled down at her, then pulled her tighter. Her thighs pressed against his, the heat of his body searing through the thin fabric of her palazzo pants. He eased her back and forth and turned her leisurely, saying, "They are not mutually exclusive concepts."

"No?"

"Nuh-uh. Let me show you."

His hand slid up her spine as he pulled back just enough to drop his gaze to her mouth. Then he lowered his lips to hers. It was a kiss of gentle confidence, polite but hungry, the kind of kiss that led to other things. Felicity felt herself shiver in pleasure, and decided that, should anyone ever again ask, she could say with confidence that she was in favor of kissing and dancing in public.

Suddenly, she stilled. Her body went rigid and she ended the kiss.

Cass looked at her with surprise. "What's wrong?"

She didn't want to freak him out or react in a way that would lead to more questions. But they were being watched. She was sure of it. Eyes were tracking their every move—cold and inhuman eyes. She beat back the deep discomfort and managed a smile. "Maybe we can go somewhere less public?"

"I know the perfect place," Cass said.

They strolled hand in hand down the pier. Cass left her for a moment to handle their bill and the waiter's tip, which gave her an opportunity to follow the energy of that stare to its source.

How could she have forgotten? She almost laughed at herself for being so blissfully unaware of her surroundings. In a marina slip not a hundred feet away was Mahaf. His huge, dark form towered over the deck of *The Aken*, stiff and unmoving. His icy stare wasn't threatening, but it wasn't friendly either.

"Ready?" Cass slipped his arm around her waist, and they walked off. He grinned down at her, "You know, Felicity, I've been thinking about it, and I believe I've stumbled on the perfect metaphor for you."

"Oooh. I love metaphors." She couldn't wait to get past the

boardwalk shops and beyond Mahaf's line of sight. "Do tell."

"You're a birthday cake."

"Hmm. How do you figure?" The glower burned into the back of her head.

"Well, you're sweet and fun and put people in a good mood the instant they see you."

"Thank you." *Yes!* Finally, they'd made the turn toward Main Street, and the glare couldn't pass through buildings. She exhaled with relief.

"But you've got a hell of a lot of layers."

She laughed and leaned against him. "Oh, Cass. You have no idea."

Ronnie finished feeding the cats and washed up the dinner dishes. It wasn't late, but she was tempted to just call it a night. It had been a rough day at the clinic, with six scheduled surgeries and a grieving family to comfort. Sitting with people in shock over the loss of their pet was her least favorite part of the job but often the most important. People sometimes felt weird allowing themselves to grieve for an animal, saying things like, "I know she was just a dog, but…"

Well, the adults struggled. The kids, not so much, since children haven't yet learned to turn away from their truths. Today, she'd sat with a dad and his two boys, both under ten, who'd cried their guts out over the passing of a goofy old Tibetan terrier mix named Leroy.

Dr. Nguyen once told Ronnie that she had a gift. She told her that it took a strong soul to simply sit with death and offer a safe place to land for the grieving. Ronnie had thanked her, but didn't bother to mention that she'd paid a high price for that gift, in civilian life and in the Marines. And Dr. Nguyen had never asked her about any of it.

Neither had the other vet techs or her community college classmates.

Maybe she'd been too hard on Tom the other day, slamming him for not asking her anything personal. Ronnie knew she gave off a general keep-your-distance vibe as she moved through life. But that was because it was better for everyone. Nobody really wanted to hear the gory details, because the details sucked.

In a way, she envied Felicity for her openhearted nature. No, Felicity didn't like everyone and she sure as hell wasn't afraid to speak her mind, but Ronnie had seen how easy it was for Felicity to connect, to enjoy other people, to laugh with them. Tonight, Felicity was out on a real date with a guy whose face lit up like a spotlight when he saw her. Ronnie had never had a man look at her like that. And it had been a long-ass time since she'd been on a real date of any kind.

Mrrraow.

Merp.

Prrrrraaaaaoooooow.

"I know kids, I know." She bent down to pat Mojo's head, scratch Circe under her chin, and rub Rick James' ear. They missed Felicity. And Felicity missed them something awful, as was evident just yesterday, when she'd sat here in the middle of the trailer and let them crawl all over her while she pretended she wasn't crying.

Shit was weird all around right now. Uncertain. Everyone was going through some kind of upheaval around here, and everything had a temporary feel to it. It was the opposite of how they'd been not two weeks ago, when the goal, though damn near impossible, was crystal clear: kill Apep and end his threat. And, boom. They did.

And nothing had been clear since.

The necklace wouldn't release. Felicity was getting bad vibes about the world, and Bethany was sensing low-vibration frequencies in a brand-new luxury apartment. Tasha was going through some kind of dark-night-of-the-middle-aged-soul drama about her house, though she was doing her best to pretend all was well.

Her phone rang and she picked up right away. "What's hanging, Mr. Moneybags?"

"Hope I'm not calling too late," Alexander said.

"Nah, it's fine."

"Niko Sweeney called me. Again. He asked for your number. Again. I must give the man points for perseverance. Anyway, I took pity on him and said I'd ask one last time."

Ronnie listened, watching absently as Melrose and P. Diddy batted around a fur ball. She really needed to clean up around here.

So how would she answer? Niko was super smart and good-looking by any measure. More important, he seemed to appreciate the difference between right and wrong, which was a trait in short supply these days. Overall, the dude was pretty impressive. So why was she hesitating?

Tom. Right. Fuck that.

"Go ahead and give him my number. Why not?"

They hung up and Ronnie grabbed one of the beers Tom put in her refrigerator.

Tubastet-af-Ankh. The cat was losing his grip, and she couldn't help but wonder if part of it was her fault. Or even most of it. If she'd kept her lips to herself, maybe he wouldn't be in such a bad place.

That kiss. It was *so* unlike her. Why did she do it? What was it about him that screwed with her self-control?

She sipped her beer, closing her eyes when a soft breeze moved through the open windows. Ronnie turned off all the lights except for the light over the sink, stripped off her clothes, and changed into a tank top and pair of sweatpants cut off at mid-thigh. An image zapped through her brain. She'd worn a tank top that night. She remembered the ink-black desert sky and the smell of her company commander, her perpetrator.

The tank top had been to blame, he'd later lied. She'd seduced him, he'd lied. Her accusation was premeditated, motivated by jealousy and incompetence, he'd lied. Every word he'd said from the witness stand had been a lie.

She hadn't let him get the *last* word, though, and that was what mattered most.

Ronnie reached her fingers down her back, ripped the tank over her head and off her body. She balled it up and threw it into the corner, grabbing a sweatshirt off the shelf.

It was getting better, no doubt about it. More than two years had passed, and the flashes came so rarely now that they were almost a surprise when they hit. These days, the memory lasted just seconds and left almost no coating of ooze on her psyche.

She heard a rapping noise so soft that at first she assumed it was the cats, enjoying their after-dinner zoomies. But the sound was steady and rhythmic, and she poked her head out to see the rescues lined up at the door, ears perked. The cats' excited reaction meant it was Felicity. But—*oh, damn*! Had something gone wrong on her date?

"Come on in!"

The door swung open. Tom stood on the stoop, body tensed and face drawn in the soft light.

Nope. A thousand nopes all strung together like nope-to-nope party lights. Nope. Nope. Nope.

Absolutely no way.

La shukran. Ni hablar. Dastet dard nakone, mamnoon. He could pick any way to say no from his fourteen non-accented languages and shove it where the Acolyte don't shine.

His knees buckled. He grabbed the door to steady himself.

"Just tell me you did not drive here."

He nodded. Then thought better of it and shook his head. "I did drive, but I wasn't drunk when I drove."

Really? How's that work?"

"Because..." He raised a stiff arm and pointed outside. "I've been sitting in my truck. Down the lane. Took me one and a half six-packs to work up the nerve to walk down here and knock."

She planned to slam the door in his stupid face—his drunk, ridiculous, tortured, stupid-beautiful face. She took a step closer to him, and her heart clenched. Guilt broke loose inside her. No, the drinking was absolutely not OK, but the trigger for it might have been that kiss.

He tilted backward in the direction of the rickety railing.

"Seriously?" Ronnie grabbed him by the shirt and yanked him inside. She corralled him to the daybed and pushed him down. "Sit. Stay. One cup of coffee and I'm getting you a ride home, understand?"

"I don't want coffee. Just beer."

"Sweet shitballs. Not happening, champ." She filled the kettle and put it on the burner.

"I didn't want the blonde, either. Nothing happened. I couldn't do it."

Ronnie spun around. Tom had slumped into the back cushion. Teena Marie curled up in his lap. Scratch and Sniff climbed on his shoulders and head. His expression was that of a lost kid.

"What blonde?"

He pointed to his neck.

"Ah. The creature who disfigured you." She put a couple spoonfuls of freeze-dried coffee into a mug. She wished it were weed killer.

Tom nodded, or rather, tried to. But the movement seemed to

make him dizzy. He listed to one side, a silly smile on his face.

God, he was pathetic. And adorable, with the cats using him as a climbing tower. And he was ripping her guts out. She wanted to cry with the unfairness of it all, of every fucking thing.

"I want you, Ronnie. Only you. You matter more than anything, do you know that? But I'm not allowed to have you."

She finished making his coffee and carried the mug over to the daybed. "Drink, then haul your sweet ass out of here."

He looked surprised. "You think my ass is sweet?"

"Slip of the tongue. Drink up."

He took a sip and made a face that might have been comical in another setting, then set the cup on the nearby booth table.

In a move Ronnie assumed he was too wasted to execute, he grabbed her wrist and pulled her down on his lap. In her shock, she failed to react fast enough and their eyes locked. She saw nothing but longing and loneliness in his expression, which she had no doubt was mirrored in her own. Her body melted into his. They fit together perfectly.

He stroked her arm, studied the raised Marine Corps emblem on her sweatshirt and reached up to touch her curls.

What the fuck am I doing?

Ronnie knew should already be standing at the opposite end of the trailer and ordering him to leave. Because there was no way she would kiss him again. Even though she felt his hard, hot thighs press into her bottom. Even though her breath had already synced with his.

Tubastet-af-Ankh raised his gorgeous unmatched eyes to hers. Everything about him was luscious—his dark and thick lashes, his generous lips, the stubble on his angular face.

"Please kiss me again, Ronnie."

It was such a polite request. It would hardly seem fair if she slapped him, crushed his windpipe, or threw him to the floor in response.

"That didn't work out so great the last time, remember?"

"All my fault."

"Yes, it was."

"How about I kiss you this time?"

"I guess it'd be all right. Just to see what happens."

Oh, God. She was going to let him, wasn't she? Fine. There would be plenty of opportunity for slapping, crushing, and throwing right after they kissed this one last time.

He smiled at her, and when his muscular arms drew her in, her spine softened and her eyelids grew heavy. He cradled her. He angled her so that he could lay her back upon the daybed. Ronnie trembled in anticipation as the searing heat of his lips hovered over hers. And then…

Her head smacked against the cushion.

She froze for a second, reached out her hands and opened her eyes. Tubastet was gone. Technically speaking.

A large tomcat with exotic black and gray markings was flopped across her belly, purring in his drunken sleep. His whiskers twitched in a dream.

She shoved him aside, which didn't even wake him up. "Yeah, that's it. I hate men. I hate cats. And I especially hate men *who turn into fucking cats!*"

Rroowaarrr, Mojo said.

Ronnie stomped the length of the trailer to the tiny bedroom and slammed the door behind her. Well, she couldn't really slam a vinyl accordion door, so what she did instead was slide that sucker closed like a badass. How unsatisfying.

Which seemed to be the theme of the evening.

Ronnie awoke before the sun, knowing that he'd be gone. And he was. But taped to the small refrigerator was a note, written in a heavy, elegant script.

Ronnie,

That has never happened to me before. I'm quite embarrassed. I apologize. I shouldn't have come over last night. Don't worry, it won't happen again.

T

She crinkled the note in her fist, unsure whether she was relieved, or disappointed, or just pissed off. She decided she was all of the above.

CHAPTER NINE

Felicity's head lolled to the side, and her warm cheek encountered the cool pillowcase. Her eyelids fluttered open. Framed in the sturdy oak trim of Cass' open bedroom window was this: deep-green rolling hills, blue sky, and lavish patches cornflower, daisies, baby's breath, and primrose as far as the eye could see, all under the midmorning sun. She languidly rolled over onto her tummy, the sheet twisting with her, and rested her chin on her arms. She felt a giant smile breaking across her face.

She was today-years-old when she knew how it felt to be adored, to be happy in a man's company while being true to herself. Gratitude flooded her. What a gift to learn this before she died. What a gift to be alive to learn it.

Oh, boy. She had it bad for Cassius Schwindorf.

"Good morning." Cass appeared in the bedroom doorway. He leaned against the doorframe and crossed his ankles. He looked as slaphappy as Felicity felt.

"How are the cows?"

He laughed. "Fairly pissed off, honestly. I was way behind schedule."

"Perhaps I should go apologize to them, since it's my fault."

"Oh, it is most definitely your fault."

"I worry that I'm insatiable."

One of his eyebrows hitched.

"Is that going to be a problem for you?"

Cass pulled his lips inward, trying hard not to smile. Why was this man so god-awful sexy? Was it because he was witty and warm and intelligent, even in dirty dairy-farm duds? Was it because he didn't seem to know he was any of those things, or care?

Felicity rolled onto her side and bent a knee. She gathered the sheet to her breasts and grinned at him.

"Three minutes." He began unbuttoning his shirt.

"Pardon?"

He untucked his shirt from his jeans and undid his belt. "I need three minutes in the shower to wash the barn off me." He kicked off his boots. "And then you'll be joining me."

"I will?"

He turned and went across the hall. She heard him turn on the water. Felicity sat up, dangled her legs over the side of the bed, and called out, "Are you bossing me around?"

"Of course not."

"Mind if I boss you around?"

"Have at it. Just give me three minutes."

She couldn't wait. Cass didn't seem bothered by her enthusiasm, and it wasn't long before they both were wet and slippery under the hot spray. Aside from the water, making love in Cass' shower wasn't all that different from making love in Cass' bed. He took his pleasure by giving her pleasure. He had no discernable hang-ups. And he let her set the pace.

It was all so wonderful that she completely forgot to boss him around. Maybe she wasn't the bossy type.

Felicity spent most of the day at Cass' place. They made pancakes together and went for a hike in the woods on his property. He held her hand on the path, telling her about his childhood and the life he'd built for himself. He left college a few credits shy of his bachelor's degree in agricultural management, and now he wanted to go back and finish. He loved his work as a volunteer firefighter and member of a civic search and rescue team.

He took her out to lunch in town, and afterward they strolled the beach like they had nowhere else to be or nothing else to do. If there was any downside to an otherwise delightful day with Cass, it was that Felicity knew she had cheated him. He had been so free and open about himself, yet she'd remained guarded. Of course, he noticed. How could he not? But he didn't push. Felicity told him more about her marriage, her teaching, and her breast cancer diagnosis, and he listened with intense interest. But when it came to her recent history, and Tom, she hit a wall.

If Cass was disappointed, he didn't show it.

It was almost two in the afternoon when Felicity said she needed to head home. The gallant Cass offered to escort her to her door, but the truth was, she was exhausted from all the excellent sex, real conversation, and intense emotional connection, and a little astounded that one man had been the source of it all. What she needed now was a nap and some space to decompress, so she'd kissed Cass goodbye and jumped out of his truck.

"I'll call you," he said.

"I hope so," she said. But then Felicity looked back at him and couldn't seem to walk away. Instead, she'd strolled over to the open driver's-side window, leaned in, grabbed both sides of his face, and kissed him again. Thoroughly.

"Thank you, sweet Cass."

Felicity hummed to herself on the short elevator ride to her third-floor apartment. If only her stupid stomach wasn't still bothering her. She popped another antacid as she stepped off the elevator, rooted around in her bag for her keys, and made her way down the hallway. She didn't notice the body slumped against her door until she was on top of it.

Blood. Everywhere.

"Tom?"

He struggled to lift his head.

Oh-God-oh-God-oh-God. "What in the hell happened to you? I'm calling 911."

His hand clutched her wrist. "No."

"But—"

"No, Felicity."

Icy tentacles of panic had already invaded her brain. She couldn't think straight. If she didn't get him help, he could die. Blood had soaked through his shirt and jeans.

Hands shaking, she unlocked her door and threw her bag into the apartment, then spun around, bent down, and grabbed him from behind, trying to drag him inside. Tom kicked against the carpet to propel himself, but he was mostly dead weight.

She got him across the threshold. Felicity shut the door, propped him up against the wall, and dropped to her knees in front of him. She tried to lift his T-shirt to see where he was hurt, but coagulated blood had plastered the fabric to his skin.

"How long ago did this happen?" She ran to the kitchen for a pair of scissors and dropped to her knees again. "Tom, answer me. What the hell happened to you? How long ago? You've lost a lot of blood."

She cut away the shirt. He hissed in agony as she peeled the fabric from his flesh. Felicity fell back on her heels in shock. She dropped the scissors. "Oh, shit, Tom."

Five deep gashes sliced across his torso at an angle, starting at one shoulder and swiping down toward the opposite hip. He'd been mauled.

"What kind of creature did this to you?"

Tom's head was tipped back against the wall. She watched him take shallow, quick breaths, but he didn't answer.

"OK, OK. I can help. I can do this." She knew his wound didn't happen in battle against Apep, but surely she could save Bastet's loyal priest? Felicity extended her hands and gently laid both palms across the lowest of the five wounds, just below his belly button. She closed her eyes, picturing the flesh mending. She opened her eyes.

No change.

She tried again, placed her hands on another wound and repeated the positive, healing thoughts. Nothing.

Tom rocked his head back and forth against the wall, eyes still closed. "Don't bother. It won't work. She won't let you."

"She who? You're hallucinating from blood loss." Felicity grabbed her cell phone from her bag.

"What are you doing?"

"I have no choice. You'll die if I don't get you to the hospital."

"No!" Tom managed to open his eyes. "Please, Felicity. No hospitals. Not for this."

She found herself dialing Ronnie instead.

"How'd the date go—?"

"Come to the apartment. *Now.* Bring the first aid kit. It's an emergency."

Felicity managed to drag Tom across the foyer and into the kitchen. She laid him on his back and placed a rolled tea towel under his head. He drifted in and out of consciousness.

Ronnie burst through the door and skidded to a stop. "Holy *fuck.*"

Ronnie couldn't manage her usual poker face. Instead, her eyes widened and her mouth opened and she let out a pitiful little cry. She turned to Felicity for answers, but Felicity could only shake her head. And that was all Ronnie allowed herself. She'd already transitioned into medic mode.

She dropped beside him, opened the large first aid kit, and pulled on sterile gloves. "Do you know when this happened?"

"No idea. He was at my door when I got home. About twenty minutes ago, I guess."

"Open all the curtains and turn on every light you have in here, OK?"

Felicity jumped up and did each of those things.

"Tom. Can you hear me? It's Ronnie."

"I tried to do my healing thing, but it didn't work. I don't know why."

"Has he regained consciousness?"

"Yes." Felicity dropped down next to Ronnie again. "I think he was hallucinating, though. When I couldn't heal him, he said something like, 'Don't bother because she won't let you.'"

Ronnie pulled out the disinfecting wipes. "At least he's stopped bleeding. His pulse is steady."

"I don't even know how that's possible."

"Well, we know from experience that he heals fast." Tom

stirred as Ronnie began cleaning one of the gashes. "He's been sliced up. Clawed. What the fuck could have done this?"

Felicity shook her head. "I have no idea, but that pattern... if I didn't know better, I'd think it was a giant cat scratch."

"Lion." Tom whispered. He attempted to sit up.

"Stay still!" Ronnie pressed his uninjured shoulder onto the marble floor.

Felicity caressed his unshaven cheek while Ronnie continued disinfecting.

"Ow."

"I know it stings. My sincere apologies." Ronnie didn't exactly sound apologetic.

Tom struggled to open his eyes, finding Ronnie first, then turning his gaze to Felicity. "You didn't come home last night. You weren't here when I checked in at noon. It's after two."

Felicity didn't understand. "And? You got bored and went to hang out at the zoo?"

He tried to speak, but his voice came out as a croak.

"I'll get you some water." Felicity jumped up just as Tom let loose with a deep groan of pain, which was followed by another of Ronnie's insincere apologies.

"Here." Felicity helped Tom lift his head and put the glass to his lips.

"These cuts aren't all that deep, but the split is wide. These really should be stitched up."

"Then do it." Tom took another sip of water.

Ronnie pulled out an aerosol can.

"What's that?" Felicity asked.

"Lidocaine numbing spray. Not that he deserves it." Ronnie sprayed the bottom wound and then opened a suture kit.

Tom took a sharp breath as she began.

"Has the spray had time to take effect?"

Ronnie shrugged as she concentrated on her work. "Sure hope so."

Yowzah. She and Ronnie needed to have a chat. Soon. Felicity watched Tom clench his teeth.

Felicity figured she'd humor him as a distraction from the pain. "So tell us about this lion, Tom."

"The *usekh*."

"Yeah, it's still stuck around my neck. But tell me exactly how you came to be ambushed by carnivorous predators."

"Not predators. The *usekh*."

Felicity straightened, looking to Ronnie for confirmation.

"I think he's saying the necklace attacked him. He sounds pretty clear on that."

Felicity snorted. "Come on, Tom." She brushed her fingers along the gold at her throat. "It's just a necklace, and it hasn't been out of my sight for a second!"

"But it's been out of *my* sight. That's the problem." Tom handed her the water glass.

Her mind went from zero to sixty. What was Tom saying, and why was it a problem that he hadn't seen the *usekh*? Was this connected with his strange daily check-ins? "You said *she* wouldn't allow me to heal you. Who's *she*?"

"Bastet. From the beginning, her command was that I must never be away from the Acolyte who wears the *usekh* for more than twenty-four hours."

"*What?*"

"It's an incentive for us both to stay close when things get dangerous and difficult, which they always do." He arched his back in pain when the needle pierced his skin.

Ronnie shook her head. "So your ever-loving goddess sliced and diced your ass because you lost track of time? That's brutal."

"The mission is brutal. Battle is brutal. You, of all people, know that, Veronica Davis of Camp Pendleton." He took several deep breaths.

"Back up." Felicity felt her blood pressure rise. "You said incentive for *both*. Does that mean the Acolyte is supposed to know this detail?"

He nodded.

She dropped his head to the floor. "So that's what your strange drop-ins were all about? And you showing up hungover at Ronnie's with Satan's own hickey? Why didn't you just *tell* me?"

He lay still, eyes closed. Felicity suspected he was faking unconsciousness. "It would have been so easy, Tom. You could have said, 'Hey Felicity, if we aren't together in the same room at least once every twenty-four hours, your necklace will try to kill me.' See how simple that was?"

Ronnie sprayed the lidocaine across the next claw mark. "I don't get what a lion has got to do with this."

At least Felicity knew *something*. "The Goddess Bastet started as a lion instead of a housecat, and it's still considered one of her goddess aspects."

Ronnie nodded. "Very fierce. I can dig that."

"May I have more water?"

Felicity lifted his head and helped him drink again. "I just don't get why you couldn't tell me what you needed."

"Ooh, ooh. I know the answer to that one," Ronnie said, tying off another suture. "It's because he can't let himself need anyone for anything, right warrior priest?"

Tom didn't answer. He kept his eyes averted. He handed Felicity the drinking glass.

Now Felicity was well and truly pissed. She let his head drop again. "So that's what this is all about? Are you fucking *kidding* me? The drinking, the meanness, the coldness, the hickey? All because you don't want to need other people? How the hell have you survived for two millennia?"

He blinked at her, his eyes empty. "You are all better off without me. I'm not meant to be in one place for this long. I hurt everyone I touch. I ruin lives."

She jumped to her feet. "All right. That's it." She placed the glass on the countertop and marched into her huge walk-in closet. She changed out of clothes smeared with the blood of the world's most stubborn, infuriating warrior priest, and returned to the kitchen. Felicity swooped down to grab her purse off the floor and gestured for Ronnie to follow her into the hallway, where she spoke in a whisper.

"I hate to ask you to do this, but I need you to stay with him until I get back. When you're done stitching, help him get to the couch so he can take a nap. Try to get him to eat something. There's soup in the pantry."

"No problem, but where are you going?"

"Portland. I need to see a lawyer about a cat."

The double mahogany doors on the nineteenth floor of KOIN Tower were bare but for an elegant gold name plate: *Alexander Helios Rigiat and Associates*. The elegance wasn't a surprise to Felicity, but the associates part sure threw her off. She'd pictured the administrator of Bastet's worldly affairs as an independent man of mystery, not a guy who ran an office. Beyond the doors she encountered a sea of plush carpet, walls of glass, and sophisticated furnishings.

"May I help you?" A sleek, young gentleman in a blue blazer greeted her from the reception desk.

"I need to see Alexander."

"Certainly. Do you have an appointment?"

"I don't need one. Tell him Felicity is here."

If the sleek dude was shocked, he didn't let on. He picked up the sleek phone on his sleek desk and spoke softly.

Felicity turned to study the large painting on the reception wall. She assumed it was abstract art, since she had absolutely no idea what it was supposed to be, and had no doubt it was worth more than Tasha's house and land combined.

"Felicity!" She spun around just as Alexander reached her. "What a welcome surprise."

"We need to talk. Now."

He produced a polite smile and gestured for her to follow him.

They walked together down an open corridor connecting several offices—the enigmatic associates, no doubt. As Felicity walked, she noticed that the occupants of those offices seemed... happy. They smiled as Alexander passed, and he responded with a little nod or wave. It was such a contrast to the attorney she'd hired to handle her divorce. The offices of William K. Schmidt, clown-at-law, had been sandwiched in a strip mall between a tattoo salon and a podiatrist. The podiatrist could have achieved the same courtroom results. Possibly even the tattooer.

Alexander gestured for her to enter his large corner suite. He spoke to his assistant as he entered his office proper. "I'm in an urgent client meeting. No interruptions, no exceptions." And he shut the door.

Before she could even get a word out, Alexander picked up a file folder from his desk. "You have perfect timing. I just learned that the judge has ordered Richard to sell the—"

"Don't care about him."

Alexander, ever unflappable, returned the file to the desktop. "Let's sit." He gestured to two comfortable-looking leather and chrome chairs in front of the wall of windows.

Felicity sat, just to be sociable, when what she really needed was some frantic pacing. It was true that her temper had cooled during the long drive, but all she wanted now was to set her plan in motion.

"Is there a problem at the apartment? Are you in need of funds? I can transfer—"

"Stop."

And he did.

Felicity took a deep breath. "Tell me about Elizabeth 'Betty' Sinclair of Midlothian, Scotland."

For just an instant, Alexander's resolute composure slipped, but then slid right back into place. "Of course. The thirtieth Acolyte. The one before Misty. A remarkable woman."

"Yes, remarkable, considering it's the first time it's ever happened in the history of Acolytes."

"What's happened for the first time, Felicity? I'm not sure I'm following you."

She leaned in closer, spoke almost in a whisper, as if sharing a secret. *"She's still alive."* Alexander didn't move. He didn't blink. She continued. "There is no death date entered in the ledger."

He matched her whisper. "A mistake on my part, clearly. I apologize for any misunderstanding it might have caused."

"You don't make mistakes like that. It's your sacred duty, right? And a little math tells me she'd only be eighty-three. Barely even elderly by today's standards."

Alexander considered that. "She'd be eighty-four, *if* she were still alive." He smoothed his already-smooth suit jacket. "You need to understand that my family maintains a confidential attorney-client relationship with each Acolyte, just as the one I now have with you. The only information that can be shared is what is placed in the Acolyte record. I'm sorry, but I can't answer any questions you may have, even if I wanted to."

"I'm terrified for him, Alexander." From the look on his face, it was clear he knew of whom she spoke. "He's suffering. He's completely isolated himself. He didn't even tell me the consequences of being away from the *usekh* for more than a day until it was too late."

Alexander paled with shock. "Dear Goddess, are the wounds grave?"

"For your basic supernatural lion mauling, yeah, I'd say they were pretty bad. Ronnie stitched him up. But I think on some level he did it on purpose. He was punishing himself for, and I quote, 'ruining people's lives.' He thinks every Acolyte has harbored Misty-level hatred toward him."

Alexander rubbed his temples. Then he raked his fingers through his widow's peak. It was the most tussled Felicity had ever seen him.

"We have to intervene, Alexander, right now."

He shook his head, but his resolve was fading. "It would be a profound violation of our standard of service."

Felicity had to laugh. "You know what else is a profound violation of standards? The necklace not releasing. The warrior priest flipping his shit because he can't return to the Realm of the Gods and then being nearly killed by the Goddess he serves."

Alexander said nothing.

"So here's what we're going to do. You'll tell me where Miss Thirtieth is. Then you'll get passports for Tom and me and arrange for two plane tickets. Because I'm going to fight for him, and you're going to help me do it."

Alexander leaned back in his chair and rubbed his palms along the leather armrests. He looked her straight in the eye. "No need for passports. She's in Los Angeles."

It was late by the time Felicity made it back to Pine Beach. When she found Ronnie alone in the apartment, a jolt of fear went through her. "Where is he?"

"Back at his place." Ronnie rose from the couch and yawned. "After he slept and ate, he said he would heal faster as a cat, so he did his thing and I carried his fuzzy butt down the hall. I figured I'd hang out here in case of emergency."

Felicity let go of the breath she'd been holding. "Thank you, Ronnie. For everything. I know it couldn't have been pleasant."

She gave a sad, little laugh. "I'm pretty sure he morphed so he wouldn't have to talk to me. Joke's on him, though, since I like him way better as a cat."

"If there's anything I can do…"

"Yeah, there's not. Did you get what you needed in Portland?"

"I did. I only hope it's enough."

CHAPTER TEN

Early the next morning, Felicity shoved a couple of apples and a pack of crackers into her bag and marched down the hallway. She knocked on Tom's door.

He answered, hair sticking up, naked except for the sheet tied around his hips. He'd removed the bandages, and Felicity could see that his sutures were healing unnaturally fast, probably from a night spent in cat form.

"Get dressed. We need to run an errand."

"What time is it?"

"Almost noon."

He rubbed his unshaven face and looked behind him out the balcony doors. "You're lying. The sun's not even up."

"Just put on some clothes."

"What kind of errand is this?"

"A life-or-death one."

"I'm busy." Tom tried to shut the door in her face, only to

discover Felicity's foot was lodged in the door jam. "I don't want to do anything. I'm tired and sore."

"I know. It won't take long, and you'll feel much better when it's over. Hurry up." Felicity shooed him inside and grabbed his wallet from the kitchen island while he dressed. She made sure it held his driver's license, then shoved it in her purse.

Tom was barefoot as he stumbled to the door and out into the hallway, so Felicity grabbed a pair of athletic shoes from the foyer closet. He yawned as they rode the elevator down. Felicity guided him through the lobby and shoved him into their waiting black Town Car.

Tom collapsed into the seat. "Where're we going?"

"Wal-Mart."

"In a fancy car with a driver?" Tom was confused.

Felicity caught the driver's eyes in the rear-view mirror and gave him a little nod.

Mercifully, Tom fell asleep about five minutes into the drive, and didn't wake up until the car came to a crawl in the midst of Portland International Airport traffic.

He squinted and looked out the car window. "This isn't Wal-Mart."

"Correct. So put on your shoes."

Felicity expected that once Tom discerned the nature of their errand, he'd put up a fight, maybe even turn his back on her and disappear into the crowd. Bastet's "incentive" must have been fresh in his mind, however, because all Tom did was look around the terminal with wide eyes. She could see his body thrum with tension.

"You good?" She placed a gentle hand on his shoulder.

"Why are we getting on an airplane?"

"Because the airplane will take us where we're going."

Tom scanned the huge overhead display of arrivals and

departures, then stared at the crowd in line for security. "And where's that?"

"Los Angeles."

He swallowed with difficulty, as if his mouth were dry. "Los Angeles? Is this about the *usekh*?"

Either Tom hadn't yet realized the significance of their destination or he didn't know. "Not directly." She produced what she hoped was a comforting smile. "But this trip will be helpful... well, that's the plan, anyway."

Tom surveyed the throng of people and uniformed employees, and shook his head. "I don't think there is anything helpful about a place like Los Angeles. Let's forget this." He took Felicity's arm and tried to pull her away from security.

At first Felicity was confused, but then it dawned on her. "You've never been on an airplane, have you?"

"No. And I don't intend to start." He pulled on her again, but she wouldn't budge.

"What's the big deal, Tom? You've used every mode of transportation known to man—cars and boats and chariots, and camels, carts, wagons and maybe even a donkey." She leaned in closer so no one else could overhear. "You travel in between *realms of existence*, for crying out loud."

He scrunched up his symmetrical nose.

"You've stood at the precipice of the extinction of humankind—goddess knows how many times—and you're afraid of an *airplane*?"

"I didn't say I was afraid. I just have better things to do than allow myself to be hurled through the sky in a tin tube." Tom crossed his arms over his chest.

"Really, like what?" He didn't answer. She put her arm around his shoulder, gave it a little squeeze, and herded him through the roped-off security maze. "You can always turn into a cat and ride on my lap."

That had the intended effect. Tom threw off her arm. "Fine. Whatever."

He didn't speak to her as they went through security and walked to their gate. Tom followed other passengers down the jetway without a word to Felicity. She had to run to catch up to him, and whisper in his ear, "You'll be fine. They have peanuts."

As it turned out, they had way more than peanuts in first class. Felicity had never flown in such luxury and cooed over every little amenity. Tom spent most of the flight clawing at the armrests, but managed to down a complimentary glass of champagne and nibble at her cheese plate.

Less than three hours later, they landed in Los Angeles, where a driver and another Town Car waited for them, just as Alexander had arranged. As they tooled through the manicured streets, Tom peered out the window and scowled. "Pretty scraggly palm trees."

"I guess, being Egyptian and all, you'd know."

He fell back into silence, just staring out the window as the sunny scenes rolled by.

"Don't you want to know where we're going?" Felicity asked.

"Does it matter?"

It wasn't long before Tom lost interest in the tidy streetscapes, closed his eyes, and let his head fall back against the seat.

Felicity studied Tom, worry rising in her throat. In the short time she'd known him—through the near-death wounds, battles, and beatings—his essence had always remained intact. The spark at the core of Tubastet-af-Ankh had always managed to shine through. But not anymore. He had no fight left in him. He'd given up.

This trip was a Hail Mary, or, more accurately, a Hail Bastet.

The driver slowed in front of a stately home that was part Tudor England and part Old Hollywood. The electronic iron gates parted, and he pulled into the semicircular drive.

When the driver opened Felicity's door, she popped out, then hesitated. "I'm sorry. I'm not sure how long we'll be."

The driver nodded. "I've been instructed to wait."

"Oh, good. Thank you."

The driver opened Tom's door next, but he didn't move. For a moment, Felicity worried that Tom would be stubborn enough to refuse to exit the car. But he pulled himself to a stand, grunting and groaning as if it were a near-impossible feat of strength.

Felicity shook her head, thinking, *oh, how the mighty have fallen.* Was this the same man who, just days ago, enjoyed a big-ass slice of German chocolate cake while Felicity nearly cried attempting the turn-squat-kick in Step Two, Defiling Apep with the Left Foot?

She urged Tom forward along the walkway. They stepped up under an arched portico framed in climbing roses and stood before a rich walnut door.

Panic flashed through her. What if this backfired? What if Betty really *had* hated him? *No.* Felicity shook it off. She knew she was right. And, she realized, if she was going to save the man beside her, this was the only way she knew to do it.

"Do you know where we are?" Felicity asked in her most soothing voice.

"No idea. And, honestly, I don't care." Tom looked down at his feet, already defeated.

That's what gave Felicity the courage to ring the bell.

A moment later, the door was opened by a petite woman in a mauve silk designer suit. When Elizabeth Sinclair of Midlothian,

Scotland, smiled, her lovely face shone with happiness.

Felicity turned to Tom. She wanted to witness the moment of recognition register on his face, the matching smile that was surely on its way.

"NO!" Tom spun on Felicity, the tendons on his neck popping. "*HELL*, NO! How could you fucking do this to me?"

He stomped off the porch.

"Tubastet!" Betty called after him, his Egyptian name incongruous with her faint Scottish lilt. He froze. His shoulders stiffened. For a long moment, no one moved—Felicity barely breathed—and then slowly, Tom turned around.

"Fine." His voice was as dead as his eyes. Felicity worried she'd made a terrible mistake.

He stepped toward the front door, his jaw clenched, his hands in fists. His eyes locked on Betty. "Bring it on. Tell me what you really thought of me, what you've waited all these years to say." Felicity could see that he braced himself for a verbal assault.

The thirtieth Acolyte primly descended the front stairs and stood before him. "Aye. I do, indeed, have something I've wanted to tell you for decades."

Tom jerked his head. "Then get it over with. You have the right. Just say it."

Betty raised her chin. She looked directly into his eyes. "Thank you." That was all she said before she wrapped her arms around his waist, rested her cheek on his chest, and held him close.

For a moment, Tom's only expression was shock. Then, slowly, he softened. He embraced her petite frame with care, then pulled her tighter.

Betty began to gently rock him in her arms with the practiced ease of a loving mother. Felicity could barely hear when she whispered,

"I've missed you, my old friend. I owe you so much. What a miracle it is to see you again."

And then Felicity watched as her fierce warrior priest, *hem-netjer-tepi* of the Ever-Living-Goddess Bastet, temple guard of Per-Bast, and the most badass man she would ever know, began to cry.

The three had been talking for more than a half hour in the gracious sitting room of Betty's historic home, with its teak-paneled walls, vaulted ceilings, and glass doors flung open to a storybook color-splash of a garden. Felicity sat in an overstuffed chair while Betty and Tom shared a small sofa.

"That's absolute *pendejadas*." Betty slurped the last of the tea from her antique porcelain cup, then plopped it into its saucer with a tad too much force.

"Um, what?" Felicity was confused.

"It's Spanish for bullshit," Tom explained, looking a bit sheepish.

"Tubastet, didn't you teach her all the good swear words?"

"As I explained, time's been short this time around, Lil Bit."

"'Lil Bit!' No one's called me that since you, Tubastet. No one's dared." Betty laughed, rich and deep, as she refilled everyone's cups. "And now that I think on it, the multi-lingual swearing may have been the most practical lesson I learned from you. It certainly came in handy when I was an ambassador."

"You were an ambassador?" Felicity had no idea.

"I was. I began working in the Foreign Office as a young solicitor. After several years I became a junior diplomat and finally Ambassador. I traveled the world. Which is to say, I became quite good at detecting the odor of *pendejadas* in a variety of exotic locales." The satisfied smile on Betty's face made her look every bit the formidable dignitary.

Betty looked over her cup at Tom. "I can't believe you allowed Misty's complaints to get under your skin."

Tom stared into his teacup with his head bowed.

"*Of course*, she hated you."

Felicity was about ready to protest when Betty held up her hand.

"We all hate you at some point, don't we?" She looked to Felicity for concurrence. "For me, let me think… I believe I began wishing for your dismemberment and agonizingly slow demise at about the three hundredth pull-up."

Felicity smiled. "It was the sit-ups for me."

Betty laughed. "I can see how that would have been a challenge for you, Felicity, not being a lassie like the rest of us." Felicity was trying to decide if she was insulted when Betty continued. "How lucky you are, I think."

"Lucky? My knees would disagree."

"Of course, they would. A grown woman's body is likely to complain, but I would venture to say not as loudly as a lassie's spirit. I was a fifteen-year-old child from the landlocked lowlands when Tubastet was sent to me. I was scared of my own shadow in those days." She smiled at the memory and sipped her tea. "I certainly resented all the effort and focus required of me. Every night I plotted my escape. I whined to my father a fair bit, as well."

"A lot, actually," Tom said.

That made Betty smile again, but almost immediately, her countenance turned serious. "That was because I didn't know what a rare gift I'd been given. I could only see the terrible responsibility, how the fate of the whole world rested on my scrawny shoulders. And I always worried that my arms weren't strong enough to swing that damned heavy lance."

"I had to get a lighter one," Felicity admitted.

"What an excellent idea! I never thought of that. And I had a terrible time with all the squatting and kicking. I still don't understand why any of that was necessary."

"Tell me about it. I fucking *hate* Step Two." Felicity froze, aware of her faux pas, and was about to apologize when Betty snickered. The two Acolytes laughed together in sisterhood.

After a moment, Betty put her teacup down and focused on Felicity. "I say you are lucky because you already knew who you were when called to serve. I'm sure you better appreciate the beautiful gifts of the *usekh* and the wisdom Tubastet so generously shares with us often-ungrateful Acolytes."

"On my good days, maybe." Felicity thought of all the times she'd cussed at poor Tom or given him a hard time when he was only doing his job.

Betty turned her intense attention to him. "Tubastet, if young Misty had lived long enough, she would have grown to appreciate all your hard work, too. But it's nearly impossible for an Acolyte to do so when in the thick of things."

Tom gave a slow nod and raised his head to meet her gaze. "I hear that. But I still want to apologize for being so hard on you, Lil Bit. I'm sorry I made you cry so many times."

"I'm not." Betty stood and walked with purpose to the wall of built-in bookcases. "Do you see all of this?" She gestured to the multitude of photos and knick-knacks on display behind her. Felicity could see fading wedding portraits and digital rotating photo frames, diplomas, military medals, awards, and even baby shoes.

"This is my life. A spectacular life I wouldn't have had if it weren't for you, Tubastet. You taught me to be brave. You taught me to trust my gut above all else, no matter where that might lead me. Do you remember telling me that?"

Tom nodded.

"Because of you, I learned to have faith in myself. Because I had faith in myself, I went to university and then on to law school. I met my Laurence there and I was blessed to have fifty-one years with him, may The Ever-Living Goddess shine her light upon the path of his departed soul."

Tom raised his cup in salute. "Ever watch over us," he added.

"We had three children, who had six children of their own and those beautiful babies bestowed upon me the sacred title of Gran. What I'm telling you is that everything I am, my whole extraordinary life, was possible only because I was the thirtieth Acolyte of the Goddess Bastet, and a student of Tubastet-af-Ankh."

Betty crossed the Persian rug with purpose and returned to her spot beside Tom. "I've always kept you in my prayers. All these years."

"Why did you think I needed prayer?" Tom appeared confused.

"Because I saw you spend so much of your time here *serving* that you weren't doing much *living*. I always thought you must be lonely, so I prayed you could find a balance, allow yourself a bit of joy. Maybe even a little love, aye?"

Tom didn't answer. He seemed lost in thought.

"Consider what I've said. Please." Her voice was sweet, but firm, and she waited until she got a nod of assent from Tom. "Excellent, then."

Betty rose. "Tubastet, would you mind if we leave you to your own devices for a few moments?"

"Of course not."

"Then, Felicity, I'd love to show you my library."

"You have your own library?" She shot to her feet, barely containing her excitement.

"I had a hunch you were a fellow bibliophile. Let me give you the tour of my favorite place in the world." She took Felicity's arm and whispered, "It happens to be very private, as well."

It took a fingerprint scan and a numeric code for Betty to open the thick door to the library. Felicity stepped inside, eyes scanning everywhere all at once, and came to stand in the middle of the most jaw-dropping room she'd ever seen. It wasn't large, but every surface of every wall was lined with built-in bookshelves. Many of the books were quite old. Some were even displayed inside locked glass cases.

"I know it's dark in here, but the low light prevents ultraviolet damage. It's climate controlled, of course, and fireproof, at least that's what the insurance appraisers tell me."

"I... I don't know what to say. I could spend the rest of my life in this room."

Betty opened a drawer in the center reading table and pulled out a pair of white cotton gloves. "Here. Enjoy."

Felicity eagerly slipped on the gloves and walked around the room, occasionally stopping to touch the spine of an obviously precious tome or pull one gently from its perch to open. She inhaled the distinct perfume only found in old books, the scent of paper and ink, leather, and time itself.

"One of the best parts about traveling the world is getting a chance to collect wonderful things. And of course, books are the most wonderful things of all." Betty put on a pair of gloves and joined Felicity, brushing her fingertips along a few nearby treasures.

"Oh my God!" Felicity had stopped in front of a glass display case holding three large papyrus scrolls. They were ancient Egyptian, but in excellent condition.

"Those are my prized possessions."

"Shouldn't they be in a museum?" Felicity cringed at the way she'd blurted that out. "I'm sorry. What I meant to ask was, where did you get them?" Felicity stared in amazement at the small portions of hieroglyphics visible along the edges of the closed scrolls.

"I inherited them. They're known as the Sinclair Scrolls." Betty moved a bit stiffly as she made her way to one of the comfortable reading chairs in the center of the room. She was such a presence, such a force, that Felicity had forgotten she was in her eighties. Their visit must be exhausting for her. But after a quick adjustment of her skirt, Betty continued. "I'm sure you know that the Acolyte is from one of the old families."

"Yes. Well, before me, anyway." Felicity gave a little laugh.

"My family predates Tubastet by at least two centuries. Obviously, Sinclair is not our original family name." She produced a wistful smile. "We picked that up sometime in the 11th century."

"Do you know what's on the scrolls?"

"Not personally, no. As many times as I've tried to learn, I can't read them. Simply not one of my gifts, I suppose. But I'm told they contain wisdom and spells. Around here somewhere is a translation my grandfather created."

Betty motioned to the chair beside her, and Felicity sat. Betty looked directly into her eyes. "Thank you for letting me see him again. I didn't realize how much I needed that."

"No, Betty. Thank *you*. You may have saved his life. Literally. He'd dug himself into such a deep hole that I was desperate."

"Sometimes we need our loved ones to remind us who we truly are. I think it's far too easy to get tangled up in our thoughts, tell ourselves stories that are as unkind as they are untrue."

"Don't I know it."

Betty pulled off her cotton gloves and leaned forward. Felicity realized her focus was on the necklace. Betty raised a hand. "May I?"

"Of course." Felicity opened another button on her shirt collar and lifted her chin.

With gentle reverence, Betty ran her fingers across the gold and its center sapphire stone. "I never thought I'd see this again, feel its power in my hands."

"Can you?"

"Just a bit. But I'll never forget what it felt like around my throat. Your visit has been quite a gift. You know, it's the first time in history that two Acolytes could sit together and have a conversation."

"Should we get a selfie?"

Betty chuckled as she withdrew her hand from the *usekh*. "I'm the oldest surviving Acolyte on record." She paused, thinking. "Naoko Mitsumoto of Kyoto, the 25th Acolyte, lived to eighty-one, which was quite a feat back in the 1600s. Probably the benefits of a diet rich in fish and seaweed. I prefer a nice glass of whiskey myself."

They laughed together.

"Felicity, pardon my directness, but I can't believe you received only two weeks of training and still defeated Apep. That's miraculous. I may be the only person who truly understands the magnitude of all you've accomplished. How lucky we are that Tubastet chose you."

Exhaustion fell heavy on Felicity's shoulders. "That is kind of you to say, but I'm not sure anybody's lucky. Things are very off kilter right now, and confusing. Honestly, I have no idea what's around the bend, or how I'll deal with it."

"I can understand your uncertainty." Betty sighed. "It's a mystery why you still wear the *usekh*. And I'm baffled as to why Tubastet is trapped here. But I do know that you have everything you need to face whatever comes your way."

"I hope so, Betty."

"In my long life, the most important skill I ever learned was how to push away self-doubt and trust my instincts, my intuition."

"Of course." Felicity smiled. "I always shoot for that, but it's hard to do sometimes."

"Oh, yes. It is quite difficult, especially in times of chaos and crisis." Betty's expression had gone serious, and she leaned in close. "Trust yourself, Felicity. It's absolutely critical."

CHAPTER ELEVEN

Tom was subdued on the return flight to Portland, but it wasn't the same old sullen crankiness to which Felicity had grown accustomed. He was pensive and calm, occasionally pointing out an interesting cloud or his fascination with the Pacific coastline from 32,000 feet. Though his wonder was almost childlike, the dark circles under his eyes were those of a man who'd been through hell. The slow and cautious way he moved indicated that he was exhausted and still in physical pain. Who wouldn't be? Just yesterday, he'd been mauled by a supernatural lion. And he'd spent today whirling from rage to tears to sorrow and back again, while reconnecting with an elderly woman he'd known only as a young girl. That kind of emotional whiplash had to have taken a toll on him.

While worrying about how drained Tom was, Felicity slipped into a deep, and thank the Goddess, dreamless sleep, waking only when she felt her body jostled.

"Felicity." Tom gave her a gentle shake. "We're almost ready to land. Wake up."

She fought back the brain fog and pushed herself up from her sleepy slump. "Sorry. I didn't mean to conk out like that."

"Clearly, you needed it. From now on, you should grab sleep whenever you can. We've got a lot of training to do." Tom kept eye contact with her while the corner of his mouth hitched up just the slightest bit.

She straightened. "We do?"

"Yeah. We do." At that, his lips curled into an almost full-fledged smile. She hadn't seen anything from him remotely resembling a smile since the morning the necklace wouldn't release. It was all she could do not to hoot and holler in relief.

"Thank you, Felicity," he said. "Thank you for caring enough to save me."

"Ha, well, you know me. Cats, civilizations, entire worlds—saving is what I do, right?"

"And you do it so well, always in your own indomitable way."

For a moment she was sure his eyes had misted. But he tapped his elbow against her upper arm and turned away, his attention back on the clouds, now glowing in the orange-pink sunset. "Look!" He pointed. "That's looks just like a rabbit."

She peered around him to see a huge cumulus floating by. "Oh, please. That's an elephant jumping into a puddle." Felicity produced a fake snort and punched Tom's shoulder. "Amateur."

It was pitch dark by the time he helped Felicity into the car Alexander had waiting at the airport. He climbed in after her and settled back against the leather. They were both mostly quiet on the long drive to Pine Beach, but as they exited the highway, he was hit by a sense of urgency. He leaned forward and gave the driver a new address, then realized he should have checked with Felicity first.

"Is that OK?"

"If we stop at Tasha's? Fine with me." Felicity gave his leg a pat. "I'm sure you're eager to check in on Little Mama's kittens, right?"

"You know me so well." Yesterday, that innocent bit of teasing would have irritated the fuck out of him. But today? Today, he felt more like himself. No, that wasn't right. The change was more significant, and though he couldn't trace it to an exact moment, he knew it came at some point between the tea. His heart-to-heart with Lil Bit had loosened the knot in him, allowing him to feel like a new version of himself.

Who wasn't crushed by shame and regret. Who felt free to make choices.

Within limits, of course. He was still the dutiful servant of the Goddess Bastet and always would be. But for the first time, he understood that he possessed more freedom than he had assumed—or wanted to admit. That was probably closer to the truth, since he realized he'd always felt safe in the limits of his duty. Those limits allowed him to pretend he had no options, which kept things easy, neat, and tidy.

And joyless.

He thanked Betty for sending up a prayer for him. She was right. He needed to find a way to serve and live at the same time. With any luck, tonight would be the start of something joyful.

When the car pulled into Tasha's yard, the only light came from the window over the sink in the Airstream. To him, it was a beacon, pointing the way.

"I won't be long," he told Felicity.

"Are you sure? I can go on to the apartment or hang out with Tasha."

"No. I just need to get something off my chest and then walk away, give us both some space. Having you out here waiting will keep me from making another stupid mistake."

Felicity gave his arm a squeeze. "Whatever you need."

Those few steps up to the Airstream door felt like the time he scaled Mount Ararat in an ice storm. He was just as cold, and just as light-headed. *Get on with it, then, priest.* He knocked twice, slightly louder than he'd intended, but that damn aluminum door was as rattly as his nerves.

Ronnie swung open the door, wholly unprepared to hide her shock at seeing him. But an instant later, she slid her mask into place. He didn't blame her. He'd given her good reason to prepare for the worst, but dear Goddess, how he hated that mask of hers. If it was the last thing he did on this trip to the earthly plane, he would convince Ronnie that she was safe with him. No mask needed.

Ronnie's eyes flew wide. "Is Felicity OK?" Her voice was sharp and low, like she was steeling herself for bad news.

"She's fine. Waiting in the car." He gestured over his shoulder.

"Great. Then I don't have anything to say to you." She tried to close the door, but he pressed his palm against the metal.

"Please, Ronnie. Ten seconds. I need you to listen for ten seconds and I'll go." He watched her consider his request, her shoulders hunching and releasing, her eyes hard. She reminded him of a fighter about to step into the ring. He waited. Time hung, suspended, as cold sweat beaded his lip.

"Ten seconds." She crossed her arms and widened her stance. "Nine. Eight—"

"I'm truly sorry. You were right. I care about you. But it's more than that. I've never felt anything like this before and—*kowai desu ne*—shit. Didn't mean to slip out of English. This is scary as hell for me."

"Korean?"

"Japanese."

"Four."

They stared at each other. Ronnie's curls formed a backlit halo around her stunning face. Her eyes sparkled, even in the dim light. But he needed to focus. He had to say something. Any words. Any language. *Just say something.* "Here's the deal. I don't know how long I have here, but you were right about that, too, because none of us knows how much time we've got to work with. All I'm saying is that while I'm here, I want to be with you. I want to spend whatever time I have with *you.*"

She didn't slam the door in his face, which was an excellent sign. But she wasn't smiling. Or responding. She looked confused.

Shit, shit, shit. He hadn't said the right thing. What even *was* the right thing? *"Solo tu, Veronica."* Goddess, he'd forgotten how to say that in English! Why wasn't his brain functioning?

Oh, right. Because this was the woman who always managed to knock him off his game, the only woman, through all the years, who'd ever really mattered.

"Only you, Veronica Davis of Camp Pendleton. I want only you."

She still wasn't smiling, but the door remained open. She shifted her weight. She dropped her arms and let them hang loose at her sides. "I'll think about it."

"Of course! I didn't mean to rush you. I'll... I'll call tomorrow." He turned and headed down the stairs.

"Cat!"

He spun around to find her smiling. It was the most beautiful smile he'd ever seen on the face of the most beautiful woman he'd ever known.

"I've thought about it."

"And?"

She gave a little shrug. "Sure."

"That's a yes?" His heart was about to spring out from his ribs.

"Sure, that's a yes. Call me tomorrow." And then she shut the door.

He climbed back into the car without a word, stunned. Had that really just happened? Had he heard her right? She was willing to give him another chance? He let his head fall back against the seat, wondering how he got so damn lucky.

The driver pulled away from the yard and headed down the lane.

"You're smiling," Felicity said.

"No, I'm not. And even if I were, it's too dark in here for you to tell." But he totally was. He smiled because she'd said yes, and now he couldn't stop smiling because *holy shit* did it feel great to smile again, to have the shame lifted, to know that he was worthy of Ronnie's time and attention. Smiling felt unfamiliar, yes, but wonderful.

Felicity yawned. "I think I'll sleep in late tomorrow. Then we can get back to training."

"That's fine. Turns out I have some important things to do tomorrow, but as soon as I get back, it'll be show time."

He couldn't see Felicity's expression in the dark car, but he heard her whisper, "Welcome back, Tubastet-af-Ankh."

Eight hours later, he was knocking at the Airstream door again—gently this time. Ronnie answered. She was dressed in a set of teal blue work scrubs and her hair was pulled up in a bundle of springy curls at the top of her head. Silver beads dangled from her earlobes and caught the morning sun.

He did his best not to smile like a fool at the sight of her because, honest to Goddess, her effortless beauty was enough to make him forget his own name.

"Hey, cat."

"Ronnie, I know you don't have much time this morning, but do you think we could—"

She grabbed the front of his shirt and pulled him inside, then kicked the door shut with her foot.

"Have a seat." She pointed to the daybed.

He sat. Cats swarmed him.

"So here's the deal." Ronnie didn't look at him as she gathered everything for her workday—her phone, her laptop, a packed lunch, a water bottle, and her keys—and shoved it all into her backpack. "I am not your typical female, not for this time and place and certainly not for any of the times and places you're familiar with."

"I know who you are. And I'm not exactly a standard-issue male, myself."

That made her smile. He saw her wrestle to contain it, but he'd hit the target. Her mask had cracked. *Hallelujah.*

"What I'm trying to say, Tubastet-af-Ankh…" Ronnie sighed, heaved the pack onto her back, and finally made eye contact with him.

He knew he must look ridiculous. Melrose had draped his chunky body around his shoulders and Valkyrie hovered from her perch on the windowsill and licked his left ear. Scratch and Sniff had decided to use his lap as a wrestling mat.

Ronnie laughed. "Well, hell. Never mind." She walked over to him, leaned in, and planted on his lips the sweetest, most honest and open-ended kiss he'd ever received in any of his lifetimes. When she pulled away, she said, "We'll figure it out as we go."

"I can work with that."

She moved toward the door. "But it's not how I normally do things."

"Me either."

She put her hand on the latch. "Not much about this situation is normal, though."

"Tell me about it."

"OK. I have to go. I'm already late."

He shook off the cats, rose, and stepped toward her. He took both her hands in his.

Then he dropped his gaze to those luscious, berry-juice lips of hers, and *he* kissed *her* this time. Ronnie mewled at the press of his mouth against hers. It was a sound of pleasure, of surrender. It was a sound he hoped to elicit from her again soon. He pulled his lips from hers, smiled, and opened the door for her.

"Have a good day at work, Veronica."

She gazed at him with unfocused eyes. "Sure. You too, cat."

She'd forgotten how much she hated sit-ups. Why in the complete hell did anyone think these were in anyway necessary for kicking ass? Tom had said something about core strength and balance, but *come on.* He'd already made her run on the beach and race up four flights of stairs like she was Rockette Balboa or some shit. If she lacked core strength and balance, she'd have fallen face-first in the sand or tumbled down the steps. Tom had even prepared her a lunch of lettuce and lean protein that tasted like the Styrofoam from whence it came. And now he expected her to do fucking sit-ups?

"C'mon, Felicity! Give it everything you've got. We don't know what danger you're about to face!"

"I..." breathing had become difficult, "...am giving it..." *ow!*

She couldn't get any oxygen, "...my *fucking all*."

Felicity collapsed onto the plush carpet of her apartment living room. "That was fifteen, right? A new personal best. Yay, me."

Tom did not look impressed. "How about push-ups?"

"I assume that's a rhetorical question, because I'm pretty sure you know my opinion on that."

"Pull-ups, then."

Still flat on her back and breathing hard, Felicity raised her arms and gestured broadly at the living room. "We seem to be fresh out of laundry poles at the moment."

There was a quick knock at the door, and before she could ask who it was, the door swung open and in swooped the rest of the goddess gang, including Ronnie, who was still in her vet tech scrubs.

"Saved by my posse!" Felicity struggled to stand and used the coffee table as leverage.

"We just came for moral support." Tasha and Bethany dropped into her oh-so-plush sofa, but Ronnie stayed standing. She locked eyes with Tom.

"Hey." Ronnie broke the silence.

"Hey. How was work?"

"Good." Ronnie nodded.

"Good." Tom nodded back.

Though she hated to interrupt their riveting banter, Felicity jumped in. "Tom's been a merciless slave driver. You came just in time, Ronnie." Felicity plopped down on the loveseat. "We're done, right?"

"We still need to focus on balance work." Tom placed his hands on the cushions and shoved the loveseat, with Felicity still on it, against the wall. He picked up the coffee table and moved it into the kitchen. "Let's work on spins and kicks."

"Ohhhh, spins and kicks are my jam!" Bethany bounced up,

pulling Tasha with her. "C'mon, Ronnie. It's time to spin and kick!"

Felicity assumed Ronnie would decline, but—will wonders never cease?—she pulled out her phone and blasted some kind of electronic dance music with a heavy beat. "Let's shake it, girls!"

Their energy was infectious, and now that Felicity's oxygen levels had stabilized, she couldn't help but join the impromptu dance party.

Bethany led them in some fun spins and low kicks as much as her advancing pregnancy would allow, while Tom watched from the safety of the far wall. Tasha attempted a double spin but lost her balance. Fortunately, Ronnie caught her, then went on with dancing.

Felicity was impressed with the athleticism in Ronnie's movements, especially the more she warmed up. That shouldn't come as a shock, of course. Ronnie had been a Marine. If what Felicity had seen on TV was accurate, Ronnie would've had to run sprints and climb walls and crawl under barbed wire to be a Marine, which required athletic skill. But Ronnie was as graceful and limber as she was strong, and her limbs moved as if they floated on water.

"Hey, I've got a good spinning kick to teach you. Stand back." Ronnie crouched low, spread her arms wide and spun quickly, kicking out so that at one point both feet were off the ground. She was airborne.

Bethany screamed. "Wow!"

"What the—?" Tasha's mouth hung open.

Felicity wasn't entirely sure what she'd just witnessed. "How do you know how to do something like that? And what *is* it?"

Tom walked to the phone and clicked off the music, his expression stern. Felicity expected him to insist they get back to sit-ups, but instead he turned to Ronnie and asked, "Butterfly kick?"

"Yeah. You know it?" Ronnie, despite the dancing and flying, wasn't even breathing hard.

Tom pushed the sofa against the opposite wall, leaving the living room wide open. "Do you know the long fist form?"

"Of course."

And before Felicity could ask what they were talking about, Tom stood with his back to Ronnie, tall and straight, and Ronnie mimicked his pose. They breathed together and raised their arms straight out from their sides and then to the front. And then they exploded into a mirrored series of moves—powerful fists slicing through the air in time with their breath, low crouches, legs kicking out, and spins. It was mesmerizing. Obviously, it was some type of martial art, but Felicity didn't have the slightest idea what kind. She was sure of one thing, however. If she attempted anything like it, she'd do a face plant into the rug.

Tasha caught Felicity's eye and mouthed, "Are you kidding me?" All Felicity could do was shrug.

Eventually, Tom and Ronnie came to a stop at precisely the same instant and returned to the tall and straight standing position that started it all. Tom spun to face Ronnie, and they each dipped forward ever so slightly in a bow, elbows out, one fisted hand pressed into the open palm of the other.

When Ronnie straightened from the bow, her whole face widened in a smile. Neither she nor Tom were the slightest bit winded, which didn't seem fair.

Not knowing what else to do, Felicity burst into wild applause. Tasha and Bethany joined in.

"So?" Tasha waited. "You gonna tell us what that was or what?"

"The Shaolin Long Fist Form."

Tasha shrugged in confusion. "What's Shaolin?"

"You've probably heard it called Kung Fu," Ronnie said.

Tom looked to Ronnie. "You're very good. Where did you learn?"

"I had an instructor in San Diego. I started after... well, after something really shitty happened and I wanted to be better at protecting myself and having mental and emotional clarity." Tom was about to respond, but Ronnie stopped him. "And where did you learn? Wait, don't tell me. From an actual Shaolin monk in Henan, China?"

"A bit farther south, in Wuhan. It was a long, long time ago, but I try to keep it up."

Ronnie nodded. "You're very good, as well."

"Hey, I'm impressed with both of you." Felicity sat on the sofa and looked up at Ronnie. "As always, too bad you're not the Acolyte."

"I think we've been over this." Ronnie sat beside her. "You totally kicked Apep's ass and whatever comes at you next, you'll do it to them too. I'm pretty effin' ecstatic that you're the Acolyte. Besides, we'll be by your side the whole time, just like we were the first go around."

Felicity gave a tired nod. "Thank you for that." She looked up at Tom. "Can we order pizza?"

"I don't see why not."

"Why do I feel like there's a catch somewhere?" Felicity narrowed her eyes at him.

"The pizza is for everybody else. I'll make you a quinoa salad." He headed into the kitchen.

"One of the six super grains!" Ronnie jumped up. "Do you have any amaranth or teff to add? I can whip up a mean lemon juice vinaigrette." She followed Tom into the kitchen, and Felicity heard them excitedly discussing the nutritional properties of farro.

Tasha shot Felicity a look. "A match made in heaven."

"Hell, yeah."

Bethany looked crestfallen. "I like quinoa. I really do. But can we still order the pizza? I'm *starving*."

CHAPTER TWELVE

Felicity was stunned at how much progress had been made at Tasha's cottage. To her untrained eyes, it seemed like a month's worth of rehabilitation had been accomplished in just a couple of days. The place was crawling with roofers, painters, carpenters, and plumbers. Vans and trucks were parked all over the property. Janson Crenshaw, the architect, had set up shop under a temporary canopy, the kind Felicity had seen at arts and crafts fairs. He waved to her when she crossed the yard. She waved back.

Bethany bounced through the front door and onto the new porch, twirling in excitement. She stomped on the treated floorboards. "Isn't it wonderful? No more squeaks! No more rotted out sections! And the steps—did you notice that they're up to code now?"

"Oh!" Felicity looked down at her feet and all around. "Yeah. It really is wonderful."

"I'm trying to convince Tasha to get a custom daybed swing built for the porch, you know, like that old swing she used to have but wider and cozier and not as janky."

"Sounds great."

"And she can get custom cushion covers and super cute toss pillows and sit out here and sip her lemonade and stuff. Wouldn't that be totally adorable?"

Felicity nodded, deciding not to burst Bethany's bubble by pointing out that no one had seen Tasha sip lemonade—with, or without vodka—since junior high.

Bethany grabbed her hand. "C'mon. I have to show you." She practically dragged Felicity through the brand-new front door and into the not-quite-finished living room, then down the hallway. They stopped in front of what Felicity had always known as Mrs. Romero's sewing room. Bethany pushed open the door. "Ta-da!"

Felicity could only stare. The cluttered and dingy room had been transformed into a sunny nursery.

"I decided to stick with pale yellow and teddy bears, since I still don't know if it's a boy or girl." She rubbed her stomach protectively, her face lit up with happiness. "I absolutely love this room, don't you?"

"It's beautiful."

And it really was. New insulated windows allowed natural light to flood the space. The oak floors gleamed and the ceiling had been scraped clean of its rough popcorn texture, a graceful light fixture now at its center. The small closet had been expanded and fit with custom storage modules, complete with dozens of tiny clothes hangers hanging from the rod in anticipation.

But the focal point of the room was the rich cherry crib—which looked vaguely familiar—and a matching changing table, rocker, and dresser. "Is this the crib you had at Rich's house? The one you showed me right before the jackals attacked?"

Bethany pursed her lips, as if stopping herself from saying

something she'd regret.

"I don't mean to pry."

"No! Of course, you're not prying. It's just..."

Felicity realized this was about Rich.

"It's not the actual, identical crib, no. I didn't think it wise to go over there and get the original. I don't know if I'll ever want to go there again."

She knew the feeling.

"But I mentioned the crib and Alexander must have overheard me, because the next thing I knew, he'd ordered one just like it for me, along with the whole set. I was so surprised!"

It seemed Alexander was full of surprises. "Well, it's just perfect, sweetie."

"Not everything's perfect."

"I know." Felicity watched Bethany lower her eyes and fiddle with the hem of her top. "I haven't really had a chance to talk with you, but are you doing all right with the whole Rich situation? Have you decided what you want to do?"

Bethany shook her head and looked up at Felicity. "I didn't have to make that decision. He made it for me by being such an idiotic jerk in the OB-GYN parking lot." She wiped her eyes and sniffed back tears. "It was hard to hear the truth come out of his mouth like that, you know? He only wanted me so he could parade me around for his campaign. Alexander's taking care of everything."

"I'm so sorry, Bethany." Felicity placed a hand on her shoulder. "It's good you've got your posse around you."

"And Alexander, who's probably a member of the posse by now, right?" Her face brightened. "I'll get him a bracelet the next time I'm at the shop!"

Mrroow! Little Mama gave a happy chirp and rubbed against

Bethany's leg.

"See? She approves of the nursery too!" Bethany scooped up the small calico and gave her a hug. "I was worried that I hadn't got the feng shui exactly right. I mean, the window isn't optimally aligned for the best red rays of morning sunlight, but I was able to put the crib perpendicular to the wall so I thought that might make up for it. Plus, I'll hang some crystals on the baby's mobile. Anyway, I brought Little Mama over to make sure the vibe was right. She knows all about what babies need, after all." Bethany gave the cat a squeeze before she gently returned her to the floor.

Without warning, the calico spun around and leapt into the air. Felicity had to react fast in order to catch her. The cat began to purr so loudly that Felicity's entire body vibrated. "Good to see you, too, my brave Little Mama." Felicity kissed her head, realizing that with all that had been going on, she'd not had time to check on the babies. "How are the kittens doing, Bethany?"

"Great! I forgot to tell you last night because of all the kung fu and everything, but I took them to the vet yesterday morning for their two-week checkup—actually, they're sixteen days old but close enough—and they are all healthy and growing *and* they're all girls! I just *knew* it!"

Meerrrruuup. Little Mama rubbed her face against Felicity's chin, neck, and cheek in gratitude, telling Felicity that she missed her.

"Of course, everyone's thriving," Felicity said, dodging an attempted rub on her mouth. "You and Little Mama are natural mothers."

"She's teaching me a lot, really, especially about patience and boundaries." Bethany refolded a baby blanket draped over the crib railing. "When Fluffy, Muffin, and Jellybean get messy, she holds them down and cleans them even if they squirm and complain. She's gentle, but firm, you know? I think she's figured out the secret to parenting."

"Fluffy, Muffin, and Jellybean?" Felicity tried not to laugh.

Bethany's face fell. She looked like she might cry for the second time in two minutes. "The names are stupid, I know, but I had no idea what to call them! I've never had a pet before. My mom said animals were dirty and carried disease, but they're actually just these cute and innocent little balls of fluff!"

"The names are sweet, Bethany. They're perfect. Just like the nursery."

She wasn't convinced. "Well, Tasha sure wasn't any help. She said she only had perfect names for *male* kittens. My gosh, you wouldn't believe what she came up with!"

"Oh, I probably would." And Felicity knew that Fluffy, Muffin, and Jellybean were a whole lot better than Fuckface, Mofo, and Jagoff.

Little Mama jumped down and exited the room.

Bethany produced a weak smile. "Anyway, I'm so thankful that Tasha decided to make this the nursery."

"Wait." Felicity cocked her head. "This was *Tasha's* idea?"

"Yeah. She's been like a fairy godmother to me."

Felicity supposed she should stop being shocked by all the ways in which her best friend had changed. Tasha was happier these days, and because of that, Tasha wanted everyone else to be happy too. "Speaking of the Divine Ms. T, where is she?"

Bethany led them out of the nursery and to the kitchen. "I don't actually know where she is, Felicity. I have to tell you, last night she was acting super nervous and sorta... I dunno... *secretive?* She left early this morning and was gone when I woke up."

Felicity checked her phone. "She hasn't answered any of my texts all day. I was hoping to talk to her before Alexander arrived."

"Alexander's coming here?"

"Any minute now."

Bethany scrunched her face, thinking. "Yeah, I can see why you'd want to give Tasha a warning about that. She's not his number one fan, for some reason."

"Not a warning, but just…" What *had* Felicity intended, anyway? To ask Tasha to be civil? She should probably save her breath. Pointing out that Alexander looked just like DDL had only caused Tasha to dig in deeper with her dislike. Felicity stepped into the kitchen doorway and got a good look at the updates. She stopped in her tracks. "This is *fabulous*!"

"I know, right? Though I still think Tasha should have taken my advice and gone open concept while she had the chance. Mr. Crenshaw was willing to knock down the load-bearing wall here between the kitchen and dining room." Bethany smacked her palm against the plaster. "But when he mentioned how it would alter the footprint and take away from the house's historical significance or something, Tasha decided to keep it as is."

Bethany glanced around the small, square kitchen, shook her head, and made this singsong pronouncement: *"Big miiiisssstaaakkke."*

Just then, Tasha walked in. It actually took Felicity a moment to realize that it *was* Tasha.

"It's a mistake? You hate it, don't you? Shit!" She raised a hand to her head. Her hair—all that long, straight dark hair that had defined Felicity's best friend for her entire life—was no more.

"No!" Felicity yelled. "Not your hair. Your hair is fantastic!"

"I love it!" Bethany agreed. "Let me see!"

Tasha demurred, tipping her head and turning around so they could see the back. "You sure you don't hate it?"

Bethany squealed. "It's super, super cute! It looks great on you."

Better than great, Felicity thought. Once she'd picked up her lower jaw from the floor, she reached out to touch the funky, silvery strands at the nape of her BFF's neck. The white-silver roots, the ones to which Tasha had been bound in servitude for the last twenty-five years, now merged seamlessly into the new whiteish-silver tone of all of her hair. That's when Felicity noticed the barest hint of muted purple in there too. "I absolutely love it!"

"The stylist said I no longer have to worry about going gray, since I'm already there. Ha! It doesn't make me look older, though, right?"

"Oh, my God, no. It does the complete opposite." Felicity threw her arms around her best friend and squeezed tight.

"Thanks, Lissie. I'm so relieved you don't hate it."

When the hug ended, Tasha smiled wide, and that's when Felicity saw the overall effect of the hairstyle. The shape of Tasha's pretty face was no longer hidden, and the light color played up her dark eyes, brows, and ever-present bright red lipstick...

Wait.

Bethany screamed. Felicity gasped.

Tasha smiled even bigger.

"My God, you did it, Tash! You got your teeth fixed! Why didn't you tell me you were going to do that?"

"Honestly, I wasn't sure I'd go through with it. On the drive there, I kept telling myself that I had better things to do with my time and I didn't need anyone's charity, but then there I was, at the appointment that Mr. McManSplain made for me, and, well, *voila*!"

"Holy shit, you're goddess-level gorgeous. That's all I've got to say."

"I second that," Bethany said. "And I hope this doesn't come off wrong, but I'm super proud of you, Tasha. You're totally worth it."

"Aww, you guys." She opened her arms for a group hug, then slowly released them. "I guess it hit me that the real reason I refused everything—the house, the teeth—was out of spite, just so I could look back and say I had turned down that bossy bastard."

"Uh, Tash…"

"And then I realized, fuck that! I was only spiting myself. Helios Riggy-ass doesn't care one way or the other and has probably forgotten that he ever offered me anything to begin with!"

"Uh…"

Tasha had delivered her address with her back to the door. She didn't know they had company.

"You're wrong, Ms. Romero."

Tasha froze. Her eyes flew wide open. "Is he standing behind me?"

Bethany scrunched up her nose and nodded.

"I do remember," Alexander said. "And I am beyond pleased that I could be of service."

Tasha spun around.

Felicity recalled how just days ago, in Alexander's office, she'd spied a crack in the attorney's decorum. But now, as Alexander laid eyes on Tasha, she saw the man's decorum crumble. For a split second, his face was a window into awe, confusion, and appreciation.

"You…" Alexander cleared his throat, collecting himself. "You look lovely, Ms. Romero. Your hairstyle is quite flattering."

"Hunh." Tasha put her hands on her hips. "Out of curiosity, do you make a habit of just walking into people's homes and passing judgment on their appearance? Would you do that to a man? Would you mosey on into his living room and say, 'Hey, dude, your hairstyle is quite flattering?'"

Felicity inserted herself between the two of them. "What brings you here this afternoon, Alexander?"

"What?" He stared at Felicity like a raccoon in a flashlight beam.

"To what do we owe your visit here today?"

"Oh. Not *here*, precisely." An impish smile appeared on his lips. He was planning another surprise, no doubt, since he was the Johnny Appleseed of surprises, dropping them everywhere he went. "So, ladies. Would you care to join me for a short stroll?"

"Ooh, a field trip!" Bethany was out the door first and gestured for Tasha to follow along.

Tasha whispered to Felicity, "Are we getting a tour of the new septic system?"

"Hey, as long as there's no calf being born where we're going, I'm good."

Tom and Ronnie exited the Airstream, together, and joined everyone on the dirt.

"Where are we headed?" Ronnie asked.

Tasha pointed to Alexander. "Ask the Pied Piper."

The crew exited the gate. Alexander led them across the lane to the old farmhouse that had once been part of the next-door dairy operation, long before the junkyard opened for business.

When Alexander motioned for them to continue onto the ancient cement walkway to the front porch, Felicity felt momentarily confused. She knew this house was here, of course, because the Wachowski place had *always* been here, and she'd passed it thousands of times over the years. Lately, she'd forgotten it even existed.

And she suddenly realized why. The house had been encased in a tangle of kudzu and hogweed, which someone had recently hacked away, leaving the clapboard structure visible for the first time in decades.

"Oh." Felicity took in the solid, square shape of the two-story house. It was appealing in a no-nonsense way, a sturdy and functional place that had been through hell but was still standing.

Tasha whispered in Felicity's ear. "I'm getting Ted Bundy vibes."

"You're *always* getting Ted Bundy vibes."

"All right," Tasha announced. "So why has the ambulance chaser summoned us all here to the Wachowski place?"

"Give it a rest, Tasha." Surprisingly, it was Bethany who said what everyone else was thinking. But she broke into a huge smile to soften the blow. "Thanks!"

"So is someone planning to restore it?" Felicity asked.

"As a matter of fact, yes," Alexander said. "Please, everyone, join me on the porch."

"You sure it will hold everyone?" Bethany frowned.

"Absolutely sure."

Once they were all on the wide porch, Bethany began stomping on the concrete surface. "Seems safe enough," she determined.

"The porch was originally wood, and, like the whole place, it will be restored to its original beauty and function."

Felicity looked to Alexander, still not sure why they were there. "So who bought it?"

"You did," Alexander said, unlocking the front door.

"I *did?*"

Tom placed a gentle hand on her shoulder and spoke softly. "I asked him to find us a place where we could live together. I hope you don't mind. I knew you'd want to be close to your Goddess Posse, and it's something I'd prefer, as well."

Felicity glanced at Ronnie, who smiled knowingly.

"Yay! We're together again!" Bethany threw her arms around Felicity and squeezed.

They all ventured inside, Felicity a bit numb with shock but aware that Tom's hand cradled her elbow. This was her house? She had a *house*?

"Alexander can make it whatever you want it to be," Tom assured her.

Felicity nodded, a lump in her throat.

Yes, it was dusty and dark and the ceiling had collapsed in places, but it was homey in an old-fashioned way. Doorways and windows were framed in a thick, carved molding that repeated on the stairway newel post design. The narrow hardwood floors were beat up, but could be salvaged. The living room fireplace was surrounded in tiny, mottled green ceramic tiles, obviously original. From what she could see, it appeared no one had ever tried to remodel the place.

"Holy wow, this is fabulous." Bethany's assessment was muffled because she held a tissue over her nose and mouth to fend off the dust.

Alexander led them through pocket doors into the dining room, with its built-in hutch and bay window, then onto the kitchen.

"How old is it?" Felicity asked.

"Built in 1918, a Craftsman four-square, Janson said. Five bedrooms, two baths, and an acre of land."

"But…"

"An inspector was here yesterday. He said it was in excellent shape for its age, structurally sound, including the foundation."

Felicity nodded, the lump in her throat expanding.

"A cleaning and repair team will be here in the morning. We should be able to make it habitable in a week or so, then we can move in the apartment furniture to get you started. Whenever you're ready, we can customize and renovate any way you wish."

"Ohhh, let me help! I'm really good at it." Bethany's eyes were pleading.

"She is, actually." Tasha admitted. "Even if I don't always listen to her suggestions."

"I still think you're going to regret not going with an open floor plan."

"Yes, I know. *Big missstaaakkke.*"

Felicity turned to Alexander. "I... thank you. I don't know what to say. I can't believe I'm going to have my own house again and I can be right next door!" She told herself she would not cry. No crying. No. But she felt a tear slide down her cheek without her permission. Fine. She was going to cry.

Suddenly, the entire Goddess Posse wrapped her in a giant group hug. Even Alexander participated, which indicated that Bethany had been right—he was a full-fledged member.

The group continued to explore the house, discussing remodeling ideas, all of which Alexander recorded on a phone app. They talked furniture, décor, and indoor/outdoor living. Even Ronnie got into the action, which surprised Felicity, since she'd never seen a hint of domesticity in her. Then again, she'd never pictured Ronnie as the flirty type either, and twice now, as they meandered through the house, Felicity had seen Ronnie sneak a look at Tom or brush her hand against the side of his leg. Sparks were flying between the two of them.

A bit later, they had all reassembled in the downstairs living room when Felicity received a text. "Oh, my God! I had no idea it was this late!" She looked up, panicked. "Cass is picking me up in under an hour. I gotta get back to the apartment and get ready. We're going dancing at The Roundabout tonight. I can hardly wait to tell him about the house!"

Tasha smiled. "Returning to the scene of the crime, eh?"

"I'm not sure that's a good idea." Tom stepped close to Felicity. "Your sense of dread is growing, and, frankly, so is mine. We've only had one training session to prepare. It doesn't feel safe."

"I'll be with Cass."

"I'm sorry, but one Roman can't protect you in these circumstances. I'll come along tonight." It appeared that Tom had made his decision.

"No thanks," Felicity said. "I don't need a third wheel harshing my mellow."

Tom looked confused and turned to Tasha for a translation.

"It's a late 1980s expression that means don't ruin my good time."

Tom nodded. "I've always felt fortunate to have missed the 1980s." He turned back to Felicity. "I promise not to damper your evening, Felicity. I can be a lot of fun under the right circumstances."

Ronnie snickered.

"I'm completely serious. I'll bring Ronnie along. It'll be a double date." He reached out and grasped Ronnie's hand, raising it to his lips for a chivalrous kiss. She abruptly stopped snickering.

Everyone had gone completely silent. Felicity half-expected Ronnie to slug him, but apparently, peace had been made. They'd reached an understanding that included public displays of affection.

"Excellent idea." Alexander gave Tasha his best smile. "I think everyone needs to blow off some steam. Ms. Romero, would you like to join me at The Roundabout?"

"Nope." She turned and walked out the front door and across the street without so much as a backward glance.

"I'd go with you, Alexander, but I'm too fat to dance." Bethany rubbed her tummy.

"You are most certainly not too fat, Bethany."

"And also, I'm kinda on Team Tasha these days. I hate men too. Nothing personal." She smiled sweetly, gave a little wave, and followed Tasha across the street.

"Maybe it's my cologne," Alexander mumbled as he headed for his car.

CHAPTER THIRTEEN

They were late. Felicity had been a bit nervous getting ready, and she'd changed clothes three times while Cass waited patiently in her living room. She was nervous because it was becoming clearer and clearer to her just how much she liked Cass. He was a sweetheart—a funny, adventurous, and hardworking man who loved to laugh. She enjoyed his company and his conversation. And for whatever reason, he seemed to think Felicity was the best thing that had ever happened to him. For all those reasons, she should be honest with him.

But where would she even begin? And what if her stomach acted up tonight? Oh, now that was an idea—she could give a combo explanation! *My stomach attacks are acid reflux caused by the stress of being the Acolyte of the Ever-Living Goddess Bastet—yeah, the cat one— and I have to figure out how to save the world, again, since I already did it once by battling a big snake, but I can feel something evil is about to strike again. But no biggie. Let's keep dancing!*

Maybe not.

"So let's see if I've got this right," Cass said a bit later, pulling his truck into The Roundabout parking lot. "Ronnie is a former Marine who's a computer whiz but works for Dr. Nguyen, the vet."

"Right."

"And what kind of consultant did you say Tom was?"

Felicity hadn't said. In fact, how Tom and Ronnie fit into her life was just another element of her ongoing omission of truth. It was getting ridiculous. Cass deserved to know about Felicity, the posse, and the mess they were in. And she would tell him. Everything. And let the chips fall where they may.

But not tonight. She just wanted one last night of laughter and music. Right before he ran screaming into the sunset.

"He's a security consultant. Former military, just like Ronnie." That wasn't a *complete* lie.

"Security. Gotcha." He pulled into an open parking spot and glanced down at her, his green eyes amused. "And he's in Pine Beach because the Pope's headed our way? The Queen of England? Or, whoa, is it Beyoncé?"

"Hey, could be. Pine Beach might be more important in the universal scheme of things than any of us realize."

He laughed. "Just promise that if it's Beyoncé, you'll get me tickets."

"Sure." She craned her neck to kiss his cheek. "Maybe a backstage pass if you're good."

When they got inside, the place was as crowded as the parking lot, but she quickly spotted Tom and Ronnie at a nearby table that gave them a view of the front door. At least she thought it was them. It was certainly Tom. He was dressed in a nice gray T-shirt and an expensive sportscoat but wore the same old brooding expression. But the woman beside him? Wow. For the first time ever, Felicity was seeing Ronnie in something other than vet clinic scrubs or her customary all-black, no-prisoners ensemble of T-shirt, cargo pants, and combat boots. Tonight she looked like an entirely different person. She wore a feminine and flowy paisley mini dress, open at the neck and tied at her slender waist, and strappy sandals. Her golden brown skin was luminous against the pale greens, golds, and browns of the dress. Her hair was down and free, wild curls framing her heart-shaped face.

But as soon as they reached the table, Ronnie grimaced and Tom's body tensed. "You're late," he snapped.

"I couldn't decide what to wear," Felicity admitted.

Cass jumped in. "Plus, I had trouble finding parking."

Ronnie placed a hand on Tom's arm before he could lodge another complaint. "Don't mind him. You know how worried he gets about you." She stood up and offered her hand to Cass.

Introductions were quick, since everyone had met before, however briefly, and Cass offered to head to the bar to buy the first round of beers. Tom volunteered to go with him, and they set off to face the crowded bar, both women watching closely.

"If he says anything to Cass..."

"He won't," Ronnie said. "He's tied up in knots, freaking out about your safety and feeling guilty that he didn't take your gut feelings more seriously from the start." Ronnie tucked a loose curl behind her ear.

"You look stunning, by the way." Felicity would have said more but Ronnie immediately stiffened and raised a hand.

"Don't make a big fuss. I know I look like a girl tonight. The expression on Tom's face was priceless." Ronnie smiled.

"I'm not making a fuss. I just think you're absolutely gorgeous. That's it. I'll never speak of it again." Felicity made the motion of zipping her lips. She managed to stay speechless for all of fifteen seconds. "But can I just mention one other thing?"

Ronnie's eyes narrowed. "But you just said—"

"I lied."

That made Ronnie laugh. Everything about her seemed softer tonight, looser and less guarded.

Felicity locked her gaze on Ronnie's. "One of the very best things that's happened to me in the last couple months is you, your friendship, your steady presence, your skill. You are an incredible young woman, Ronnie." Felicity lapsed into silence, not sure how to continue.

"Just spit it out, Felicity. I know you're buttering me up for something."

"I don't want to see you hurt." Shit. That was cringe-worthy, and not at all premeditated.

"Then look away, Felicity, because I *will* be hurt." Ronnie held her head high, her jaw resolute.

"Sorry," she mumbled. "It's not my place to…"

"But I knew that going in. He's leaving and there's not a damn thing I can do about it."

Felicity reached out and took Ronnie's hand.

Ronnie nodded. "Yep. It will hurt like hell, probably the worst hurt I will ever feel in this lifetime, which is saying something."

Felicity kept her touch gentle, remained silent, and thought how surreal it was to be having such an intense heart-to-heart while "Honky Tonk Badonkadonk" blasted all around them.

Ronnie leaned in. "But here's what's important: whatever time we have, however short it is, it will be worth it. *He's* worth it." Ronnie closed her eyes and quickly turned away.

But Felicity had already seen the beginning of tears, and her heart ached for Ronnie.

"Ladies, it's time to shake your moneymakers."

Cass grabbed Felicity's hand and before she knew it, she was two-stepping across the floorboards to the "Boot Scootin' Boogie." She felt bad leaving Tom and Ronnie at the table alone, especially with Ronnie feeling so vulnerable. Tom wouldn't know what to do with himself at a country western dance club, and she had a hunch this wasn't Ronnie's preferred musical genre.

But when Cass leaned forward and gave her a quick kiss, she decided to let Ronnie and Tom work things out for themselves. This might be her last, pre-confession night with Cass. She would enjoy it, if it killed her.

Ronnie hated first dates. Granted she and Tubastet had kissed and shared some pretty intense experiences at this point, but this was their first time out in public as a couple. Or was that just a cover? Was it even a real date? They were here to protect Felicity, right? Maybe that would explain why he hadn't looked at her, but instead stared at the dance floor where Cass twirled Felicity. She should go home. Clearly, she was making Tubastet uncomfortable.

Stop it, Ronnie told herself. There were plenty of descriptive words that applied to her—cautious, methodical, stubborn—but *insecure* sure wasn't one of them. She didn't date much because there were few men she thought were worth her time and energy. And even those never amounted to anything. She was just so tired of the bullshit, the awkward-bad sex, the regrets.

But the man beside her was different. Her feelings for Tubastet were already stronger than anything she'd ever felt before, and the truth of that had made her overly sensitive. She needed to pull herself together.

"The 25th Acolyte lived in Kyoto."

Ronnie glanced around, not even sure Tubastet was speaking to her. But then he turned his mismatched gaze her way, and his focus was so intense that it left no doubt.

"Behind her father's house was a small meditation garden edged by a row of Sakura trees. I was sitting beneath one on a particularly pleasant spring day, just staring at the pink blooms against the pale blue sky. I spotted a single, solitary blossom that was absolute perfection. It was simple, elegant, a miracle of nature. And as I studied that lone cherry blossom against the sky, I knew that it was the most beautiful thing I'd ever seen and likely ever *would* see. And that held true for a long time. Right up until tonight, when you opened your door."

Ronnie swallowed hard. "I... uh... thank you."

"I came to understand the meaning of beauty during my time there. And I learned something else I'll never forget."

"What's that?"

"I'm allergic to seaweed. Hives everywhere, eyes swollen shut. Sickest I've ever been in all my days." He looked dead serious, right up until he laughed. And Ronnie laughed with him.

They talked and talked. At one point, Ronnie's abs were sore from laughing. She'd long ago lost track of Felicity and Cass on the crowded dance floor, but assumed they were still out there somewhere, twirling and do-si-doing the night away. Which was fine with her, because it turned out Tubastet was one hell of a storyteller, and Ronnie figured the longer he talked, the less she'd have to say about herself.

But eventually, with one arm around her, he traced his finger along the crescent scar on her right arm and asked how she got it. She was relieved that she could tell him the truth, and launched into the saga of Bodhi Milliken, her first love, the skateboard bet gone bad, and how it ended in a broken radius and a broken teenage heart.

Tubastet had just launched into a story about a donkey accident in the Chilean Andes when Felicity plopped down into the chair across from them. She was a happy, sweaty mess.

"Where's Cass?" Ronnie asked.

"Getting us some waters. Why aren't you guys dancing? C'mon, it's great!"

"It's been a while since I've been out dancing." Tubastet admitted.

"Ooh, do tell." Ronnie tucked herself tighter into his arm, and he stroked her shoulder.

"About sixty years ago, in a hole-in-the-wall jukebox joint in Nicosia, Cyprus."

"Wait." Felicity used her fingers to check her math. "You must have been with Betty, right?"

"Yes. It was the night before we faced Apep." Tubastet looked down at Ronnie, a sad smile on his face. He buried his nose in her curls for an instant before he went on.

"All hell was about to break loose in the Suez Canal. We were there to rendezvous with the ship captain taking us across the Mediterranean Sea. And the Brit who ran the place…" He stopped and shook his head, laughing. "Betty and I ended up dancing to 'Blue Suede Shoes' by Carl Perkins minutes before we gathered the ritual weapons and headed out."

Just then, Cass returned with their waters. "What did I miss?" he asked.

"Just a boring, old war story," Tubastet said.

"Excuse me. Be right back." Ronnie rose from the table, pulled a couple of twenties out of her small purse, and headed across the dance floor to the DJ's booth.

By the time she'd made it back through the crowd to their

table, whatever song had been playing came to an abrupt halt, and these words echoed from the rafters: "Well, it's one for the money..."

As Carl Perkins's bluesy voice blasted over the speakers, Ronnie reached her hand toward Tubastet. "May I have this dance?"

He didn't hesitate, just grabbed her hand and pulled her out onto the dance floor. She wasn't sure what to expect from a two-thousand-year-old Egyptian priest, but it wasn't that he could move like a rockabilly superstar. She could barely keep up with him. Sure, she'd known he was a beast on the battlefield and had mad martial arts skills, but he spun her around so smoothly that it took her breath away. Their eyes locked together, and for an instant, Ronnie felt like they were the only two people in the whole world.

When the song reached its ending guitar chord, he twirled her one last time and pulled her to his chest for a gentle kiss.

Ronnie's lips tingled, along with some of her other parts, and it was all she could do not to pull him into a dark corner and kiss the hell out of him. She'd told Felicity the truth. *It is absolutely worth it. He is worth it.*

They danced a bit more and surprised themselves by attempting several line dances. They weren't very good but that was beside the point. Ronnie felt like she was floating.

An hour later, all four of them headed to the parking lot. Ronnie overheard Felicity ask Tubastet if she had permission to go home with "her Roman." If Cass heard the strange question, he didn't react. She watched Felicity and Tubastet exchange whispers that seemed just shy of an argument until he finally nodded his agreement.

Felicity ran off toward Cass's truck but immediately turned around and raced back to Tubastet. Ronnie heard her say something about *serving* and *living* but missed the context. Then Felicity got in Cass's truck and they pulled out.

"What was *that* about?" Ronnie walked with him to his truck. "What did she say to you?"

Tubastet helped her climb up into the cab and even buckled her in, giving her a quick kiss before he closed the passenger door. He climbed behind the wheel and turned the ignition. "Felicity reminded me of something a very wise person once said." He turned to her and smiled. "Should I ever get the opportunity, I think I'd rather show you than tell you."

They were mostly silent on the ride back to the Airstream. Ronnie did a lot of looking out the window, and he did his best to keep his eyes off her and on the road.

He wanted Veronica Davis more than he'd ever wanted anything or anyone in his long, lonesome life. And it wasn't his call to make. It was all up to her. He'd certainly hinted at what he wanted, but he wouldn't blame her if she fell short of welcoming him into her bed. He was skilled enough to draw out the pleasure until they were both exhausted, but once the pleasure had passed, there would be no upside for her. Only loss.

He risked a quick glance at her silhouette. So calm. So fierce. So much beauty. He pulled his gaze away and gripped the wheel. The truth was painful, and Ronnie's time on the mortal plane was short. She deserved only the best from it, a sustaining love and commitment, someone to share the arc of that lifetime with her. She deserved a man who would be there the morning after, and every morning after that.

He was not that man.

Unable to help himself, he glanced her way again. Her lithe and strong limbs glowed bronze in the faint dashboard light. Her neck's arch was graceful. In the course of his duties, he had known hundreds of desirable women, all remarkable in one way or another.

But none had the rare mix that Ronnie possessed: beauty and courage, intellect and determination, a blow that could kill and a heart that could forgive.

He'd stared too long. She turned to him, eyes shimmering with tears.

"Ronnie—"

"Shhh." She raised her finger to her lips. "We're about five minutes away, right?"

"Yeah."

"My mind is made up, and I don't want you trying to change it. I don't want to hear whatever bullshit you've prepared for the occasion."

All right then. At least she'd spared him the additional five minutes of torture. "Understood."

They drove past the farmhouse, lights blazing in every window. A dozen vans and trucks were parked outside, which meant Alexander had his troops working night and day getting things ready. Then they drove through Tasha's gate. He stopped the truck in the gravel near the Airstream and put it in park.

"I really had a wonderful time with you tonight," Ronnie said.

"I told you I could be fun."

The corner of her mouth hitched. "That remains to be seen, cat." Ronnie opened the passenger door and hopped out. She waited a moment and leaned inside the cab again, an elbow resting on the open door. The neckline of her dress opened to reveal the silky-smooth rise of her breasts. "So? You coming in, or what?"

"Am I?" His heart just about jumped from his chest. He couldn't think straight, probably because all the blood had just drained from his brain.

She straightened, rested one hand on a hip. "I'm inviting you in, but you have to promise me there'll be no talk of your duty or necklaces, posses, battles, steps, weapons, or anything else about your priestly obligations."

He nodded and turned off the engine. His mouth had gone as dry as the Arabian Desert. "What precisely do you want, Ronnie?"

"You. Just Tubastet-af-Ankh, the man."

"Then that's what you'll get."

He followed her up the rickety aluminum steps to the trailer, enjoying the view of the satiny skin at the back of her thighs. He'd never touched her there, not skin on skin. He imagined he'd encounter smooth velvet and hard muscle. He could barely wait to find out.

He followed Ronnie inside. It was dim, with only the tiny light above the tiny sink allowing them to see where they were going. Twenty-two gleaming eyeballs were trained on them as they entered, however.

"Sibni f-haali." His direction was quiet but firm, and the cats obeyed, scattering to the daybed, where everyone found a comfortable spot and went unnaturally still.

Ronnie turned, smiling. "You sure do have a way with puss—"

His mouth claimed hers. There was no warning and no warmup, and she responded with the same urgency that now pounded through his veins. Her hands scrabbled to remove his jacket and shirt and unbuckle his belt. She shoved one hand up under the shirt, spreading her slender fingers wide and resting her hot palm against the flat of his belly. She stayed there for a short moment before she journeyed down, down, to the zipper of his jeans.

All the while the kiss deepened. Her lips parted beneath his, welcomed him, asked for more.

It didn't surprise him that it would be like this, more of a conflagration than a controlled burn.

He let his hands slide down her back and he grabbed her ass, lifting her, her legs opening to grip his waist. Still, the kiss did not break. He turned her until he could gently set her down on the booth table, and only then did he come up for air, pulling back just enough to see her, all of her.

She glowed, her throat and breastbone exposed to him as she breathed hard.

"I want you so damn bad, Ronnie."

She tipped her chin. "I'm yours. Come here." She pulled him toward her, but instead of kissing him, she dodged his lips and nuzzled the side of his neck. At first, he couldn't figure out what she was up to. Until he felt her bite his neck, right where that damn hickey had been. Fine. He deserved it and could take the joke. She kissed away the sting, made a soft murmuring sound, and then bit him again. Harder.

"Marking your territory?"

"Maybe," she whispered.

"My turn."

He dropped to his knees and tugged off her sandals, one at a time, setting them under the table. Her bare legs hung in front of him now, loose and slightly parted, an invitation. He placed his palms on the tops her feet, slid them up and encircled her ankles with his fingers. Soft, strong, *his for now*. He leaned in and left a string of kisses on one ankle, then the next. He slid his hands up and around, caressing her calves as his lips brushed along her skin.

She moaned. He looked up to see her head fall back, her eyes close, and her lips part. She was uncoiling, opening, letting the mask fall away, just for him, and his heart constricted. In his mind he heard the words: *I love her*.

He continued with his exploration, his fingertips sliding up and over her knees to her inner thighs.

"Yes," she whispered, as much a plea as appreciation. She grabbed his hair, tugged, then stilled. She rested her hands on the top of his head. A benediction. Permission.

His for now.

Moving farther still, his tongue sizzling against her hot flesh, his hands pulling her wide so that he could feast on her. He found her core, the tiny strip of fabric useless. He ripped away the pointless undergarment and tossed it over his shoulder.

She was hot and sweet, and he tasted her, savored every drop, took all of her into his mouth until he felt her shatter against him.

He was up. He grabbed her, his mouth crushing hers as he carried her to the small bed. Unfortunately, his shoulder caught on the accordion door and ripped it from its tracks. Ronnie burst out laughing.

"I have a feeling we'll be breaking a few more things before this night is over," he said, still cradling her in his arms.

"You know the old saying, 'If the trailer's rockin', don't bother knockin'.'"

"What?"

"I saw it on a bumper sticker once."

He tipped back his head and laughed, lowering her to the bed. Then he felt her hands grasp him through his jeans, and things got dead serious.

Ronnie clutched at him, pulled him as tight as she could, not at all worried that she was too much for him, too strong or too demanding. Tubastet, the man, was her match in every way that mattered. He'd spent the last several hours making sure she knew that and would never forget it. And she wouldn't.

She rolled with him again, straddling him now, luxuriating in the sensation of each and every place their bodies met. He was all the way inside her, the connection complete. His hands moved like water, trailing along her thighs, hips, waist, breasts, neck. She'd lost track of how many times they'd brought each other to orgasm, how many times he'd made her fall apart in his arms. By now, she'd heard his moans and groans of pleasure in more languages than she could count. She'd found every scar on his warrior body, too, and kissed away each painful memory he carried.

He'd let her do it. It was the greatest gift he'd given her that night.

Suddenly, his eyes flew open. He locked his gaze with hers and grabbed her hips. "Ronnie," he said, his voice ragged with emotion. He'd done so well all these hours, never mentioning it once, but when he'd said her name just now it was all there, too raw to ignore—the sadness, the love, the yearning. He thrust inside her, hard, and she slipped under again.

She let herself be rocked, pulled under until she drowned in those mysterious, mismatched eyes of her lover. The wave of ecstasy struck with such force that she cried out, trembled, and collapsed on top of him.

She came to sometime later. Her head was tucked into the side of his neck and she breathed him in. He smelled like incense and hot earth, like her. He smelled of the elixir the two of them had created together. He stroked her back with feather-light touches.

That's when she realized the side of his neck was wet. So were both her cheeks, her lips salty with the flow. Whose tears were these? Hers? His? Both?

It didn't matter. She left a gentle kiss on his throat and stretched out on top of him, the length of her body in perfect alignment with the length of his.

His arms encircled her. She was warm. She was safe. She was alive again. And she fell asleep.

CHAPTER FOURTEEN

It was the silence that woke Ronnie. Early mornings in the Airstream were usually the time for catting around, with stirring, scampering, mewling, grooming, and zooming. These sounds were soothing to her, proof that all was right with the world and another day was on its way. But this morning, there wasn't a creak or a skitter to be heard.

Which meant...

She rolled over in the small bed and Tom was there, awake, propped up on his elbow, watching her. She reached up to brush a fingertip along the curve of his always-so-serious face. "You're still here."

"I am."

"The Airstream's still standing."

"I'm as shocked as you are."

They both chuckled. Ronnie glanced at the broken accordion partition, then at the destroyed bed.

"So, uh," she said, "did you do something weird to the cats?"

A crooked smile spread across his handsome face. "I just asked them to be quiet so you could sleep a while longer."

"That was sweet of you."

"I know."

Ronnie laughed. "So how long have you been awake and staring at me?" She stretched her arms over her head and pointed her toes, noting that Tom took in the length of her naked body with a look of hungry appreciation.

"Not very long. I enjoyed watching you sleep. So peaceful and lovely." Tom slowly leaned in to place a tender kiss on her lips.

"Mmmm. Nice." She raised her arm and cupped the back of his head, pulling him in for another.

Ronnie's cell phone rang.

Tom sat up quickly, grabbed her phone from its spot on the small shelf.

"Ignore it. Come back." Ronnie attempted to yank the phone from his hand so she could throw it across the room, but he held it just out of her reach.

"It's too early for calls." Tom said.

"Exactly! Ignore it."

"It could be an emergency." Tom checked her screen and scowled. "It's Niko Sweeney."

"See? Ignore it!" But Tom put the phone in her hand instead.

Ronnie sat upright, irritated, and answered the call. "Hey Niko, I'm sorry I never called you back. I've been super busy." She shot a look at Tom, who smiled.

"Can't blame a guy for trying. Look, sorry to call so early, but something's happened that you need to know about." She could hear the anxiety in his voice.

"What's going on?"

"I already called Mr. Helios Rigiat. He said I should call you immediately."

"Why?" Ronnie glanced at Tom again, and the sense of alarm she felt was reflected on his face.

"Viper Apps has just gone live again," Niko said.

Ronnie threw the sheet from her body and jumped up, grabbing some sweats and a T-shirt from the tiny closet. "*How is that possible?* Talk to me, Niko." She pulled the shirt over her head, then switched the phone from hand to hand so she could shove her arms into the sleeves. "Please explain to me exactly how the hell that could have happened. We crushed the servers."

"Technically, *you* did the crushing, and I don't know yet how it happened. Obviously, there was a backup hidden somewhere, maybe in the Cloud. It's gonna take some digging."

Ronnie rammed one leg into the sweats, then the next, and yanked them up to her waist. Her eyes shot to Tom. He was sitting straight up, leaned against the back wall, his arms limp at his side. She couldn't decipher that blank look on his face. Was he *jealous*?

"Is there an IP address, Niko?"

"On a VPN via proxy server."

"Shit. Well, of course. Thanks. Keep me posted." Ronnie disconnected, turned to Tom. "Viper Apps has just gone online again."

Tom jumped out of bed and reached for his jeans. "We have to find Felicity."

"On it." Ronnie called up her Favorites menu and tapped on Felicity's name. She listened as it rang, then rang some more, before it went to voicemail. "She's not picking up. Let me try the location finder for her cell. It should work since that used to be my phone."

"No. I had her turn it off for safety." Tom was fully dressed.

"Do you know where Cass lives?"

Ronnie shook her head. "No idea. Some dairy farm somewhere."

"That doesn't narrow it down much." He headed for the door. "Keep trying to reach her, and I'll see if Tasha knows."

Ten minutes later, Tom, Ronnie, Tasha, and a very sleepy Bethany were gathered in the kitchen of the double-wide. Tasha had started a pot of coffee and was getting mugs from the cabinet. Tom had Alexander on the phone.

"Wait," Tom said. "Alexander, I'm putting you on speaker. Tasha, please spell that again."

Tasha sighed, then repeated the spelling of Cass' last name for the third time in as many minutes. Only louder. "S, as in Sam…"

"Got it," Alexander said.

"C-h…"

"Uh, huh."

"W-i-n…"

"Yep."

"D-o-r-f."

"To recap," Alexander said, "all you found was a PO box, no physical address? And his number is unlisted?"

"Right," Ronnie said. "That's common around here. And he doesn't do any direct retail sales, so he doesn't have a web presence. I'm thinking the county assessor's office or the state Department of Agriculture might be the quickest route to finding him."

"Give me a minute. Call you right back." Alexander hung up.

Bethany yawned and said, "I knew a Schwindorf family back in Lehigh Valley, Pennsylvania. I wonder if they're related?" She had all three baby kittens snuggled on her lap, tucked into the fleece of her robe.

"Sorry I don't know where the farm is, gang. I just can't remember." Tasha pulled out the sugar bowl and a handful of spoons, setting them on the table. "My dad was friends with Cass' dad back in the day. I know it's around Tillamook somewhere, but there are dozens and dozens of them."

Tom tapped his fingers on the tabletop. "Alexander will get the address."

Tasha poured three cups of coffee and set them out. She handed a cup of herbal tea, no sugar, to Bethany. "What's the big rush, anyway?"

"Yeah," Bethany said. "Thank you, Tasha. Why can't we just wait until Felicity gets home?"

"She needs to know about Viper Apps—*now*." Tom glanced around the room. "You all know how she's been sensing something coming? Well, I think this is the start, and honestly..." Tom held Ronnie's gaze. "This was why I didn't think going out last night was a good idea. She may already be in danger."

Tasha took a big gulp of coffee. "Well, then you better hope she turns on her phone real soon, because it'll take at least twenty minutes to drive to the farm. A lot of dangerous shit can happen in twenty minutes, as we all know. Maybe you should get started and be halfway there when Alexander calls with the address."

"I know!" Ronnie stood from the table and looked down at Tom. Oh, he was going to *haaaate* this suggestion, but it might be their best hope. "Tubastet, you need to transform."

He set his mug on the table, visibly tense. "Why?"

"For the psychic link. Felicity has a connection with her cats, right? So why not with you if you're in cat form? And anyway, you said you're able to communicate with Alexander when you're a cat, correct?"

"Correct."

"Can you do the same with the Acolyte?"

"I've never had to."

Ronnie nodded. "Now's the time to try."

Tom remained quite still, then eventually agreed. "I'll do it." He reached out for Ronnie's hand and gave her a private smile. "Not sure I have enough energy after last night, though."

Ronnie got lost in those sultry, mismatched eyes of his, then leaned down to plant a kiss on his lips. She intended it to be sweet, but almost instantly, the sweetness morphed into the same kind of hunger they shared the night before, which was entirely inappropriate.

"Close your eyes, Bethany," Tasha said. "I don't think you're old enough to see this."

"The kiss or Tom turning into a cat?"

"Ha!" Tasha said. "I still say the cat thing is a joke."

Ronnie broke the kiss, winked at Tom, and touched the scratchy whiskers on his cheek. "Go for it."

Tom went to the couch. He sat with his feet on the floor and his palms pressed together before him, eyes closed. Ronnie heard him whisper the incantation, followed by a deep inhale. A strange light shimmered through the double-wide, and when it vanished, a large grey and black cat with unusual markings perched on the cushion.

Ronnie heard a crash and turned to see that Tasha's mug had slipped from her hand and hit the tile floor. Tasha's giant bug eyes stared at the newest addition to their cat collection. "What the fuck did I just see?"

Mew! Said one of the kittens.

Bethany squealed. "He looks so snuggly as a cat. Can I hold him?"

Ronnie placed a hand on Bethany's shoulder. "We should give

him some space, let him focus on Felicity."

Tasha shook herself out of her stupor and began cleaning up the coffee and broken ceramic. As she reached for the broom, she mumbled to no one in particular. "I knew he said he could do it, *theoretically*."

"He's the most gorgeous cat I've ever seen," Bethany cooed.

"I have to agree with you on that one." Ronnie just couldn't stop staring at the cat that was Tom. He was so regal, upright and still, his eyes closed. This was how she'd first met him, a beautiful, brave creature who was so much more than he appeared. Ronnie's heart swelled. She had to fight back tears, which wasn't like her at all. But he really was the most gorgeous cat she'd ever seen. And for just a little while longer, he was hers.

It was happening again.

The thing gnawed on her organs and jabbed at the underside of her skin as it took over her body. She saw the long, blonde hair tangled against her shoulders and falling against her bruised breasts. She tried to run. She couldn't. She tried to scream. No sound came from her mouth. Her phone! Oh God, if she had her phone, she could call for help. Where was it?

She stretched out her hand, the long purple nails now broken and jagged, but she couldn't reach what she so desperately needed. She was a prisoner. She had no power. She was terrified. There was no hope for her, was there?

Suddenly, one of her cats appeared. No, not one of her cats. It was a tomcat. No, it was Tom *as* a cat, sitting majestically in front of the Airstream. The image made her hot with rage, but why? She wanted to shoo him away, smack him, call him names, but before she could do any of those things, she heard him whisper one word:

"Come."

Felicity sat bolt upright in Cass' bed, fighting for breath. The sun was just coming up.

"Is everything OK?" Cass stroked a soothing hand down the length of her naked back.

"What?" She spun around to look at him. She wasn't sure how to answer. Everything was not OK. She'd had another damn nightmare, and it had been the most bizarre yet! And her stomach hurt, worse than yesterday.

"Felicity?" Cass sat up next to her, the covers falling down the front of his body. She stared at him. He looked worried.

Then she remembered Betty's advice to trust her gut. And so she would. Simple as that. If Tom were calling her, no matter how odd the circumstances, she would go. "Cass, I'm sorry but I need to leave. Right now. I can't explain it, but something's wrong. Can you drive me to the Airstream?"

"Of course."

Cass never questioned her or asked for details. He simply pulled on his jeans and a shirt, grabbed his boots, and helped her into the truck.

"I hope everything's all right, Felicity."

"Me too. Thank you, Cass."

"For?"

"Everything. Another wonderful night. For trusting me. For being the real, honest you."

"I..."

She waited for him to finish, but he seemed to change his mind. Then he smiled and took her hand in his. He held it the whole drive back.

The instant they pulled through the gate, Felicity kissed his cheek and jumped from the truck. She prayed he wouldn't insist on helping, and, thank Goddess, he didn't. Cass put the truck in reverse, hesitated, then gave a nod and backed out of the yard.

Tom, Ronnie, and Tasha came running from the double-wide and across the gravel and weeds to reach her.

"I'm sorry, guys," Felicity said. "I know it's super early. I hope the sound of the truck didn't wake you. I just had the weirdest feeling you needed me. Well, that Tom needed me, and that he was here."

Tom stared down at her, his brow furrowed. "You turned off your phone, Felicity." He shook his head in disapproval.

"I, uh, I was busy." She felt scolded, like a seventh-grader caught roaming the halls without a pass. "What's going on?"

Ronnie stepped forward. "Viper Apps has gone back online."

Before Felicity knew what hit her, she doubled over in blistering pain. It originated from the same location as her usual stomach cramps, but with about a thousand times the ferocity. She couldn't breathe. Her head swam.

"Lissie!"

Tasha's voice sounded so far away. Felicity's vision went black and fuzzy at the edges. She lost her balance. And suddenly, she felt herself being bundled into Tom's arms. He ran with her into the double-wide and lay her on the couch. Reflexively, Felicity pulled her knees tight to her chest and rolled onto her side in the fetal position.

"We need to get her to a hospital." She felt Ronnie grab her wrist to check her pulse. "She's clammy and her heart rate is elevated."

"I knew she was having stomach problems, but the antacids seemed to be helping." Tasha set a cold compress on her forehead, but it brought no relief. Felicity curled herself tighter, willing the pain to subside. It didn't.

"No," she croaked out. "I'm all right. Just give me a minute."

"Breathe, Felicity," Ronnie said.

The initial spasm of pain eased enough that she could get some air into her lungs.

"You're not all right." Tom's voice was firm.

That was true, she knew, as another strong spasm overtook her.

"Oh, my heavens, Felicity!" It was Bethany, rushing to the couch. She dropped to her knees. "I was in the bathroom. I mean, I'm always in the bathroom." She gently touched Felicity's cheek. "Are you sick?"

"We're taking her to the hospital."

"I said *no*!" Felicity opened one eye to glare at Tom. "Why is it all right when *you* don't want to go to the hospital but not when *I* don't want to go? I just need my antacids. Somebody get me my antacids."

"I know what you really need!" Bethany popped to a stand and rushed back to her bedroom. A moment later she returned holding a burning bundle of white sage and a long feather.

"Sweetie, that's not going to do anything." Tasha spoke through gritted her teeth.

"She's under spiritual attack. This will sever any connection or attachment. Just because you don't believe in it, Tasha, doesn't mean it's not real. Please, everyone, step aside."

Felicity smelled the pungent smoke waft all around her head and did her best not to throw up. As Bethany used the feather to direct sage along the length of Felicity's body, she watched tendrils uncurl on their way to the ceiling.

"Yep," Tasha said. "That smell would chase away pretty much anything, real or imagined."

Tom said, "I'll pull up the truck."

Ronnie said, "We won't all fit. I'll get the Jeep, too."

And suddenly, Felicity bolted upright, gasping.

"Lay back down, Lissie."

"It's gone!" Felicity took several deep breaths.

"What?" Ronnie checked her pulse again.

"It's gone. The pain is gone." Felicity gently prodded her still tender stomach, but the spasms had completely stopped.

"You're welcome." Bethany blew out the smudge stick and gave her head a little I-told-you-so swivel.

"So it was just gas, then." Tasha said. "Right?"

"Not." Bethany took her supplies back to her room.

Everyone sat, Ronnie still beside Felicity on the sofa, and Tom and Tasha pulling up dining room chairs to be nearer to Felicity.

Ronnie leaned in close. "Do you think the news about Viper Apps brought it on?"

"I don't know. Could be, but it might be just a coincidence."

"I don't believe in coincidences," Tom said. "Someone or something has accessed backup files that Apep hid before he became a slab of flesh in a canopic jar." He got up and began pacing. "Now the Ever-Living-Bastet's Acolyte is under attack."

"You believe in Bethany's crap?" Tasha looked surprised.

Tom stopped. "I turn into a cat. I don't judge."

"Hunh," Tasha said. "Maybe I should've just let her feng shui the hell out of my living room."

Bethany bounced back into the conversation. "Sorry! I had to pee again. I always have to pee. I'm either peeing or eating or crying at commercials for treatment of moderate to severe psoriasis." She plopped down into a chair. "I mean, seriously, I don't even feel like myself anymore. It's like an alien creature has taken over my body, you know?"

Everyone laughed. Everyone but Felicity, who sat rigid, icy fear slicing through her veins.

"Uh, Tom?"

"Yeah?" He sat down again.

"What if Apep didn't put his piece of flesh in a canopic jar and hide it somewhere, like he usually does. What if he stuck it inside a human body?"

"He couldn't do that. A living human has *ka*, the life force, which would act as a barrier to such an attack."

"OK, so what about a dead body?"

"It doesn't work like that, either. Once the *ka* has left the body, it is inanimate, despite what those ridiculous mummy movies try to tell you. Dead is dead. Apep's flesh would simply decay along with the dead body."

Ronnie nodded in understanding. "So no Apep zombies running around. At least we've got that going for us."

Felicity knew she was onto something, and persisted. "What about an almost-dead body? You know, one that's substantially weakened, just moments from death?"

Tom frowned in concentration. "I suppose in theory it could work. But Apep would have to be at the exact right place at the exact right time to insert his flesh at the instant between life and death. It would be a matter of milliseconds."

"Where would he find someone at the moment of death?" Ronnie asked. "A hospital?"

"Or the scene of a car accident," Tasha offered.

"A hospice? Oh, this is making me sad. Can we change the subject, please?" Bethany pulled a tissue from her pocket.

That was when Felicity was certain. "Tom," she said, straightening on the couch. "Misty had long, blonde hair, didn't she?"

"Yes."

"What did her hands look like? I mean, the night she died. Do you remember?"

"Her *hands*?"

"Yes. Think. Her hands, wrists, fingers, nails..."

"Well, she'd just missed another training session to get one of her manicures. She insisted on getting these long, purple nails, which were hideous, and I tried to tell her that long nails were only going to get in the way of her defeating Apep. As with everything else, she didn't listen."

Purple nails, just like the dream. It required all of Felicity's concentration not to hurl all over Tasha's carpet. She held up a palm. She needed a moment.

"What is it, Lissie?"

"It's Misty."

Tom stiffened. "What are you talking about? Misty's dead."

"Listen to me, Tom. I started having these wild nightmares the day the necklace wouldn't release. I dreamed there was something under my skin, in my belly, crawling around and eating away at my organs."

"Oh, *hell*, no," Ronnie said. "How many times did *that* happen?"

"I've lost count, really. I assumed it was stress and exhaustion, but now—" Felicity glanced around the room at her posse, all staring at her with concern. "I think Misty and I are connected somehow."

Tasha dropped into a chair.

Finally, something made sense to Felicity. As strange as it sounded, she knew it was the truth. "I'm having these nightmares and stomach pains because I'm linked to Misty, who is in physical anguish."

Tom leaned in toward Felicity. She could feel his whole body thrum with alarm. "Misty can't feel anguish, Felicity. She's *dead*."

Felicity took a deep breath, knowing this was going to be hard for him to hear. "No. Misty wasn't *completely* dead, Tom. Apep doesn't need to wait to regenerate a body because he's using Misty's."

Tom looked sick. "No. Impossible. I held her as she died. I took off the *usekh*..." His voice trailed off and his eyes went wide.

"What?"

"I... oh, no." He scrubbed his hands over his face and when he looked at Felicity, his expression was tortured. "I had to force the *usekh* loose, pry it off with the ritual dagger. It wouldn't release fully on its own and Apep was about to strike. I was mortally wounded. I had no choice." He blinked, shell-shocked. "I thought she was dead. I had no choice."

Ronnie reached out and took one of his hands firmly in her own. "We know you had no choice. You did what you had to do to save the world." Tom tried to pull away but Ronnie held on. "You didn't do this, Tubastet. This is *not* your fault." Tom gave a barely perceptible nod, though he didn't appear convinced.

Felicity touched his arm. "How could the link between us have formed? Do you know, Tom? Is it because she so recently wore the *usekh*?"

"I don't have any idea. Wait..." He thought a moment. "The blood," he whispered.

Tasha hooted with laughter. "Blood? You're going to have to be more specific, since there's been a lot of blood around here lately."

Tom shook his head as if he were angry with himself. "Maybe there was still a trace of Misty's blood on the *usekh* when I put it around Felicity's neck."

"That could have formed a link between us?"

Tom shook his head. "I don't know for sure. Maybe."

Felicity leaned back, exhausted but determined. She looked at her posse around her. "OK. Now we know. We know why the *usekh* is stuck around my neck. We know what we have to do. Everything's going to be all right."

Tom exploded, jumping from his chair. "How can you say that? Misty's soul is being held hostage in her own body! Because of me."

Felicity stood and got right in his face. "Misty went to fight him of her own free will, against your explicit instructions. Tom, *you* had no choice, but *she* did."

"But because of her choice—"

"We deal." Felicity interrupted, then fell back to the couch. "Because of her choice, we will now have to deal with what we have to deal with."

"What do we have to deal with?" Bethany looked horrified.

"It's simple. We defeat Apep, again, and then we rescue Misty."

"But," Tom's voice was barely more than a whisper, "I don't know *how* to rescue her. I know nothing about how to free her from Apep's control or get her safely moved on to the netherworld while she's stuck in a state between life and death."

"That's OK," Felicity said. "I know someone who does."

CHAPTER FIFTEEN

Cocoa powder was everywhere—dusted in her hair and on her eyelashes, smeared on the sleeves of her blouse, and dumped on the tops of her sneakers. Ordinarily, this side effect of baking wouldn't be an issue, but in this mostly white apartment, it caused Felicity anxiety. Well, to be honest, it was the baking itself making her anxious. She was no schlub in the kitchen, but she wasn't Martha Stewart either, and after so many baking-free years in the Airstream's miniscule kitchen, she lacked the confidence she'd once had. The cake layers were now in the oven, but she knew the hardest part, the actual cake assembly, still lay ahead.

"Hey, Lissie, I brought the cake plate!" Tasha walked inside the apartment without bothering to knock. She was followed closely by Bethany.

"Hello!" Bethany chirped.

Both stopped when they got a good look at her.

"Shouldn't the chocolate go *inside* the mixing bowl?" Tasha perched on the barstool near the island.

"Ha, ha." Just then, Felicity noticed that she'd managed to fling flour and cocoa all over the floor and counters as well, probably when she revved up the hand mixer at too high a speed. She was out of practice. Rookie mistake. She really needed to pull herself together before she tackled the double fudge frosting.

She made a mental note to never again put this much pressure on herself in the kitchen. Usually, desserts weren't life and death propositions. It was downright nerve-racking knowing this cake had to be good enough to save the world.

"Your enthusiasm alone is going to make this cake delicious," Bethany said, displaying one of her big, earnest smiles.

That's when it occurred to Felicity that Bethany Hume, her ex-husband's pregnant child bride, had become one of her all-time favorite people. Which was just weird.

Tasha held up the delicate china cake plate for inspection. "This is what you wanted, right?"

"Yeah. I need something fancy. Presentation will be key. But you're sure you don't mind if it goes missing? Because I'm pretty sure we won't be getting it back."

"Nah, that's fine. It's just something my mom grabbed at a yard sale a few years before she passed. I've never even used it. You're lucky I remembered where I'd packed it away in all the chaos."

"Well, it sure smells yummy. Are we getting a taste?" Bethany gave her expanding tummy an unconscious caress.

"I'll bake another one for you later. This one is a form of bribery."

Tasha looked confused. *"Bribery?"*

Felicity wiped some of the cocoa powder off her face with a dish towel. "Technically, I guess it's more of an offering than a bribe."

Tasha grimaced. "Do I want to hear the details or should I just leave it be?"

Felicity came around the island and gave her best friend a quick hug. "I'd prefer not to say much more, in case this turns out to be a spectacularly stupid idea and nothing comes of it. But, don't worry, it's not risky or dangerous or anything."

"Riiiight," Tasha said, eyes narrowing. "Because putting a cake on a fancy platter isn't usually a risky or dangerous undertaking."

"Yes!" Felicity smiled. "Exactly!"

This was so risky, so potentially dangerous, that Felicity was stone-cold terrified. Her hands shook as she held the top-heavy china cake plate in front of her, making slow progress down the long municipal pier. She tried to tell herself that her fright was irrational. Ridiculous, even. She had nothing to fear from Mahaf, the ferryman.

This time would be different than her first visit to *The Aken*. This time, instead of arriving empty-handed, she would make an offering of this delicious, three-tiered, chocolate fudge feast of the senses. And this time, she wouldn't just stroll on up the gangplank and board the ferry without permission.

Felicity stopped as close to the ramshackle ferry boat as she thought prudent, then mustered up her courage. She wasn't the same scared ninny she'd been the last time she was here, after all. She knew what she was doing. Mostly.

"O, wise Mahaf! I come seeking guidance."

Silence. Felicity worried that he wasn't home, but then realized there was nowhere in Pine Beach an eight-foot-tall supernatural ogre could go without causing mass hysteria.

"Who dares disturb my peace?" The loud bellow shook the pier and caused her hands to tremble wildly.

Mahaf appeared on the deck. He loomed over her, bigger than she remembered. Bigger and angrier.

Felicity cleared her throat and tried to speak in a voice that was as strong as it was deferential. "It is I, the Acolyte of The Ever-Living Goddess Bastet, daughter of Ra." She knew name-dropping was big with the ancient Egyptians, so she added that bit of flair. She hoped it wasn't too much.

His huge figure leaned forward and he nodded. "I know thee. You have fought valiantly, though the balance is not yet restored."

"I know, wise Mahaf, ferryman of the dead. That's why I come to you, bringing this humble offering." She lifted up the cake.

He stared suspiciously.

"It's a homemade chocolate cake."

He stared some more.

"It's the best I could do on short notice."

Suddenly, his stern face softened. "Indeed, I see you have made this with your own warrior hands, hands steeped in the blood of your enemy."

Felicity wondered if that was a good thing, because it didn't sound the least bit appetizing.

"I accept your offering."

Whew. It *was* a good thing.

"Come." He turned away as if expecting her to follow him aboard. But she wasn't sure she could make it up the plank while holding the top-heavy cake plate. "O, wise Mahaf!" she called. "Would you mind holding this while I climb on board?"

He grunted, took the plate, then lifted his chin toward a worn wooden table on the deck. When she was seated, he handed her the plate again, and she carefully set it on the tabletop. He remained standing.

"Acolyte, what did you name this?"

"Chocolate cake."

He studied it a moment, then dipped one of his sausage fingers directly into the fudge frosting, scooped out a large blob, and carried it to his mouth. He slurped.

She waited.

Again, he dipped, scooped, and slurped. Then he nodded, holding is finger aloft as he made this pronouncement: "Choc-o-late. Yes. A worthy offering." He looked down at her. "Ask your question."

"O, all-seeing Mahaf, I believe the former Acolyte called Misty McAlpine of Clackamas, Oregon, has not yet crossed into the netherworld."

His answer was immediate. "She has not."

"But she should have, right? I mean, she *should* be dead."

"Indeed, you are correct."

"I believe Apep holds her *ka* hostage. I need to know how to release her."

Mahaf tipped his head as if listening to something she couldn't hear. Eventually, he glanced down at her once more. "You must bring her to the Threshold of Death, and she must choose to cross."

"Threshold of Death?"

"She cannot be forced. It must be her choice to leave her earthly body and send her *ka* to the *Duat*."

"But how—"

"I have provided the answer you seek." He snatched up the cake plate, turned his back to her, and walked away.

Felicity knew better than to overstay her welcome. She stumbled down the gangplank and practically ran back along the municipal pier, all the while repeating the instructions to herself like a mantra: "Threshold of Death, her choice to cross, send her *ka* to the

Duat...Threshold of Death, her choice to cross, send her *ka* to the *Duat*..."

"What the living hell is a Threshold of Death?"

Tasha seemed particularly cranky that evening as they all gathered in the double-wide, but Felicity figured it had more to do with Alexander's presence at the table than the complexities of life and death in ancient Egyptian philosophy. Tasha sat at one end of the table taking notes with a pen and paper, while Alexander sat at the opposite end taking notes on his computer. In between were the rest of the posse and a pile of deli sandwiches that only Bethany seemed to be enjoying.

Tasha's irritation might be linked to the noise, as well. The windows were closed, but they'd had to talk over the nonstop clanking and banging from all the construction and cleaning activities at the cottage and farmhouse. The racket was giving Felicity a headache.

Alexander stopped clicking on his keyboard and looked up. "I think Mahaf is referring to a tomb entrance. Don't you, Tubastet?"

"There's some big old marble tombs at the Pine Beach Cemetery up on High Ridge," Felicity said. "Couldn't we just sneak in there and use one of those?"

Tom shook his head. "The texts are more specific. It would have to be Misty's tomb, one prepared for her."

"Exactly," Alexander said. "The tomb provides a passage to the netherworld only for the individual to whom it belongs."

"Then we'll build Misty a tomb and get her to enter it." Ronnie was in full-on Mission Objective mode. "That's totally doable."

Felicity swallowed a bite of turkey and swiss on rye but barely tasted it. Something about this didn't seem doable at all. "Hold up," she said. "What about the piece of Apep that's inside Misty? Won't we need to complete the Six Steps of Overthrowing Apep on Misty before she crosses over?"

"We could do that." Tasha jotted it down.

"Actually, I don't think we can." Tom leaned forward, concentrating. "I think Apep is safe as long as he's inside Misty. Each of the six steps must result in direct contact with his flesh, just like last time."

"Oh." Felicity understood. "So Misty's body is acting as armor then, protecting him."

"Exactly."

"So how do we get Apep *out* of Misty so she can go through the door?" Ronnie asked.

Everyone lapsed into silence, stumped.

"Wait!" Felicity sensed a plan coming on. "Alexander, you said the tomb is only a passage for its owner."

"Correct."

"And, Tom, I know from you that Apep is exiled here, unable to leave this world."

"Also correct."

"Then if we get Misty to step through the door to her tomb, Apep would be unable to go through with her!"

Tom's eyes opened wide. "Yes. That's right. He would be forcibly expelled from her body."

"That sounds gross," Bethany said, munching on a corn chip. "I mean, Apep's not a whole... *thing* anymore, right? Only a piece of him is inside Misty. So what will be expelled?"

Just then, Alexander's phone dinged with a text message. He picked it up and grimaced. "Damn."

"What?" Ronnie asked.

"It's one of my sources. The Watts Bar Nuclear Plant just repelled a backdoor attack into their operating system. The attacker used an employee ID to gain access."

Felicity looked to Tom. "That has to be the handiwork of Viper Apps. No coincidences, right?"

"At least he was stopped." Tasha tried to hide her horror, but Felicity saw the fear in her eyes.

Ronnie shook her head. "It's only a matter of time until he succeeds. Even with everyone on alert."

"Then we have no choice." Felicity nodded with finality. "We act now. We set up the tomb."

"Maybe we can rig up a plywood shed of some kind." Ronnie tossed her half-eaten roast beef sandwich onto her plate. No one seemed to have much of an appetite anymore.

Except Bethany, who chomped down on a gherkin and chewed with enthusiasm.

"Here it is." Alexander had been reading something on his computer screen and spun the laptop so that everyone could see. "The tomb must have four solid walls coordinating with the four cardinal directions."

"Does plywood count as solid?"

"I don't think so, Ronnie." Tom rested his hand on her forearm and managed a weak smile. "I think we also need to come up with four magic bricks to place at the corners, is that right?" Tom checked with Alexander.

"Yes. That's right."

"Sorry I don't know more about this." Tom shrugged, looking a bit lost. "Bastet's not a funerary deity."

"Ronnie, are you gonna eat that?"

"It's all yours, kiddo." She slid her plate toward Bethany.

"I assume we'll need the correct hieroglyphs on the door and surrounding walls," Tom said.

"And dancing," Alexander added. "Dancing is required in the funerary procession, along with live music. I need a *Book of Coming Forth* to double-check all this." He turned the computer back his way and started clicking again.

"What's that and how come I've never heard of it?" Felicity assumed that by now she'd read everything there was on ancient Egypt.

"It's also called the *Book of the Dead*."

"That's not what we called it." Tom looked offended. Ronnie gave his hand a squeeze.

Alexander quickly turned his laptop to face outward again. On the screen was an elaborate painted papyrus. "Here it is."

All right, then. The *Book of the Dead*, Felicity knew. "We'll need to choose appropriate spells from the book, I assume?"

Tasha checked her notes. "Do I have all this right? We need a solid tomb lined up with the cardinal directions, some magic bricks, lots of hieroglyphs, live music, dancing, and a couple of decent spells."

"Exactly, Ms. Romero. Well summarized."

Tasha blushed a little at Alexander's compliment. Felicity couldn't remember the last time she'd seen Tasha blush.

But Tom was glowering. "We're running out of time. Where are we going to get a solid structure to use as a tomb that is perfectly aligned north, south, east, and west?"

"Tasha's kitchen."

Everyone turned to Bethany, who had just finished her third sandwich. "I've checked. For my crystal work. You need to know these things. They're important."

"Uh, my kitchen just got fixed up. My living and dining rooms aren't even finished yet."

"Tasha, it would just be a little ritual paint on the walls that we'd easily be able to paint over." Tom gave her one of his rare smiles.

"I'll repaint it myself."

"And I'm happy to help, Ms. Romero."

"Tash, I'm not sure we have any other options. Time is running out." Felicity hated putting her best friend in this position again, especially now. For the first time in her life, Tasha cared deeply about her family's homestead. It had been a marvelous transition to witness, but now they were asking her to let go of the controls again.

Tasha lowered her gaze, and Felicity could see the wheels spinning. Just then, Little Mama jumped up onto Tasha's lap, one of her kittens dangling from her mouth, and before Felicity could intervene, Little Mama dropped the fuzzy baby onto Tasha's thighs. The little fuzz bundle—it looked like the one Bethany had named Jellybean—climbed up Tasha's shirt and began rubbing against her face.

Felicity thought about rescuing the kitty, but decided to let the encounter between her BFF and Jellybean take its course.

Tasha raised her head and looked around the table. She gently pulled Jellybean's needle claws from her shirt and, as if this was something she did all the time, began stroking the little kitten's head.

Felicity saw the instant Tasha gave in. "Fine. We'll paint over it. Just don't get any hieroglyphs on my new granite countertops. Or the stainless steel appliances. Or the tile floor. But other than that, fine. Do what you have to do."

Felicity leaned over and gave her a big hug.

"But how are we going to get Apep-inside-Misty to come to Tasha's kitchen? Felicity are you gonna eat that?"

Felicity passed her plate to Bethany and wondered whether the ultrasound had been mistaken and she was carrying twins. Or triplets.

"I know!" Ronnie practically screamed with excitement. "We send out a formal invitation!"

"What?" Tom looked perplexed.

"Well, think about it. Apep taunted Misty when she was alive and she went right to him. And Apep still needs to kill the Acolyte, right?—no offense Felicity—and destroy the necklace. So we just say, *come and get it*. He wouldn't be able to help himself."

Felicity perked up. "And Apep doesn't know that *we* know he's inside Misty. He thinks we're unprepared."

"Exactly."

"But, Ronnie, how do we get him a message?"

"I'll ask Niko to help. We'll back-trace how Viper Apps went live again in the first place, isolate an IP address, and send a message—an *invitation*—that he can't refuse."

Tom nodded. "Neal—"

"Niko."

"—won't need to come here. We'll use Alexander's offices. I'll be there to help."

Tasha glanced at Felicity, and she knew exactly what her BFF was thinking. Tasha was right—Tubastet-af-Ankh was jealous.

Ronnie only smiled.

"You're growling, priest." Alexander dropped down into the chair beside him.

"You need your hearing checked."

"Hissing, then?"

He pulled his attention from Ronnie and Niko what's-his-face, who were huddled over the computer in Alexander's private office. They'd been at it for more than two hours at this point. He had no idea why it was taking so long. All they needed was to back-trace an IP address and send Apep the simple message they'd all agreed upon: "The Acolyte still wears the *usekh*."

"I don't hiss," he told Alexander.

"Of course not."

It certainly had taken a convoluted process to settle on such a straightforward message. Ronnie had advocated for them to taunt Apep into action. Tasha wanted to leave Apep no choice but to show himself. Felicity insisted that they not reveal they knew Apep was using Misty's body. And Bethany wanted to smudge the double-wide to raise the frequency to a harmonious one-mind state of consciousness.

Tom had wanted a beer. Desperately. But he'd abstained.

And now, at this moment, Tom worried about what it was that Niko wanted, because the dude had just leaned even closer over Ronnie's shoulder to point out something on the screen. Ronnie nodded enthusiastically.

He forced himself to turn away.

"Doing OK?" Alexander asked.

"Great." He looked out the wall of windows to the street nineteen stories below. Skyscrapers still fascinated him. Another miracle of technology that modern people didn't seem to appreciate.

"How's Felicity's place coming?"

He indulged Alexander, though his friend no doubt knew exactly how the renovation was progressing. "I'm not sure how you pulled it off, but it's already been painted, polished, and landscaped."

Alexander chuckled as he checked his smart phone. "The roof's scheduled for tomorrow. Once the plumbing and electric pass inspection, the movers will come. I know Felicity is anxious to get in."

He nodded.

"Does she seem anxious to get settled?"

Alexander may have been intent on small talk, but he was more interested in Niko's right hand, which now rested on Ronnie's shoulder.

Alexander leaned in and spoke quietly. "It's not the Middle Ages anymore, Tubastet. You can't simply declare a woman your property, kidnap her, and whisk her off on horseback."

"Don't be ridiculous." He knew Alexander was teasing, but he failed to see the humor in the situation. He couldn't take his eyes off Ronnie no matter how he tried. A skyscraper perspective of the Pacific Ocean had nothing on her. She was magnificent. And he had no idea how much time he had left with her. "Anyway, you bought me a pickup, not a horse."

Alexander gave his shoulder a friendly punch. "I'm happy for you, Tubastet. Truly. She's incredible. You deserve some happiness while you're here."

He gave his friend a sideways glance. "Ah, yes. But it's the 'while you're here' part that's the problem, right?"

"Yes." At least Alexander didn't try to sugarcoat it.

Just then, Niko let loose with a shout. "That's it!"

Ronnie sat back in her chair, her face awash with victory. Her eyes found his. "We did it, cat. Message sent."

He wanted to share in her celebration, but what was there to celebrate? Now that the message had been sent, Apep would answer. The battle would be upon them. He looked to Alexander for reassurance. "Are you sure this will work?"

His laugh was soft. "We've gone over this. I'm not sure of anything except that this is our best shot. All the pieces must fall together seamlessly from here on out."

"You know what, Alexander?"

"What?"

"Sometimes, I wish you'd just bullshit me. Make up some fairy tale, pat me on the head, and tell me everything will be fine."

Alexander cocked his head, considering. "That's not part of my sacred duty to the Ever-Living Goddess and her warrior priest. Besides, you'd kick my ass if I lied to you."

"Yeah. I would."

Home. Such a simple, glorious word.

The morning light shone through her spotless windows as Felicity strolled from room to room, touching the just-delivered furniture arranged to her specifications. Most was from the apartment, but Alexander had once again worked his magic. Several new pieces had been rushed over, including a large dining room table. She'd asked for something that could accommodate all six of them with room for a highchair once Bethany's baby arrived.

Counting the chairs made her realize that soon there would be an empty one, when Tom had gone. Felicity pushed aside that melancholy thought. First things first. They had to win the battle with Apep before she could indulge in melancholia. Until that time, for however long they had, they could sit together here as a family. Her family.

That made her smile.

The doorbell rang. Probably another delivery. She knew there were still rugs, lamps, bed linens, and window treatments on the way. To think…if anyone had told her a couple of months ago that today she'd be living in her own castle, she'd have thought them nuts!

Felicity rushed to the front door, dodging the obstacle course of yet-unpacked boxes. She grabbed the doorknob and opened, then immediately kicked herself for not using the peephole. Peepholes had been invented for just such an occasion, and the next time she damn well better use the one in her front door because there stood Richard Hume, Esquire.

He stepped across the threshold without being invited.

"Where's Bethany?"

"No idea. Did you try across the street where she's staying?"

"Of course, I did. I banged on the door for ten straight minutes. I figured she was avoiding me."

Felicity took a deep breath. "Look, I'm busy. Just leave a note on Tasha's door or something." She attempted to shove the door closed on him, but stopped. "Wait. How'd you know where I lived?"

"I watched you work with the delivery guys while I was staking out Tasha's place."

"You were staking out...?" Felicity shook her head. Unfortunately, she'd dropped her guard just long enough for Richard to push his way inside. She watched him wander around, touching her newly painted walls and spotless furniture with his clammy hands. As soon as he'd gone, she'd be asking Bethany to smudge the living fuck out of this place.

"How'd you afford this house and all the pricey stuff?"

"I have a badass fairy godmother." Felicity went into her kitchen to finish unpacking. Richard followed. She checked the clock and decided she'd give this little Welcome Wagon visit ten minutes before she threw him out. She knew Richard Hume. She knew how his ego operated, and she knew if she tossed him out now it would only ignite a fire under him, inspire him to greater heights of inanity. So she'd give him ten minutes to shoot his clever barbs and deliver his zingers and make a general ass of himself, and *then* she'd kick him out.

"Oh. So that's why you lured Bethany here. You've tricked her into giving you all her money?"

"She doesn't have any money, you idiot." Felicity lifted a heavy box and set it on the kitchen counter, allowing herself a moment to appreciate her strength. The truth was, she could beat Richard to a pulp if she wanted to, and maybe even do some push-ups afterward.

Or not.

"But she has access to *my* money. That's it, isn't it? I'd better double-check all my accounts. You're getting even by brainwashing Bethany and stealing my money!"

"First of all, Dick, half of the money in your house is *my* money. I've been nice letting you live there rent free, but my lawyer says he's rectifying that situation, with interest."

"Speaking of your lawyer, how can you afford such a fancy-schmancy one? And where'd you get that tacky gold necklace?" Rich pointed accusingly. "You look ridiculous in it, just so you know."

"I inherited it."

"From who? You don't have any rich relatives, unless it's just cheap-ass costume jewelry." His eyes narrowed, suspiciously. "I don't understand what's going on with you, Felicity."

"First of all, it's *from whom*, as in, *from whom did you inherit the cheap-ass costume jewelry*. Second, you never understood what was going on with me, Rich, because, in all the years we were together, you didn't want to. And now, I don't have the time or inclination to explain a damn thing to you."

She picked up a razor-sharp box cutter, and Rich flinched reflexively. She almost laughed. But, as much as Rich's smug face made a tempting target, she only intended to use it open the box.

Alexander had offered to have a team unload everything, but Felicity liked the idea of putting her new dishes away in her new kitchen.

"You've really fucked things up for me, Felicity. I had to meet with the *Pine Beach Gazette* editorial board alone. Then I had to attend the Chamber of Commerce dinner stag, without my young, attractive wife, who's gained a few pounds, true, but she's still hot. Do you know how that looked to voters? I'm running for mayor on a family man platform! And I'm a man without a family!"

"Your concern for Bethany's welfare is touching." She lifted a stack of plates and set them on the counter above the dishwasher.

At that moment, Mojo rushed in and gave a loud *merroew*! Last week, Ronnie had taken Mojo to work with her and had him neutered. He was still bitching and moaning about it.

Scratch and Sniff came galumphing down the stairs like a herd of buffalo. She smiled as they slid across the wood floor and wrestled their way into the kitchen. Just that morning, Felicity had moved all the cats over to the farmhouse and fed them breakfast. The new mudroom was now cat central, large enough that all eleven were able to eat together peacefully, which was a first-time-ever event. Felicity had so much room now that she'd bought four fancy robot cat boxes she planned to place strategically throughout the house. Alexander's team had installed a cat door, too, so they could come and go, though deep-down, Felicity hoped they'd start staying in the house more often. She always worried about cars and coyotes, especially with the wanderers like Little Mama. Of course, Little Mama and her babies were safely—and in Felicity's humble opinion, *permanently*—living with Tasha and Bethany.

In one fluid leap, Mojo landed on the counter beside her. His meow this time was louder and seemed more urgent, and for about the five-thousandth time she wished she understood what he was trying to say.

"God, Felicity. How many of those dirty things do you have now? Aren't you tired of being a crazy fuckin' cat lady?"

"You say that like it's a bad thing." She slowly turned to Rich and looked him straight in the eye. "Never underestimate the power of a crazy fuckin' cat lady."

He rolled his eyes.

She picked up a table knife, spun it expertly in her hand, and faked a jab at Rich, who stumbled backward. It was all she could do not to shout, *Fell the foe with thy knife, asshole!*

He looked terrified. "Are you threatening me?"

"No, I'm putting away my flatware. You're the one who barged into my home and started accusing me of brainwashing your innocent, almost-ex-wife."

"You and your trashy best friend are keeping her from me!"

"I assure you, if Bethany wanted to see you, she'd see you. In fact, why she ever wanted to see you in the first place is a complete... well, who am I to criticize? It's all ended well, though. She's come to her senses." Felicity turned her back on him and returned to loading the dishwasher. "You know, she's one of the loveliest young women I've ever known—smart and insightful and kindhearted. We've become close friends. In fact, she sees Tasha and me as role models. It's so sweet."

"Role models?" He looked like he'd stepped in dog doo. "I... don't understand any of this. You've changed, Felicity!"

"How nice of you to notice." She shut the now-full dishwasher door and set the machine to medium wash with heated dry. She turned to face Rich. "Now, I think we don't need to see each other in person again. If you need anything, contact my lawyer, who, conveniently, is also Bethany's lawyer. I'm sure you can find the front door. Goodbye, Rich."

He appeared to be perched on the edge of a retort. Of course, he was. He lived to have the last word. But this time, he kept quiet, turned, and walked from the kitchen. Moments later she heard the front door open, then promptly slam shut.

P-Diddy and Circe rushed in, meowing loudly. What was going on with the cats today?

That was when she heard a blood-curdling scream. From Rich.

She ran to the front door and flung it open, only to stare in shock.

The house was surrounded by crocodiles.

Huge, terrifying, man-eating crocodiles with rows and rows of sharp teeth and thick, knobby skin. They crawled through the new landscaping, swished their tails down the barely dry concrete walkway, and lumbered up the porch steps. These were Nile crocodiles. She'd certainly seen enough illustrations and photos in all those reference books she'd studied. And as the name might imply, Nile crocodiles were not native to Pine Beach, Oregon.

"Get it off me!"

Only then did she note that a smaller specimen, likely a juvenile, had made it onto the porch and chomped down on Rich's Gucci loafer-clad foot. She winced. That had to hurt like a sonovabitch, and she wouldn't wish that pain on anyone, not even a sonovabitch like Rich.

"Don't move if you want to live. Keep your hands up high!" Felicity rushed back in the house, grabbed her iron lance, and returned in a matter of seconds.

She first beat back a fifteen-foot-long croc on its way up the porch steps. It retreated with a loud hiss.

"Help me! Save me, Felicity!"

She spun on the balls of her feet and brought the flat of the lance down hard on the small crocodile's head. It quickly released Rich and spun toward Felicity. She held it off with the weapon.

"Get in the house, *now*! I don't want your blood causing a frenzy. Call 911." She kicked out and hit the snout of another large croc and used the lance to shove the juvenile out of the way so Rich could get inside.

He was momentarily stunned, watching Felicity battle back one croc after another. "What the hell's going on with you, old girl?"

"For fuck's sake, get inside!"

He recovered his senses and limped toward the door, moving as fast as his wounded foot would allow.

She bludgeoned one more crocodile and kicked the small one down the steps before maneuvering to the front door and escaping inside, ensuring that the door was latched securely behind her.

Felicity heard a meow and turned to see all eleven cats perched around the room. Thank Goddess, they were safe.

Mojo let go with another loud wail of complaint.

"Yeah, you did try to warn me and I'm sorry I didn't understand. I'll have to work on that."

She watched Rich on the phone with an obviously skeptical emergency operator. He'd wrapped his bleeding foot with one of her brand-new tea towels.

She pulled out her own phone and dialed. "Tom!" she said. "Apep got our message."

It took more than an hour for the sheriff's department and animal control to clear a path for the paramedics to get to poor Richard.

By that time, Felicity had provided some first aid on his punctured foot and healed the two spots that were bleeding heavily. She *might* have been able to heal the whole wound, since Rich had been attacked by Apep's crocodiles, but there were two reasons why she didn't. First, it was a serious injury, one better left to medical professionals. Also, she didn't want him to learn of her new talent. Felicity sighed with relief when Rich got carried out to the ambulance, crying like a girl, and was taken away.

It took another two hours for Oregon Zoo handlers and fish and wildlife officers to arrive and then catch and load the animals for transport. Their view was that the sixteen *Crocodylus niloticus* converging on Felicity's house was an inexplicable event. Felicity, of course, kept the explanation to herself.

"Seems you've got an illegal breeder nearby." A sheriff's deputy later met with the posse as everyone safely assembled in Tasha's yard. "There's big business in the reptile trade, you know. But don't worry. We'll find them and shut the operation down."

Sure, Felicity thought. *You go do that.*

Once the deputy thanked them for their assistance and left his card with instructions to call should additional reptiles appear, he and the remaining first responders drove off. Felicity was relieved that Cass and his volunteer unit hadn't responded to the call. The last thing she needed was to explain away yet another strange twist in her life. He had to be suspicious at this point, with the random catastrophes, the non-romantic, half-naked roommates, the sudden financial windfalls, and the woo-woo nightmare messages from beyond.

"What next?" That was Alexander, who'd arrived just in time to see the last of the crocodiles carted away.

"We prepare for Apep's imminent arrival." Felicity spoke the words with far more confidence than she felt.

"I'm almost done painting the tomb in the kitchen. I got a lot done yesterday," Bethany said proudly.

Tasha nodded. "I haven't looked. I have a feeling I don't want to look."

"I'll start on the hallway now." Bethany rushed back into Tasha's now-beautiful home.

"Goody." Tasha looked green around the gills.

Felicity patted her BFF's shoulder. All things considered,

Tasha had been a good sport.

"I've tracked down the ancient instruments we'll need," Alexander said. "I just have to pick them up from the collector near Salem. Anyone want to ride shotgun?" He turned to Tasha.

"Oh, gee. Sorry. Ronnie and I are stuck on shopping duty." Tasha practically yanked Ronnie toward her car.

"I'll go with you, Alexander. Just give me a few minutes to protect the farmhouse." Tom turned to Felicity. "I'm sorry. I really should have put up the Eyes of Horus sooner."

"Hey, things have been crazy. And none of our reptile friends got inside the house, right? So go do your wacky *Wadjets* and then keep Alexander company. I have four bricks to paint." A moment later, Felicity waved as both cars set off down the lane.

Well, then. That was that. This was really happening.

They could do this. *I can do this.*

Oh, Goddess, at least she hoped so.

CHAPTER SIXTEEN

Felicity completed her assigned task and was back at Tasha's by early afternoon.

"Hey, you're good at that!" Felicity watched as Bethany stood on a ladder and copied in tempera paint the images that Alexander and Tom had chosen. It was all much brighter than she'd anticipated—shades of red, blue, green, gold, black, and yellow all over the hallway walls leading to the kitchen and around the kitchen doorway.

"Did you finish painting the bricks?" Bethany asked.

"All four, but they're not nearly as colorful and elaborate as all this. Look." Felicity pulled one of the bricks out of her big canvas bag. "Just white paint slapped on a regular brick. So boring I wonder if they'll actually do what they're supposed to." Felicity pointed to the corner by the kitchen sink. "This is south, right?"

"No. South is the corner near the stove."

"Right. Gotcha." Felicity took her tote into the kitchen and her jaw fell open. Bethany worked fast. Most of the walls of the brand-spanking-new kitchen, with its solid maple shaker cupboards and its granite countertops, were now covered by admonitions and instructions for a dead person to safely traverse the underworld. And not just any dead person. Misty's name was scrawled out in fancy hieroglyphs at several prominent locations.

Tasha would have an absolute, all-out shit-fit when she could finally bring herself to look in the kitchen. The new drywall and its two coats of carefully chosen Tawny Taupe now looked like an ancient Egyptian back alley, every surface scrawled with bold incantations. The term shit-fit might not even cover it.

Felicity put each of the prepared ritual bricks in its appropriate corner of the room, reciting the short incantation Tom had written out for her. She felt stupid. She really didn't know what she was doing and hoped her little part would fit into the larger picture and that, somehow, it would all work. After she placed the fourth brick and finished reciting, she had a moment of panic. Had she placed the bricks in the wrong places? Maybe she should have a do-over.

She reached down to pick up the brick in the north corner and found it wouldn't budge. She tried another brick and found that it, too, was firmly planted in place. OK. Maybe that meant things were going according to plan. Felicity looked around at the perfectly aligned walls and thought they glowed a bit. Then they seemed to pulsate, and Felicity felt like they were moving in on her.

She wasn't ordinarily claustrophobic, but there was no denying that standing in someone else's tomb—one that seemed to be *activated* in some way—was fairly creepy. Perhaps it was time to get out. Felicity slipped through the kitchen doorway.

"Hey, Bethany. You know what I just realized?"

"Hmm? What?" She added shading to the scarab beetle's antennae.

"I just realized that it's a good thing Tasha didn't agree to the open concept kitchen. It's the only room we could find that was a perfect configuration for the tomb."

"Huh. Interesting. Hey, Felicity—I just love painting all these little animals that have special meaning. Look at this cool bug!" Bethany gestured to what she'd just finished.

"That's a sacred scarab. It's the hieroglyph *kheper*. It's very important since it means the essence of existence itself."

"Uh-huh." Bethany was not particularly interested in the deeper meaning of existence and was already happily on to painting a bird.

At that moment, Tasha and Ronnie returned, clutching several shopping bags.

"Had to go to three stores, but we finally got six dark shower curtains to cover the—" Tasha dropped her bags. "What's all this shit all over my hallway walls?" She looked to Felicity. "Is the kitchen like this, too? I should've looked. No, I shouldn't have looked. Don't tell me."

"Well…"

"I thought it was just going to be a few symbols. But this is… it's… it's…"

"Perfect?" Felicity offered.

"It's… more than I'd anticipated." Tasha looked queasy.

"But it's great, isn't it, Tasha?" Felicity nudged. "Bethany has done a great job, hasn't she?"

Tasha took a few breaths. "Super great."

Ronnie moved closer to examine the details. "I'm impressed, Bethany."

"Super impressed." Tasha's dull repetition made Felicity want to elbow her out of her stupor. Yes, it was jarring. It certainly didn't fit in with her muted color scheme. But that was the point. It had to be attention-getting. It had to beckon. It had to be everything the modern dead person would want on their safe journey to the afterlife. It was what had to be done.

"Tasha, if this doesn't work, and Apep triumphs, you won't have any walls to worry about. You won't be alive to worry about your walls. You understand what I'm saying?"

Tasha nodded. "Super understand."

"Did you already finish the kitchen?" Ronnie asked.

"Yes, ma'am," Felicity reported. "Tomb walls are painted and bricks are installed." But as Ronnie poked her head in to see for herself, Felicity grabbed her arm. "I wouldn't go in there if I were you. The installation of the bricks has activated something." Felicity produced an apologetic smile and before she could explain further, Alexander and Tom rushed in.

"We have the traditional instruments and Tom wrote out the spells." Alexander balanced several wooden carrying cases.

"Here's everything you asked for, Felicity." On Tasha's new hand-hewn dining table, Tom placed each of the familiar weapons along with the extra items Felicity had requested. He placed a case of bottled water on the seat of one of the matching chairs.

Tom pulled three sheets of paper out of his pocket and unfolded them with care. "The first spell from the *Book of Coming Forth* is called Opening the Path." Tom handed the page to Felicity. "I didn't bother giving it to you in the original Ancient Egyptian."

"Smart man." Felicity looked it over. It seemed simple enough.

"Here is the second spell. It's called Passing the Dangerous Coil of Apep."

Alexander nodded. "We think that one will help loosen Apep's grip on Misty."

"Got it." It was fairly short, so Felicity felt confident she could read that one aloud without any problem. Maybe the contents of *The Book of the Dead* weren't nearly as daunting as she'd feared.

Tom handed her the final sheet of paper. "This is the most important spell. It's The Releasing of the Four Winds."

"Does that correspond to the ritual bricks Felicity installed at the four directions?"

"Exactly!" Tom smiled at Ronnie's question. "It gives the dead person the breath of life so that they may gain entry into the Underworld." Tom grabbed Ronnie's hand and gave the inside of her wrist a quick kiss.

Felicity was struck by a pang of sadness. As eager as they were to defeat Apep once and for all, then free Misty, their success would bring on Tom and Ronnie's final parting. She pushed away the thought and forced herself to focus. "What are the instruments?"

Alexander bent down and opened the first case. "This is the sistrum." He held up an odd rectangle with inner metal discs. When he grabbed the bottom handle and shook it, it released a sound like bells. He opened the next case and gently lifted a delicate C-shaped stringed instrument. "This is the lyre." Finally, he produced a long double-pipe. "And this is the shepherd's flute."

"And how many instruments do we have to play to make it an official funerary procession?"

Tom and Alexander shared a questioning look. Finally, Tom answered. "You know, I think just one instrument might work as long as there's a melody. But we'll need at least two dancers."

Alexander nodded. "Right. The funerary texts are very specific in that *dancers* is plural."

Ronnie picked up the sistrum, gave it a rattle. "Not much melody in this, but I guess one of the dancers could shake it."

Tasha pulled her little notebook out of her purse. "I can shake the sistrum since Bethany and I are the dancers, plural." She made a brief note. "Lissie has to do the spells and the actual defeating of Apep, plus she's pretty tone deaf, so music making is out for her."

"I wouldn't say *deaf*, Tash. Tone challenged, maybe."

"Uh-huh." She checked her notes again. "Tom and Ronnie are on battle duty, doing all that sparring stuff if it's needed to move Apep down the hall close enough that we can yank down the curtains and reveal the tomb decor. So I guess that leaves Mr. Lawyer here with the actual music man duties."

Alexander looked panicked. "I, uh, can't play the lyre or the flute."

Tasha couldn't hide her scowl. "Well, that's inconvenient for the whole saving the world thing we're trying to do here, *Alex*."

"And you, Tasha? Please, regale us with the tale of how you've mastered these ancient instruments." For the first time ever, it sounded as if Alexander had come to the end of his patience.

"Perhaps," Felicity interrupted, "it doesn't have to be *exactly* as written." She searched the room for concurrence. "I mean, we all remember how we improvised the last time, right? Does anyone play *any* kind of instrument?"

Everyone shook their heads. Everyone but Alexander, who shuffled his feet and said, "I used to play lead guitar in a college band."

Tasha laughed. "Ooh! A kumbaya cover band?"

Alexander's eyes narrowed. "Rock and roll. Unfortunately, I have yet to find a hard rock remake of 'Kumbaya,' but, Tasha, since you're obviously a renown composer and arranger, perhaps I can commission you for the job."

"Look at my ibis!" Everyone stopped arguing and turned toward Bethany, who smiled wildly from her perch on the ladder.

Felicity watched Alexander take a deep breath and smooth his hair, then give all his attention to Bethany's work.

"That is truly impressive," he said. "You have a real artistic flair, Bethany."

Tasha helped Bethany descend the ladder. "Watch that last step, sweetie."

"Actually, a guitar should work," Tom said. "It's in the same string family as the Egyptian lute. Do you know any of the classic tunes?"

"If by classic you mean Zeppelin and Clapton, yeah, I've got you covered."

"Know any ABBA?"

Alexander ignored Tasha.

Tom looked unconvinced, but Felicity jumped in. "It'll work, Tom. It doesn't have to be one particular ancient Egyptian song. It will be *music*. It will have a melody. And Bethany and Tasha will be the two dancers, plural. So it will fill the bill. Bethany's almost done painting all the required images. Ronnie will hang the shower curtains that'll hide everything until we have Misty inside her tomb. Once Misty steps down the hallway, then I'll begin the spells."

"It's a solid plan, cat," Ronnie assured him.

Tom gave her a sideways glance. "It's our *only* plan, so solid or not, it's got to work."

Alexander had an acoustic guitar delivered within the hour, but his usual calm assurance was gone, as was his formerly impeccable suit jacket, which now lay crumpled on the floor beside him. He studied the guitar as he played it, as if reacquainting himself with the mechanics.

Since Felicity couldn't help him with that, she pulled out her copy of the spells and went over them again.

Bethany tugged Tasha over to Alexander. "Have you decided what you're going to play? I want to prepare some really great dance steps, so it'd be good to know the vibe in advance, and the beat, of course."

"The beat." Alexander looked up, terror in his expression. "In all honesty, I have no idea what I can still play, Bethany. It's been twenty years since I picked up an acoustic."

"I'm sure you can come up with something great," she replied. "I have complete confidence in you."

Tasha opened her mouth, but Bethany cut her off. "No more snark, Tasha. Now is not the time. We're all aware of your issues with men stemming from choosing emotionally unavailable partners. Your heart chakra is blocked. We get it. But tonight, we need to work together as a team. No more sarcasm and no cutting comments. Everyone will do their individual best and then encourage others to do their best too. Got it?"

"Uh, OK."

Bethany smiled. "Awesome. You're the best." She dragged Tasha to their assigned place near the kitchen to start working out dance steps.

As Felicity slipped the written spells into her back pocket, she noted, yet again, that Bethany might be young and hormonal, but she was a bomb-ass goddess.

"Push hands!"

Felicity turned in the direction of Ronnie's voice to see that she and Tom were standing close together, facing one another, knees bent, moving their hands and wrists in tandem to create a slow-motion dance. One of them would push forward and the other would retreat, and then vice versa. But the movements didn't look uniform or predetermined. They had to be communicating some other way, Felicity decided. "Is that more Shaolin?"

"Tai Chi," Ronnie answered. "It helps us get attuned to each other."

"We're letting our bodies listen to each other's intentions," Tom explained. "It's called *ting jing*."

Felicity decided that should anything *ting jing*-related come her way in the future, she'd take a hard pass. She wasn't sure she wanted anyone listening to her body's intentions. Felicity took one more look around the house. They were as ready as they'd ever be, right now. She just hoped they wouldn't have to wait much longer to spring into action.

There was a knock at the door.

And she couldn't breathe.

This was the moment they had prepared for, the beginning of the beginning, and a wave of doubt had already washed over her. She couldn't go there. She wouldn't allow it. What was it Betty had said to her in the library? *You have everything you need to face whatever comes your way.*

"Everyone get in your assigned places!" Tom ordered.

Alexander, with guitar and rumpled jacket, moved to the hallway outside the kitchen. He put the guitar strap over his head. "Music ready."

Tasha grabbed the sistrum and then took Bethany's hand. They positioned themselves just in front of Alexander, and the two shared a nod. "Dancers are ready too."

Felicity stood in her assigned spot in the middle of the room, out of immediate striking range of someone at the door but directly in their line of vision. "Acolyte ready."

Tom took a visible breath and swung the front door wide.

Misty stood on the threshold, apparently alive except for...

A rush of icy doom smacked Felicity between the eyes. No. The figure in the doorway was *not* alive and she wasn't Misty. The eyes assured her of this. They were lifeless. Utterly inhuman. They did not belong to the Acolyte from Clackamas. They belonged to something not of this world. To Apep.

The girl's body still carried the wounds of that horrific battle in the Shanghai tunnels. Her long, blonde hair was matted with dried blood, and those purple nails were broken and filthy, just as she'd seen in her nightmare. Felicity supposed the reason the young Acolyte hadn't healed much since that fight was because, well, she was mostly dead. Misty's skin puckered and oozed along her arms and legs, scarlet stripes gruesome against her pale skin. Those marks told Felicity all she needed to know about the brutality of that clash, and how hard her predecessor must have fought.

But this was not Misty who now swaggered into the room. It was only her outer shell, kept alive to serve as a vehicle for the chaos serpent, who now had complete control of the former Acolyte's youth, her strength and agility, and her endurance.

Felicity swept her gaze to Tom. Her teacher stood frozen in shock, as if he couldn't comprehend what he was seeing. Well, that was fast—just seconds in and it was clear they'd been overly confident. The truth was, they were wholly unprepared to face this enemy, whatever *this* was.

"Still enamored of the lower class, I see, Tubastet-af-Ankh." The voice didn't have the silky-smooth resonance of Apep's, but neither was it that of a teenage Acolyte.

Felicity observed Misty—*no, not Misty!*—scan the room with a robotic disconnection. It was terribly disconcerting, and possibly something that Apep planned to use to his advantage. It was imperative that she get it through her skull that this thing wasn't Misty. Wasn't even a person. Misty was long gone and could not be saved. It was too late.

Felicity felt the essence of Apep, that cold and slinking cruelty, suck all the oxygen out of Tasha's living room. She felt his ugliness brush up her spine like a deviant caress. She shivered at the violation, a wave of nausea rising. But she would not let him use her own emotions against her. Not this time. She might not grasp the entirety of the power he wielded in Misty's body, but she knew his playbook, knew what had to be done, and knew exactly where she would need to begin.

Felicity stilled herself. She dropped her shoulders and relaxed her chest. She gathered up her energy, let the *usekh* amplify it, and purposefully directed the force outward, repelling him.

That *thing* spun around, knocked off balance, and focused its dead eyes upon her. "You still around, old gal? I admit I was quite surprised to get your message. Did you enjoy my friends?" The creature let loose with distorted, grisly hack of a laugh. It cut off suddenly, and the dead eyes honed in on the necklace around Felicity's neck. "I really thought you would have given the jewelry back to the cat by now."

Without warning, the entity executed a turn-squat-kick that connected with Tom so hard it sent him flying. *Oh shit.* This was bad. Tom had trained Misty for battle, and that had been a textbook-perfect Step Two move, Defiling Apep with the Left Foot, executed with impossible speed by a young, strong body now under the control of a supernatural evil. Not a good combination.

The entity faked a kick in Felicity's direction, and she jumped back reflexively. The hacking laughter echoed through the room.

"Well, if we're going to do this again, then we might as well get started. Go ahead…" the mostly dead teenager/chaos demon waved a dismissive hand in Felicity's face. "Start the steps so I can finish you off and be done with it. I will destroy the *usekh* even as it lay on your throat. All the more satisfying, really."

The creature smiled at Felicity, and her stomach dropped. She could see so much of the real Misty underneath Apep, a once-happy girl who loved makeup and Instagram and resented anyone telling her what to do, which made her exactly no different than any other teenager on Earth.

What a tragedy. What a loss. Felicity paused, reminding herself: *this is not Misty.*

"Would you just get on with it?" The Apep creature rolled its dead eyes. "Hurry up! Spit on me, old gal. Let's go."

Admittedly, it was tempting. She wanted to smack the smirk right off that vacant face. But that was exactly what Apep wanted, for her to expend her energy on a useless attack. To battle him while he was invulnerable inside Misty's body. The only outcome of that fight would be certain defeat for the Acolyte.

Felicity caught Tasha's eye and gave a tiny shake of her head, *not yet—they aren't close enough to the hallway.* She began to slowly walk backward, hoping to draw the thing closer to the kitchen.

But it didn't move. It just cocked its head to the side as if listening, and suddenly straightened again. "Oh, I hope you don't mind. I brought company!"

And the room exploded in a blast of glass and screeching. Felicity ducked and threw her arms over her head, peeking just enough to see... *vultures?* Yes, vultures. They'd smashed through the windows and poured through the open door and even swept down the chimney.

Oh, for the love of Alfred Hitchcock! "Birds!" Felicity howled. "Are you fucking kidding me?"

"Oh, my God, the new windows!" Tasha's complaint came

from somewhere behind her.

And these were not just any birds. They were hideous holdovers from the dinosaur age, something no cat could take on, as Apep surely knew.

The giant raptors swarmed the room, circling with their huge wings slicing through the air, their cackles and screeches deafening. In the chaos, Apep-Misty grabbed one of the new, hand-carved chairs and swung it at Tom. It broke apart against his back, which sent Ronnie running into the fray.

Felicity grabbed the first remotely weapon-like item she could find—which turned out to be a booklet of paint swatches. She rolled it up and started swinging wildly, hitting the vultures with samples of Swiss Almond Beige and Warm Winter White.

But her efforts were less than effective, and a sharp talon sliced down her cheek. *Shit! That burned!* A powerful hooked beak clamped down on the necklace while another pecked at her throat. One of the flying dinosaurs pulled at her hair. A huge and ugly icepick of a mouth snatched the flimsy paper out of her hand.

Just then she noticed a piece of two-by-four lumber resting near the front door and made a run for it, but before she could reach it, a little calico face peeked in through the jagged window glass.

No! It was Little Mama. "No, baby girl, run away!" Felicity screamed, but the small cat didn't seem to hear or care. She leapt through the window, fur all fluffed, tail straight, ears flattened and ready for battle.

Her cat paws had barely hit the floor when a vulture dive-bombed her, clutching at her with its talons but failing to get a solid grip. Felicity's heart stopped. She screamed at the little cat, screamed and screamed, but her voice got drowned out by the otherworldly hissing and cackling of the birds. This was a horrible nightmare, the absolute worst she could imagine, and she couldn't move fast enough. She watched in terror as the vulture pecked a chunk of fur and flesh out of Little Mama's throat.

Hell, no! She wasn't losing another cat to Apep's evil! Absolutely not! He was fucking with the wrong cat lady!

Felicity got her feet moving and scrabbled across the room, ignoring the clutching talons and snapping beaks that tore at her. She batted away the vile birds as she fought on, finally reaching Little Mama's collapsed body. Felicity dropped to the floor, curled herself over the small calico cat and nearly cried with relief that the kitty was still breathing.

Felicity touched her fingers to the tear at the cat's throat and watched as the gash began to mend. *Oh, thank you, Goddess! Thank you for letting me do something for Little Mama that I couldn't do for my Boudica.*

She was overwhelmed by a fresh wave of grief for her dear little one-eyed Boudica. It hurt to breathe. Tears burned her eyes, and blood poured down her cheek from the talon gash. She couldn't move, could only offer her own skin and bones to protect Little Mama from the attacking vultures and pray it was enough. She felt helpless. Powerless. An all-consuming wave of despair pulled her under.

Just then, a vulture yanked at her hair, ripping a hunk from her scalp. She heard Tasha scream. How could she turn this around?

By remembering who she was. By going to battle for what was right. That was the only way out of this for anyone. The old Felicity might be scared and unsure, but the Acolyte she'd become was bold and confident, strong enough to beat back the shadow of grief. The Acolyte could take on these old feelings of inadequacy that threated to swamp her, flip them around, and burn them as fuel.

Felicity, the Acolyte, could fend off the vicious vultures and the supernatural evil entwined with Misty. She would save her friends. Her world. And her cats. Yes. That was what she *must* do.

But how? Her legs were leaden and her heart was shattering. Boudica was gone and another dying feline lay in her worthless arms. Felicity swiped at her tears and tried to stem the blood pouring from her face. She couldn't. The cut was too deep and the blood rolled down her cheek and along her jaw, dropping onto the small bundle of fur she held. *I'm a fucking mess, polluting everything I touch.* She tried to clean the blood from Little Mama's soft calico fur, but only managed to smear it from head to toe.

Meeeruup. Little Mama's voice was barely audible, but she wriggled against Felicity's hands. She was alive!

What the hell? It almost seemed as if Little Mama was heavier than she'd been just a moment before. That was ridiculous, of course. Cats don't instantly gain five pounds for no reason—only menopausal women do that!

But it was, in fact, happening. Now, the cat was at least ten pounds heavier in Felicity's arms. Then heavier still. The cat weighed at least twenty pounds by the time Felicity lay her on the floor. Within seconds, Little Mama had become so huge that Felicity had to yank her hands out from under her before they were crushed.

What-the-catastrophic-fuck is going on?

Little Mama's legs lengthened. Her paws swelled and her claws thickened and grew, sharp as knives. Her chest expanded along with her neck and head. The rest of her followed in suit—back, haunches, tail—inflating like some strange feline balloon. Little Mama jumped to her feet. She didn't seem to be in any pain or distress, but there was absolutely no explanation for any of this!

The once-petite house cat turned to face Felicity. Her eyes were no longer their usual yellow but had mellowed into a rich copper-gold.

As Felicity watched—astonished—as the brown, red, and white patches in her fur faded completely, leaving her coat a sleek and uniform tawny color, stained by the bright smears of Felicity's blood.

And suddenly, Little Mama opened her mouth to *meow* again, but she emitted a house-shaking *ROOOOOOAR*.

Before Felicity could react, another vulture swept down, talons outstretched for her face, but Little Mama leapt up and swatted at the offending bird, sending it tumbling across the room to slam into a wall, feathers flying. Still, the cat grew.

In the next instant, a fully grown lioness bounded around the room. She pulled vultures down from midair with dagger-like claws and flung their carcasses out the shattered window. She ripped them to shreds with her carnivorous fangs.

Felicity heard another scream—maybe Bethany this time—but whether it was about the dive-bombing vultures or the huge lion now crashing through the living room, she wasn't sure.

Felicity's mind flashed with an illustration from one of her library books. It was a depiction of an early image of Bastet, with the head of a proud lioness, before the good old boys downgraded Bastet to domestic cat status, turning the ruthless hunter into a petted pussy.

Fuck that.

Felicity stood tall, the blood running down her face, and allowed the power of Bastet—the original, untamed beast—to flow through her arms, legs, belly, and chest. She refused to be beaten down, reduced, and caged. Not by anyone, or anything, ever again. She would simply not allow it.

The big cat stilled. She stood very near the Apep and Misty entity, watching it battle with Tom and Ronnie. Felicity assumed the lioness was about to attack, but instead, the magnificent feline turned her large, copper eyes to Felicity, as if awaiting her orders.

Felicity shook her head. In her mind, she told her: *No. Apep cannot be destroyed that way.* And the not-so-Little Mama turned away and resumed hunting the few remaining vultures, leaping through the front window in hot pursuit as they tried to escape.

Felicity's first thought was that at least she no longer had to worry about a coyote getting Little Mama. Her second thought was that she really needed to be more careful about where, and upon whom, she bled.

CHAPTER SEVENTEEN

Felicity kicked a dead vulture aside and did a quick sweep of the battlefield. Feathers floated through the air. Every bit of fabric had been shredded—carpet, clothing, furniture, drapes. Tasha, Bethany, and Alexander were vulture-battered but still standing at their stations in the hallway by the kitchen. Felicity quickly joined them.

Tom fought on, beating back the Apep-Misty entity with Ronnie at his side. Though pecked and scratched and more than a little bloody, the two fought with perfect trust, their movements synchronized. Felicity recognized some of the Shaolin moves from the night in the apartment, one rapid-fire punch, spin, and kick after another.

But the body of the former Acolyte was supercharged by the presence of Apep and moved with incredible strength and speed, holding off Tom and Ronnie like it was child's play. Felicity suspected that Tom was holding back, hampered by the remnants of his guilt and thrown by the idea of warring with his own Acolyte.

Ronnie was unconstrained by either, and charged again and again with laser-focused ferocity. Her moves had gone far beyond sparring and were now full-contact assaults.

Tom and Ronnie made progress, moving their grotesque opponent down the hall in tiny increments, pushing it closer to position. Step by small step, strike by strike, the two managed to maneuver Apep-Misty toward Felicity, almost, but not quite, within range of the makeshift ritual tomb.

Suddenly, the entity landed a hard blow that sent Ronnie flying, and as Tom rushed to protect her, he was downed by a brutal kick to his side, precisely at the site of a nasty scar. But of course, Misty would know that, Felicity realized. She knew exactly where Tom's body was the weakest. She'd trained with him for three years, heard the stories of his past battles, past injuries and accidents. Misty would know he preferred to lead with his left foot, to block with his right arm, and to spin counterclockwise.

But why would Misty's consciousness lash out at Tom? And then Felicity remembered all the hatred and resentment contained in those texts and emails. Even almost-dead, Misty's fury lived on, which meant their enemy was a spry, highly trained killing machine fueled by a preternatural evil and white-hot desire for revenge.

Great.

The creature spun away from where Tom and Ronnie had fallen, quickly smashed another chair, and yanked off a leg that had splintered to a dagger-sharp point. It hurled the javelin straight at Bethany.

"NO!" Tasha screamed.

Alexander was already airborne. He stretched out, using the length of his body to shield her, and the spear pierced his shoulder. He crashed to the floor on his side, then scrabbled to rise up on his knees.

Tasha crouched beside him. Felicity saw a quick exchange of words but couldn't make out what was said. Tasha nodded, then shocked the hell out of Felicity by wrapping her hands around the chair leg and ripping the spear right out of Alexander's flesh. Then she balled up his jacket to put pressure on the wound.

Felicity had to make something happen. Apep-Misty wasn't yet in the perfect position for the ritual, but Alexander was wounded and Tom and Ronnie were barely conscious. She had to act.

Felicity shouted, "Now, Bethany!" It took a moment for Bethany to pull herself together, but slowly, she began the steps of the dance. Alexander nodded to Tasha that he was all right, so Tasha let go of the jacket and yanked down all six shower curtains in rapid fire succession to reveal the decorated walls of the fake tomb. She then joined Bethany in the dance, shaking the sistrum in time to their movements.

Apep-Misty tipped its head, puzzled.

Alexander, blood dripping down the length of his arm, scooted back to his spot in the hallway and grabbed the guitar. He leaned against the wall, propped the instrument on a knee, and played with far more skill—and volume—than Felicity thought possible. For an instant, she believed she recognized the tune, but she couldn't place it. It hardly mattered.

Felicity rushed to the kitchen door, pulled the first spell page from her pocket and began to recite loudly. "O, you Soul, greatly majestic, behold, I have come that I may see you! I open the netherworld that I may see my father Osiris and drive away darkness!"

With those first words, the air around them began to change, to tingle and expand.

The Apep-Misty amalgamation faced Felicity, teetering, slowing its movements in charged air. Suddenly, Felicity doubled over in anguish—a lightning bolt of pain ripped apart her stomach. *Dammit.* Somehow, she'd linked up with Misty again and could feel her internal struggle.

Felicity took a deep breath and continued reading from the piece of paper shaking in her grip. "I have come that I may see my father Osiris, that I may cut out the heart of his enemy Set!"

The pain grew in Felicity's gut, stabbing and tearing at her insides. The Apep-Misty entity stumbled toward her.

"NOOOO!" The voice that exploded from the thing was more Apep than Misty, and the body lurched toward Felicity and the tomb, two steps forward, one step back.

"I have opened up every path which is in the sky on earth. O all you gods and you spirits, prepare a path for me!" Felicity felt a shuddering in the floor beneath her feet. She peeked over her shoulder to see that the kitchen doorway was shimmering, the space turning a dark blue.

Apep-Misty moved disjointedly, out of sync with itself, as the two beings inhabiting the single body worked against each other. Felicity had backed up and now stood just before the kitchen threshold. She only needed to coax them a few steps farther. At that moment, Bethany and Tasha danced into view, twirling and flitting around them, Tasha shaking the sistrum vigorously, greatly agitating the hybrid creature.

"The spell has worked and the way is open—" Felicity didn't finish her announcement. The entity lunged at her, grabbed her throat with one hand and the *usekh* with the other.

"Now, you die Acolyte, and I take what is *mine.*" That voice was Apep, full and true, and the unnaturally strong hand at her throat squeezed. Tighter. Tighter. Felicity clutched at the hands around her throat, but couldn't loosen them at all. Her eyesight dimmed. She struggled to take any breath. She felt her life force being wrung from her body. But in a flash, all was cleared. She gasped and blinked back at the light.

Tom had pulled the beast from Felicity's throat and held it steady before the doorway. Bethany and Tasha danced, closer to the thing in Tom's grasp, upping the intensity of the twirls and flourishes as Alexander played even louder. In a surreal moment, Felicity realized that she *did* recognize the tune. It was ABBA's "Dancing Queen," and Tasha and Bethany had started singing along.

"*You can dance…having the time of your life!*"

The kitchen doorway's shimmering blue responded to their dance and the music, its color now a deep, rich sapphire. They discoed their way over to help Ronnie, who was struggling to shake off her injuries.

The Apep-Misty monster lunged for Felicity again, but its mouth opened and a high-pitched, nasally wail escaped. "*I haaaate yoouu!*" Misty was in total control in that moment, fueled by the rage she harbored for her former teacher. It staggered away from Felicity toward Tom, who remained just out of reach. "You made me miserable! You were so *freakin' mean*! I can't believe I ever thought you were hot!" It kicked out wildly, barely missing Tom's crotch.

Felicity felt a shooting pain that took her breath away, and when she looked down blood had splattered on her paper. She raised a shaking hand to her face to find her nose was bleeding now, too. Her gut twisted and her head swam. Misty was fighting the internal Apep, hard, which was good, but Felicity wasn't sure how much more her own body could take. She needed to get Apep out of Misty's body *now*. It was time for the second spell, Passing the Dangerous Coils of Apep, which should give Misty the upper hand.

"O, you waxen one who takes by robbery and who lives on the

immobile ones..."

Apep-Misty swung around to confront Felicity, ignoring the hard blows Tom was landing to its gut, chest, lower back. "Stop!" That was Apep, and he shoved his fist at Felicity's face. But the internal battle being waged inside the body had slowed its movements, made them jerky and imprecise, and Felicity was able to evade the punch.

"I will not be immobile for you! I will not be weak for you!" Felicity could barely get out the words of the spell, feeling blood ooze from her left ear now, too, and run down her already bloody neck.

"I HATE YOU!" That was Misty again, and the body lurched back to Tom. The pain in her head was so brutal that Felicity collapsed to her knees on the floor. She could not keep going like this. She knew that. She had to take drastic action before she passed out.

As Tom and Ronnie struggled to keep the powerful Apep-Misty away from her, she crawled on hands and knees to the table that held all her weapons. But it wasn't the lance or knife she needed. It was something far more powerful.

She grabbed what she was after and used the table to pull herself to a stand again. Bethany and Tasha stopped just before they reached her. "Are you all right?"

Apep-Misty cried out and surged forward, the doorway shimmer fading fast.

"Keep dancing!" Felicity screamed. "Don't stop! You have to keep dancing!" As they did, she heard Alexander segue into "Stairway to Heaven," which seemed appropriate.

Felicity wiped the blood from her mouth and nose with the back of her hand, and stumbled in reverse toward the kitchen door, clutching her weapon. She must continue her spell. "Your poison shall not enter my body!"

She finally reached the doorway, the pain blinding now. "If I am not weak for you, suffering, you shall not enter my body!" She took a deep gulp of air, and at the top of her lungs she shouted the last line of the second spell: "For I am Ra at the head of the abyss!"

For an instant there was only silence, and Felicity could feel the battle raging in the dually occupied body. The pain was beyond unbearable. She was blacking out. She had to stay on her feet. "Misty! You can be free! Come through the threshold!"

"She will not! I control her!" But Apep's voice had weakened.

"Misty! Look over here!" Felicity cried. "Look what I have!" The body jerked toward her, jerked away again, then swung wildly until it faced Felicity straight on. That's when Felicity raised her arm to display the ultimate weapon.

Misty's cellphone.

"MY PHONE!" With a surge so strong it jolted Felicity from head to toe, she felt Misty take control of the body and then rush headlong toward Felicity. "Give me that!"

She had to time this bit perfectly. Felicity waited two more seconds. She balanced on the balls of her feet, holding the phone as steady as she possibly could. The purple-nailed hand of the mostly dead Misty reached out—nearly touching the screen—and Felicity whipped the phone through the glowing blue vortex and into the kitchen. Even through the shimmer, the phone was clearly visible as it lay on the newly tiled kitchen floor.

"NOOOOOOOOO!" The cry of despair was delivered in a voice equal parts Apep and Misty, and together the entity plunged into the blue membrane. Immediately, the body convulsed, then froze on the threshold. It rose up, its feet leaving the ground. It writhed and twisted, and Felicity's agony spiked. She collapsed to her hands and knees but watched as, finally, with one last excruciating spasm, a slick and bloody mass was expelled from between Misty's shoulder blades, flying from her back into the living room.

As the body—fully Misty now—propelled into the kitchen, the homunculus remains of Apep rolled across the floor and stopped directly between Felicity's hands. Tom and Ronnie scooped up the ball of mucus-covered flesh and wrapped it in a bathroom towel.

Felicity watched Misty retrieve her precious phone. She cradled it like a broken doll. For a moment, Misty was clearly shocked and confused, but that didn't last long. She looked up and through the doorway to Tom. She tried to run out of the kitchen but only slammed into the shimmering blue membrane, solid as brick.

"I hate you!" she screamed at Tom, her face scarlet with rage. Ignoring Misty, Tom took Felicity gently by the arm and helped her to her feet, steering her to the table. There, her weapons were laid out. Tom clutched the bloody remains of Apep in his hand. Out of the corner of her eye, she saw Ronnie step in front of the kitchen door, stance wide, expression fearless as she guarded the former Acolyte.

"Keep playing the music! Keep dancing!" Tom called out to Alexander, Bethany, and Tasha. "As long as you continue, Misty is contained."

"OK, OK!" Tasha responded. "But how much longer does this go on?"

"I have to pee again!" Bethany said.

Alexander launched into "Layla."

Tom leveled his gaze at Felicity. "Quickly, Acolyte. You are about to accomplish what has never before been achieved. It is time to destroy the final piece of the once-immortal Apep."

Felicity grabbed one of the water bottles from the table, took a huge mouthful. Tom held the hideous blob of flesh out to her and she spit the water across its bloody skin. "Be thou utterly spat upon, O Apep." And the burning began.

Tom lowered the bundle to the floor. Felicity placed her left foot against the towel shroud. "Rise thee up, O Ra, and crush thy foes!" Her fatigue crashed into her, and she almost lost her balance. She was so close. She could not falter now.

"YOU DESTROYED EVERYTHING!" Misty was standing right up against the blue membrane, looking past Ronnie, her eyes burning into Tom. He kept his back to her, focused on Felicity, but she could tell that the words hurt him.

Tom handed Felicity the light lance. Felicity simply tapped the point against Apep's burning flesh. "Horus has taken his lance, thrusts into Apep!" She really didn't really want to skewer the decaying tissue, like some sort of evil shish kebab, and luckily, she didn't need to. The internal burning intensified and spread, engulfing most of the bundle.

"YOU MADE MY LIFE HELL!" Misty was louder now, if that was even possible, and Felicity wanted to tell her to shut the fuck up, but she stayed focused on her important work.

She picked up the long fetter and simply wrapped it around the towel. She cleared her throat and tried to speak clearly. "They who should be bound are bound!"

"I WISH HE'D KILLED YOU INSTEAD!"

Felicity couldn't help but flinch. They were still connected, and even though it had faded greatly, Felicity felt Misty's own pain cut into her heart.

Tom, his jaw clenched, handed her the knife, and she was so exhausted she barely had the energy to slice it across the smoldering terrycloth. "Seize, seize, O butcher, fell the foe with thy knife!"

Felicity had a flashback to this point in their first battle, when Apep had turned into that giant, grotesque snake. She was relieved to see he was in no shape to do that again. There was only the barest movement from the towel-wrapped flesh.

"I'D KILL YOU IF I COULD, YOU KNOW THAT?!"

Felicity's stomach churned violently, feeling Misty's anguish. She quickly turned away and vomited all over what was left of Tasha's new carpet. Oh, Goddess, she just needed this to be over.

Tom handed her the bottle of water, and gave her a quick hug. "You're doing an amazing job. We're almost there." She took a few small sips.

"FUCK YOU, TUBASTET-AF-FUCKING-ANKH!"

Felicity grabbed a long lighter from Tom and touched it to the cotton. With what felt like her last breath, she croaked out, "Fire be in thee, O Apep. May the Eye of Horus have power over the soul and the shade of Apep!"

And before her eyes, the little, towel-wrapped homunculus burst fully into flames.

Even Misty was finally silent as they all witnessed the great God of Chaos disappear into a pile of ash for the very last time.

CHAPTER EIGHTEEN

Felicity relieved Ronnie at the kitchen doorway. She stared into the furious eyes of her predecessor. "It's time to go, Misty. You know that." She tried to keep her voice gentle and sympathetic, since she knew the pain Misty was in.

"I hate him." At least Misty had stopped screaming. Now, as she faced Felicity, her voice was small and weak. And wrenching.

"I know." Felicity nodded in sympathy.

"He was so mean!" Big, fat tears rolled down her forever-young, forever-disfigured cheeks. "I hated him."

Felicity looked directly into the dying, tortured eyes. "Did you?"

Misty angrily wiped at her tears. "I lost. I lost the battle and it hurt. It hurt so much!" Misty was sobbing now, struggling. "And now I'm ugly and scarred. I'm going to be ugly and scarred forever! I hate him for that."

Right then, Felicity knew what had to be done. She lifted a

hand and pushed it through the glowing blue curtain, hoping this would work. Her hand tingled, but Misty's physical pain had faded enough that Felicity was able to concentrate.

Misty watched suspiciously but didn't move away. Felicity brushed her fingertips along Misty's cheek, then her throat, and directed her touch along the remains of the jagged wound. Next, she pushed her other hand beyond the veil and brushed her palms down the length of Misty's blond hair. She moved her palms down Misty's arms, wrists, all the way to the tips of her purple nails. The wounds were wiped away, as was the blood and filth.

Misty looked at Felicity in astonishment and dared to touch her now healed throat. She ran her hands through her hair. "How did you do all that?"

Felicity didn't answer, but spent the next few moments touching every mark, scratch, and scrape she could find. When she was done, it was as if Misty McAlpine of Clackamas, Oregon, had never stepped foot in the Shanghai Tunnels.

She only wished she could as easily heal the wounds the young woman carried inside.

Misty stroked her clean and unbroken skin, over and over every place where there had been a cut or a gash. Then she looked up at Felicity, shocked. "I'm not ugly anymore."

"You are beautiful, Misty."

It was Tom. He stood beside Felicity, and she had no idea how long he'd been there.

"And I'm sorry," he said. "I know it doesn't change anything, but I need you to know that I am sincerely sorry for the pain I caused you."

Misty wiped at her stream of tears and stared at Tom with such vulnerability and longing that Felicity almost turned away. "I loved you," Misty whispered.

"And I loved you."

She shook her head. "But... not like I loved *you*."

"No," he said, his voice gentle. "Not like that."

With one last smoothing of her hair, Misty turned to Felicity. "I'm ready." She stepped into the center of the kitchen.

"Now, Felicity," Tom said. "The last spell."

Felicity looked down at the text that would send Misty into the Underworld. She read aloud: "To the Door of the west wind: Ra lives. Osiris is triumphant."

A wind picked up in the kitchen and began to swirl around Misty. Her hair went flying.

"To the Door of the east wind: Ra lives. Osiris is triumphant."

The wind intensified, whipping around Misty with such force that cabinets opened and their contents were dumped on the floor. Anything not nailed down on the new countertops went flying.

"Do we have to keep dancing? I really, really have to pee!" Bethany looked desperate.

Ronnie stepped up, tapped Bethany on the shoulder, and began dancing next to Tasha. "I got it. You go." Bethany scrambled down the hall toward the bathroom, and though Ronnie was clearly exhausted and hurting, she kept dancing.

"Hey, Alexander, do you know any Rihanna?"

"Sorry, Ronnie. How about The Beatles?"

"Go for it."

As the wind swirled, Alexander launched into "Here Comes the Sun."

Felicity looked into the kitchen and witnessed Misty's form fade from view. At the same time, Felicity's energy returned, and she heard it in the strength of her voice with the next line of the spell. "To the Door of the north wind: Ra lives. Osiris is triumphant!"

And the whole damn house shook. Tasha stumbled in her dance steps. "Oh, shit." Wind barreled from the kitchen and churned through the rest of the house.

Felicity squared her shoulders, ignored the wind now hammering directly in her face. "To the Door of the south wind: Ra lives. The bolts are drawn, and they pass through this foundation. Osiris is triumphant!"

As Felicity shouted the final words, the swirling wind picked up what remained of Misty and spun her. In the next instant, she was gone.

But the wind was not. It seemed to be gaining force.

Bethany returned. Tom signaled that Alexander could stop playing and Tasha and Ronnie could stop dancing.

"Is that it?" Bethany sounded hopeful.

"Of course, it is, right Lissie?" Tasha rested her hands on her knees, panting. She shouted over the wind. "It has to be! Tell me it's over!"

It was clear that all of them had reached the limit of their endurance. Unfortunately, it appeared the wind had just gotten started.

The gusts scattered Apep's ashes, sent vulture feathers swirling, and tipped over the remaining chairs. Plaster tore away from walls and wood lathe cracked, twisted, and sheared off. Ceiling fixtures crashed and appliances shuddered. The wind yanked already-shredded draperies clean off the rods and tore through the remaining intact windows, sending shards of glass flying through the air like see-through guillotines.

"Get behind a door!" Alexander screamed. "Everyone!"

Tom grabbed Ronnie and pulled her with him into the guest

bedroom, slamming the door shut just as a blast of wind embedded daggers of glass into the wood.

Alexander reached for Tasha, but a fierce gust swept her into the kitchen, beyond his grasp.

Felicity pulled Bethany through the nearest door, which happened to be the empty coat closet. "Hurry, Alexander!"

He hesitated, still searching for Tasha in the churning vortex. "Stay alive!" he shouted. *"I will find you!"* Just then, a rush of air knocked him off his feet. He scrabbled through the debris to the closet, then rose to hold the door shut against the chaos.

The house shook and the gale roared, battering what they could not see, lifting up the very floor beneath them. Things crashed and thudded and toppled over, but Felicity dug in and held tight to Bethany while Alexander used all his weight to keep the closet door from flying open. Still, the wind pummeled and shook the hundred-year-old Sears, Roebuck do-it-yourself wood and hinges, the only thing keeping them alive.

"What's happening?" Bethany cried, covering her ears.

"I don't know!" Felicity tried to keep the panic out of her voice, but failed.

On and on it went. There was no way to know how many minutes the frenzy lasted, but when it finally did end, it was so abrupt it was jarring. One second the house was a screaming terror and the next it was utterly silent. After a few moments of quiet, Felicity signaled for Alexander to open the closet door. They all staggered out. Felicity blinked and tried to focus. Yes, the wind was gone.

And so was the front of the house.

At that moment, Tom peered out of the bedroom door. "Everyone OK?"

"I think so," Felicity said. "You guys?"

"Good."

"Tasha?" Alexander called for her, listening for a response. "Where are you, Tasha?" He raced into the kitchen, throwing aside debris to make a path.

Felicity followed, gingerly picking her way across the mess. She looked around but didn't see any sign of her best friend. She shoved down the growing panic as Alexander began pulling on already-open cupboards and the laundry room door. Nothing.

"*Tasha!*"

Alexander yanked on the wooden pantry door, but a giant split ran down its center and the jagged wood was jammed into its molding. Tom joined him in the effort, and the two finally ripped the broken door from the frame.

Tasha was inside. She sat curled into a ball, shoved into a corner on the pantry floor, an open bottle of wine in her hand and a box of extra toasty Cheez-Its spilled at her feet. She took a long, shaky swallow. It was not her first.

"Tash, you OK?" Felicity knelt beside her and looked for wounds. "Are you hurt? Tasha! Talk to me."

"I'm absolutely fine. Everything is fine." Tasha took another swig. "Thank you for asking."

"Excuse me." Alexander urged Felicity to move aside. He knelt down and scooped her—and her wine bottle—into his arms.

Tasha crooked her elbow around Alexander's neck. She smiled at him. And in a dreamy whisper she said, *"You found me!"*

Alexander stood. As he carried Tasha toward the porch, she shouted, "Hey, look! I got open-concept after all!"

CHAPTER NINETEEN

Felicity's hands had gone numb. She shook the circulation back into them and leaned over Alexander again. "Your shoulder should be good as new. Now let me see your hands."

Everyone was seated in a line along the top step of what remained of Tasha's porch. Felicity had treated one person at a time, healing whatever wounds could be identified. Bethany had a gash on her left thigh and a twisted ankle. Tom had another broken nose, a broken wrist, and a broken rib. Ronnie had a contusion on her left shin, lacerations on her forehead, a busted lip, and a broken pinky finger. Felicity had already wiped the Cheez-It dust from Tasha's chin and plucked a few deep splinters from her hand, but other than that, Tasha was fine, just as she'd said. Felicity still couldn't get over how her BFF yanked the wooden spear from Alexander's shoulder in the heat of battle.

"My shoulder is already healed. It's like nothing ever happened!" Alexander rotated and stretched, amazed.

"But your hands are a mess of cuts and blisters. Let me see them."

"I hadn't played guitar in years."

"I thought you were the bomb, Alexander." Tasha, who was propped against him, gave him a shy smile. "The ABBA was a rock-solid choice, too." She offered him her wine bottle.

He smiled in return, grabbed the bottle with his newly healed right hand, and took a long gulp. Felicity finished up with his left hand, stood up straight, and stretched.

"All right, then. Looks like your attorney hands are once again as smooth as a baby's bottom."

"You know, this would be a neat skill to have on the battlefield," Ronnie pointed out.

"Maybe that's why I have it, or, have it while I'm in the *usekh*."

"Was there really a lion?" Tasha wondered aloud.

"I saw that too!" Bethany's eyes got huge. "It was terrifying!"

"Yep. There really was a lioness." *A fierce, brave mother cat who came to help us in battle.* Felicity kept that part to herself. She stared out across the yard, hoping Little Mama was safe.

"That's a new one, isn't it Tubastet?" Alexander turned to Tom.

"It is, indeed. Of course, everything about these last few weeks has been new." Tom sat with Ronnie, holding both her hands in his.

"But where did the lion come from, Lissie?"

"Oh, you know how it is with me and cats, Tash! They just show up. I'm a feline magnet."

She caught Tom's gaze. He raised an eyebrow at her, a signal that he knew she wasn't telling the entire truth.

"And now we have another visitor," Ronnie said.

Felicity turned to see Little Mama herself crawl out from under the Airstream, once again in calico cat form. Felicity was hugely relieved to see her, and had to laugh when Little Mama stopped in the middle of the yard to preen and meow as if she knew she was the talk of the town.

Bethany rose from her spot on the top step and went to the kitty. "There you are, Little Mama! What are you doing out here in the dark when your babies need you, you silly little thing?" She scooped the undercover lioness into her arms and carried her back to the double-wide. "Yes, I know you're weaning your kittens, but still, you know how Jellybean gets when she can't see you!"

Tasha sighed. "You know, I've really come to love those little fuzzy mofos."

A comfortable silence settled over the exhausted group as they watched the sun complete its daily round. When darkness fell, it was like a soothing blanket placed on Felicity's frayed nerves. She felt her shoulders release and the feeling return to her overworked hands. She felt herself begin to relax.

Until Tom stood up and said, "It's time."

The stars sparkled above them as he and Ronnie walked to the far edge of the yard. He wanted some privacy to say what needed to be said before he said goodbye.

Ronnie clutched his hand in hers and looked up at the velvet sky. "Show me where you'll be."

That made him laugh. "What do you mean?"

"Which star? Which one is where you'll be?"

"It doesn't work like that."

She turned to him, serious. "I know. But I want someplace to look so I can picture you looking down, remembering me."

He pulled her into his arms and spun her around so they were both looking in the same direction. He extended his arm and pointed high. "That one with the whitish-blue glow. That's Rigel. It's one of the brightest stars in Orion. That's where I'll be. Do you see it?"

She nodded, but when he looked down at her face, her eyes were closed.

"That's officially our star."

"Will you tell Bastet?"

"Absolutely." He gently turned Ronnie to face him. "I'll tell her everything about you."

"Like what?"

"Like how you're a tireless warrior. A loving friend. A talented healer. And an excellent kisser."

They stood like that a moment, face to face, drinking each other in. Tom wanted to remember every nuance of her lovely face. The way her soft lips curled into a smile. How her rich, brown eyes could see through all his bullshit and find something worthwhile at his core. He heard the words tumble from his mouth as if his tongue had a will of its own: "I'd stay if I could. For the first time ever, I'd stay. For *you*. If there was any way at all..."

"I know."

"It's my sacred duty, Veronica. To serve however I'm commanded. Even though Apep has been defeated, there will be other battles for me. Bastet is one of the ancients charged with keeping the balance of the universe, and I—"

"We've been over this, Tubastet-af-Ankh. I get it. I understand the meaning of duty and I know why you have to go. I don't *like* it, but I accept it."

He took a deep breath, deciding to speak before he lost his nerve. *"Tha se agapao—"*

"In English. Just this once."

He tenderly cupped her face. "I will love you forever."

"I will love you forever, too."

He kissed her then. It wasn't a passionate kiss, but one of melding, as if he could absorb enough of her to last into eternity. He wanted to remember her feel, her softness underneath the armor she wore, the way she yielded, the way she tasted. He wanted the kiss to be one of thanks, one of gratitude for all that she'd given him. But he was simply overcome by grief, and had to pull away.

"I want to stay." In fact, he wanted to beg the Goddess, howl at the universe, scream into the night, throw a petulant tantrum to satisfy his rage and longing. But he didn't. He was Bastet's faithful warrior priest and would do whatever she needed of him. He would serve however she commanded. That had been his solemn vow. Forever.

He kissed her gently one last time and then forced himself to let her go. He walked across the yard, a chasm in his chest where his heart once beat. He went to the others who gathered near the remains of the front porch. Alexander stood with Tasha, Bethany had rejoined them and stood beside Felicity. Felicity stepped toward him and handed him the ritual knife. He wanted to say something to her, but he couldn't. He couldn't utter another goodbye. He could barely breathe.

Felicity turned around, lifted up her hair so he had unobstructed access to the back of the necklace. For once, she was silent, and he was profoundly thankful. He slid the thin blade under the back of the *usekh*, mumbled the correct words and...

The necklace released.

He heard everyone gasp in relief. Everyone but him.

He gently lifted the circlet of gold still warm from her skin. Felicity turned to face him and gave him a little smile. "Thank you for everything, my dear friend."

He could only offer a curt nod before sliding the gold and jeweled collar around his own neck. He felt it immediately conform to his body. Yes, this was right. This was correct. This was his sworn duty.

The necklace clicked into place.

Felicity had no words. Her emotions swirled and clashed and almost overwhelmed her. She was hugely relieved—joyous even—to finally be free of her twenty-four-karat prison. Though she always knew she'd miss Tom, only now did she understand how much the loss would hurt. Watching him say goodbye to Ronnie had been one of the most achingly sweet exchanges she'd ever witnessed.

And now, after the necklace clicked into place around Tom's throat, it began to glow. Tasha reached out and grabbed Alexander and Bethany's hands, squeezing tightly. Felicity took a few steps away from Tom, but stayed near, and Ronnie silently moved closer. As they all watched, the light glowed brighter and brighter, surrounding Tom completely, until it grew so intense they had to cover their eyes. Felicity could feel its heat on her face beneath her hands. And just as it seemed it couldn't get any brighter or hotter, it was gone.

Felicity struggled to get her eyes to focus and adjust to the shocking absence of light. But when she could finally see clearly, Tom remained where he'd stood, right in the middle of the yard.

He looked dazed.

The *usekh* unlatched with a loud *pop!* and fell to the dirt at his feet.

Ronnie took a step toward him.

"No, stay back." Tom picked up the necklace and put it around his throat again. This time it didn't conform or even latch. It just hung in his fingers, a dead, cold weight.

Felicity rushed forward. "Are you all right? Is there something wrong with the necklace?" Felicity took it from his hands and felt it warm to her touch. A gentle tingling spread up her arm and the center sapphire glowed a bit, as if beckoning her to put it on again.

Nope. Been there and done that. She shoved the necklace back toward Tom.

He laid it against his throat once more, his eyes wide and his mouth slack. He shook his head. "The *usekh* just awoke again for you, Felicity. It's cold and empty when I touch it."

And Felicity knew.

"OH, MY GOD!"

"Lissie, what?" Tasha started to rush over, but the ever-cautious Alexander held her back.

Felicity didn't answer. She took the *usekh* from Tom, and it immediately heated up yet again. "Hell, no," she mumbled, searching for somewhere, anywhere, to set it down. The dirty ground didn't seem right for a priceless, indestructible, magical artifact, so she ran over to the little aluminum table on the Airstream's rickety porch and placed it in the center. It didn't seem to mind.

"Tom!" She rushed back to him. "Turn into a cat."

"What? Why?" He remained slightly dazed.

"Just do it." Felicity insisted.

"But—"

"Please. Trust me."

Begrudgingly, Tom brought his palms together, touched his forehead, and chanted the short incantation.

Nothing.

He raised his face, eyes flashing. "I don't understand this."

"Don't you?" Felicity reached out and took both his hands in hers. "You're free. Bastet has freed you from her service."

"I'm free?"

"Welcome home."

"I'm free!" This time it was not a question. Tom whirled around and Ronnie, who was already running toward him, let loose with the most un-Ronnie-like girly scream anyone had ever heard. She jumped. Tom caught her. They spun together, his arms clasping her as she hung on in a tangle of arms and legs.

"I just love a happy ending." Bethany leaned against Tasha, sniffling. Alexander put an arm around each of them and pulled them close.

Everyone enjoyed their moment to smile, laugh, sigh, or cry happy tears. But that's all they got—a moment.

Felicity heard it first. It began as a low rumbling, like a train in the distance. And the train kept coming. Louder. Deepening into a reverberating boom that shook the ground like thunder.

Tasha whipped her head around to glare at Felicity. "What now? Seriously. What the apocalyptic fuck is it *now*?"

Perhaps Felicity had been too quick to choose a simile, because this sound was not *like* thunder. It *was* thunder. She looked up at the perfectly clear night sky. "Hunh."

Then the thunder crashed and rolled across the yard, and a blinding streak of lightning stabbed straight down from high above. The bolt moved with laser precision, striking Bastet's necklace on the table.

The *usekh* exploded. Shards of gold and jewels sprayed skyward in an orange blaze, lighting up the darkness all around them like Fourth of July fireworks.

Felicity stood frozen in disbelief. And then she watched in horror as thin, jagged blue lines of—was that electricity?—zapped along the remains of the metal porch and sizzled up the sides of the

Airstream.

The lines swarmed and crackled and crisscrossed, spitting and hissing, until the entire trailer was wrapped in a network of living, static threads. The Airstream began to reverberate with a strange hum that grew louder and louder and...

Tom grabbed Felicity's elbow and yanked her away from where she stood. "RUN!"

Felicity ran as fast as her depleted body could carry her toward the double-wide on the other side of the yard. Out of the corner of her eye, she saw Tasha running with Bethany and Alexander in the same direction.

They were almost there when a huge explosion detonated behind them. The concussive blast knocked everyone off their feet, and Felicity slammed, shoulder first, into one of the concrete blocks of the double-wide's foundation.

It took her a moment to catch her breath. She struggled to sit, finally managing to pull herself upright, and leaned back against the vinyl siding. She glanced around to see that everyone else was still in one piece too, despite having the wind knocked out of them.

Felicity's gaze tracked to where, just moments before, the Airstream had been trapped inside an electrical net. Now, there was nothing but a blob of smoking black ash forming an Airstream-shaped silhouette in the dirt.

"Wow." It was Bethany who spoke first. "What a freakish accident!"

Five heads turned toward sweet, naive Bethany. Tasha took her hand and gave it a gentle pat. "That was no accident."

"Tom," Felicity licked her dry lips. "I thought Bastet's *usekh* was indestructible."

"It was."

She let that information sit for a moment, absently touching her throat. She found only a normal, naked, middle-aged neck, no trace remaining of the warm gold that was once a part of her. And though Felicity was no longer the Acolyte, she was smart enough to know that a piece of the puzzle was missing.

"Why would Bastet destroy the *usekh*, Tom?"

"She wouldn't." His expression was blank. "In fact, she couldn't."

Felicity looked at her dazed and depleted posse, slumped against the double-wide where the blast had thrown them. They'd believed this was over, that they'd been triumphant. Maybe not.

"So, if Bastet couldn't destroy the *usekh*, what could?"

Tom hesitated a beat. "Nothing good."

A gentle rain began to fall. Droplets hissed as they hit the Airstream-shaped scar in the earth. Steam swirled, rising from hot ash.

And Felicity thought she heard someone laugh.

THE END

The Cat Lady Chronicles continue...

Book 3: CATACLYSM, May 2022

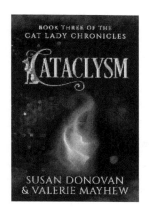

A cat lady in her prime…

Former middle school English teacher Felicity Cheshire stunned everyone when she battled back an ancient god of chaos and saved humanity from destruction. All she wants now is to curl up in the sunshine and grab a well-deserved nap with her rescue cats.

A malfunctioning piece of mystical jewelry…

When the gold and sapphire necklace that started all her troubles won't release from her throat, it's clear the danger is far from over. Worse still, her warrior priest trainer is stuck on earth and experiencing a midlife crisis two millennia in the making.

A world on the brink… again.

Felicity and her Goddess Posse of BFFs learn they must hunt down and defeat a horrifying new foe. On the way, they must deal with gray roots, swollen ankles, an unfortunate hickey, and an Airstream full of cats. Felicity may be stronger and wiser this time around, but she's sticking with one hard and fast rule: no sit-ups.

Coming Soon:
    CATACLYSM, Book 3 of the Cat Lady Chronicles

ABOUT THE AUTHORS

SUSAN DONOVAN

Publisher's Weekly has called Susan's books "the perfect blend of romance and women's fiction." She is a *New York Times and USA Today* bestselling author of novels from St. Martin's Press, Penguin USA/Berkeley Books, HQN, Amazon, and Hachette, along with several self-published works. Susan is a former newspaper reporter with journalism degrees from Northwestern University. She lives with her posse in New Mexico.

VALERIE MAYHEW

Formerly a writer of paranormal television (*The X-Files, Charmed*) Valerie is now sowing mischief of the normal kind as a college writing instructor. She lives in Los Angeles with her husband, who writes horror, her children, who can be horrors, and more cats than she cares to admit. Valerie survived four years of the drama program at The Juilliard School, where she received her B.F.A.

Catch up with the cat ladies at:
www.catladychronicles.com

Made in the USA
Columbia, SC
21 June 2022